Praise for *Madness in Miniature* 1

"Margaret Grace is skillful in bringing the clues together in this intriguing mystery.... The family relationships and love bring this series to life. *Madness in Miniature* is another successful, enjoyable mystery in my favorite series by this prolific author."

—*Lesa's Book Critiques*

"Summer gets lively when Gerry and her granddaughter, Maddie, deal with another murder, this one coupled with an untimely earthquake. Grace's seventh cozy entry combines a love of miniatures with traditional sleuthing."

—*Library Journal*

"*Madness in Miniature* is a wonderful cozy starring a dynamic amateur sleuth team. The case is fun, but takes a back seat to the interesting look into town relationships, especially with the schism caused by the dispute over the pros and cons of the new superstore."

—*Genre Go-Round*

"Intriguing plot. I liked the way the miniature theme worked into the story.... This is a good mystery with a lovable kid. The relationship with her grandmother is a delight."

—*Bookloons*

"As befits a traditional mystery, Margaret Grace plays fair, doesn't have any gratuitous blood and gore, and fully develops her characters.... HIGHLY RECOMMENDED. It would make a great family film."

—*I ♥ a Mystery*

Manhattan in Miniature

Manhattan in Miniature

A MINIATURE MYSTERY

Margaret Grace

2015
PERSEVERANCE PRESS / JOHN DANIEL & COMPANY
PALO ALTO / MCKINLEYVILLE, CALIFORNIA

Copyright © 2015 by Camille Minichino
All rights reserved
Printed in the United States of America

A Perseverance Press Book
Published by John Daniel & Company
A division of Daniel & Daniel, Publishers, Inc.
Post Office Box 2790
McKinleyville, California 95519
www.danielpublishing.com/perseverance

Distributed by SCB Distributors (800) 729-6423

Book design by Eric Larson, Studio E Books, Santa Barbara,
www.studio-e-books.com

Cover design and illustration by Linda Weatherly S.

10 9 8 7 6 5 4 3 2 1

LIBRARY OF CONGRESS CATALOGING-IN-PUBLICATION DATA
Grace, Margaret, (date)
  Manhattan in miniature / Margaret Grace.
    pages ; cm. — (Miniature series)
  ISBN 978-1-56474-562-0 (softcover)
  1. Porter, Geraldine (Fictitious character)—Fiction. 2. Grandparent and child—
Fiction. 3. Murder—Investigation—Fiction. 4. Miniature craft—Fiction.
I. Title.
  PS3563.I4663M36 2015
  813'.54—dc23
                                                    2014018192

To my husband, Richard Rufer

Acknowledgments

THANKS as always to my dream critique team: mystery authors Jonnie Jacobs, Rita Lakin, and Margaret Lucke.

My gratitude also to the extraordinary Alameda County DA Inspector Chris Lux for advice on police procedure. My interpretation of his counsel through more than twenty books should not be held against him.

Thanks to the many writers and friends who offered critique, information, and inspiration; in particular: Gail and David Abbate, Sara Bly, Nannette Carroll, Margaret Hamilton, Diana Orgain, Sue Stephenson, and Karen Streich.

Special thanks to Meredith Phillips, my meticulous and helpful editor and inspirational co-crafter in the world of miniatures.

My deepest gratitude goes to my husband, Dick Rufer, the best there is. I can't imagine working without his support.

Manhattan in Miniature

Chapter 1

I NEEDED A new refrigerator; there was no doubt about that. But I didn't expect to have so many choices. I stood in the appliance section of the store, in front of the current selection of models. Should I buy the tall, white two-door or a similar style in black with an ice maker? I was also attracted to a French-door arrangement in a wood-like shade, and the bottom-drawer-freezer stainless steel model next to it. I had already ruled out the old-fashioned one-door in avocado green that reminded me of my first kitchen in the Bronx back when Ken and I were newlyweds. I wasn't planning on redecorating to that extent.

In the end, I decided to buy them all, including a boxy yellow throwback with its motor on top that had fallen behind the others. You could never have enough appliances to fill all your dollhouses or miniature room boxes.

"What about the restaurant-kitchen room box we're making, Grandma?" Maddie asked. "Shouldn't we buy two of the big stainless steel fridges so we can put them side by side?"

"Good idea," I said, as Maddie threw another silvery fridge into the wire basket she carried. Maddie was my mini-Sherpa in more ways than one.

We headed for the checkout counter at SuperKrafts, Lincoln Point's first crafts store. My English-teacher background had finally stopped rebelling at the gimmicky spelling, and I was able to enjoy the store's great collection of supplies for lovers of crafts of all kinds. Maddie and I had a clear shot at every shelf and bin of merchandise, with few other shoppers, most of whom were focusing on supplies for Christmas ornaments and fabric stamped with sleigh bells or Santa and his reindeer. I'd convinced my eleven-year-old granddaughter that earlier was better on a Saturday so close to Christmas if we wanted to beat the crowds. We stopped on the way to checkout and admired the new decorations to celebrate all the December holidays.

I was glad to be done with the Thanksgiving theme, which had been carried out with six-foot-tall turkeys, massive ears of plastic corn, and giant cornucopias. I doubted anyone ever called an oversized pilgrim "cute." Maybe I'd offer to help decorate next year and add a miniature Thanksgiving table to the mix. Why anyone preferred larger-than-life to smaller-than-life was beyond me. When an item was enlarged, so were its warts and imperfections. But shrink the world into a scale of one inch, or less, for every real-life foot, and you had nothing but cute. Like the seven refrigerators I'd be taking home today, all under six inches in height. I couldn't wait to stock the one-inch freezer shelves with half-inch cartons of ice cream.

Jody, today's sales associate at SuperKrafts, peered into our basket. "Do you need any stoves or sinks to go with?" she asked.

"We have a ton of those," my granddaughter answered, emptying the basket onto the counter. The assortment of little wooden, plastic, and metal refrigerators, toppled out, joined by a few accessories Maddie had picked up for her own miniature project. "I'm doing a skating scene," she explained. "These pipe cleaners are for the trees. And Grandma and I are making a mini-restaurant where you can see into the kitchen in the back. That's why we need these." She pointed to the stainless steel fridges. "I'm making the tables out of cupcake holders, the ones where all the pleating looks like a tablecloth."

Too much information, I figured, but Maddie supplemented her explanation with hand gestures until Jody nodded her appreciation.

Jody ran our items across the magic red scanner, pausing now and then for a judgment of "cute," or "adorable," supporting my theory of miniatures. I was ready to write a check for the amount displayed on the screen, when a loud voice interrupted the transaction.

"Hold it, Jody." The directive came from a woman in a red apron that clashed with her chemically enhanced hair color. Bebe Mellon, my friend and the store manager, rushed down an aisle toward us. "Don't forget to give Gerry the special discount," she ordered.

"Goody," Maddie said, as if she herself had toiled for the money we'd spend.

"Your grandma earned it," Bebe said, ruffling Maddie's red curls, a shade darker than Bebe's, but home grown. "We probably wouldn't even be in business if it weren't for her."

"Thanks to Skip, not me," I said, giving due credit to my homicide-detective nephew for straightening out some problems that had befallen SuperKrafts in general and Bebe in particular, during its early days in town.

While Jody wrapped and bagged our purchases and Maddie gave a running commentary on the use of each item, Bebe pulled me aside. "Guess what, Gerry. I've been invited to staff the SuperKrafts booth at the big show in New York City. It's the biggest crafts fair on the East Coast. They get, like, three hundred vendors from all over the world. This year Corporate wants us to highlight the expanded miniatures sections in their regional stores. Like ours." Bebe waved her arm toward the area of the store where Maddie and I had spent most of our time.

"That's very exciting. What exactly will you be doing?"

Bebe's face lit up as she answered. "My partner and I will be setting up our display, of course, and we'll be part of all the raffles, like almost every hour during the day. A lot of lucky people will win room boxes. And, of course, we'll be selling supplies, with special deals for crafts groups and small, independent crafts stores. Plus there will be workshops." She took a deep breath, but her excited demeanor didn't go away. "I'll be teaching a session on making a lighted Christmas room box." She took a well-deserved breath and smiled. "See why I'm so wired?"

Bebe had weathered a tough life and had come by this new job honestly. I was happy things were turning around for her. I tried to match her enthusiasm with a big hug. "It sounds like a lot of fun, and what a vote of confidence in you."

Bebe nodded. "Uh-huh. Even though I haven't been with SuperKrafts that long."

"I can see why you'd be excited."

She leaned in closer to me. "Yeah, but the fair is next weekend. Truth is, I was just supposed to help their New York person out with ideas and reports about what customers in California were asking for, but she got sick and they asked me to step in since I already know all the ins and outs. So, I was their second choice. Or maybe even third." Bebe shrugged. "I don't care, though. It's a chance to meet the bigwigs and see Manhattan at Christmas time." Bebe drew a deep, happy breath. "And if I do well, who knows what's in store. Ha, ha. Get it? What's in *store*?"

"Good one," I said, and laughed, to prove I got it. I made a move to rescue Jody from my granddaughter and steer Maddie home, but Bebe wasn't finished.

"It sounds like a lot of fun, right?"

"It certainly does," I said, with the sincerity of a native New Yorker. Now living in a snow-free zone of California, about forty miles south of San Francisco, I could only dream of the days when I'd skated on real ice in Central Park, window-shopped on Fifth Avenue, stood in awe when the Rockefeller Center tree lights came on. The words to an endless album of holiday songs ran through my head, and I could almost taste the first snowflakes on my tongue. "You can't beat the holidays in the Big Apple," I said, aware of a dreamy quality to my voice.

"Great," Bebe said. "So, you're in?"

"Excuse me?" Between my merry but confused daydreams and my rush to claim Maddie and be on our way, I'd thought I'd misheard Bebe's last comment.

"I know it's kind of last-minute. Well, okay, it really is last-minute. We'd have to leave in three days. This coming Tuesday. But, as I say, it's my chance to make a good impression. And it's definitely a two-person job."

"You mentioned you had a partner? Someone from the company, I assumed. Someone already in New York."

Bebe rubbed her hands along the front of her apron. "I was thinking of you, Gerry. I just left a message on your machine, then I looked out my office window and realized, here you are. It's meant to be."

I laughed at her joke. "I don't think so."

"I'm serious, Gerry. First of all, they're seriously understaffed in this busy season and I can't just take pot luck on the kind of help they'll give me. I told them I had the perfect solution to this last-minute glitch. They've agreed to fly you out with me. Especially once I mentioned that you're the best at this kind of thing, very experienced. You've been running crafts fairs and raffles around here since I've known you. Right?"

"That's true, but—"

"So you'll come?"

I scratched my head. To help me absorb this sudden invitation? "Bebe, I can't just pick up and—"

"Why not, Grandma? Please, please. Say we can go!"

We? I glanced down at the pleading look in Maddie's eyes. How much longer would she be clamoring to spend time with her grandmother? And how many more opportunities would I get to introduce her to the Rockettes before she became a preoccupied teenager, with daily mood swings and major shifts in interest, too grown-up for a show that featured a dance line of long-legged women with antlers on their heads? And what was so important in my life that it couldn't be postponed a week or two? I was hooked.

"Yes, we can go," I said.

Chapter 2

AS WE WALKED toward my car in sunny California, Maddie researched the weather in New York City (right now, overcast and forty-three degrees) and the top not-to-be-missed sights in Manhattan. She toted our refrigerators and odds and ends of furniture in a medium-size plastic bag with a loop handle, thus freeing her thumbs to work her smartphone. I always found it amazing how much one could spend in a miniatures store and still need no help carrying out the purchases.

I was reeling over my quick decision to participate in a crafts fair three thousand miles away, a week from today, and so close to Christmas that it wasn't too early to set out Santa's cookies. Maddie, on the other hand, was ready to discuss what we needed to buy for the trip (lined gloves, nonslip boots, and matching scarves and caps, among other things) and how to break the news of the journey to her parents (with a youthful confidence that assumed they'd be thrilled to send their daughter off to the big city). If I didn't know better, I'd have thought Maddie knew about this change of plans weeks ahead of time.

"I'll only have to miss a few days of school, and, you know, the teachers don't really cover anything new right before vacation," Maddie explained. "We'll just be making stupid presents and cards—"

"Like the ones you give me?" I asked, chuckling, trying to stop her flow.

"Except for the ones I give you," she said, hardly breaking her rhythm. "Plus, I'd be learning about holidays around the world and singing Christmas carols in Spanish or French or something," she noted.

"I thought you liked all that."

"Instead of reading about the way other people celebrate, I'd rather go somewhere and see for myself." New York as a foreign culture? I supposed she wasn't far off. "While I'm away I'll make a journal of my trip, improving my writing skills." The way to a retired English teacher's heart, even though I saw through her clever manipulation. "That's what the other kids have to do when their parents even take them skiing at Tahoe. Then they share with the class when they get back." Maddie grinned and puffed out her bony chest as much as she could. "I'll be telling them about a real trip. Across the whole country in a plane."

I smiled as I recalled that New York City, the Bronx in particular, had played a major role in Maddie's initial venture into miniatures. For a long time she was only about kicking a soccer goal, not about choosing a dollhouse sofa or making mini-desserts from polymer clay. The first project to attract her attention was a model of the apartment where Ken and I had spent our first years. He was an architect and applied his talents to a beautiful replica of that six-hundred-square-foot space. The illness preceding his death interrupted the work and that dollhouse lay unfinished for some years though I worked on dozens of others. Maddie had lured me back to it, and to the land of the living, by asking to finish it with me. My fondest wish had come true—that my preteen granddaughter would somehow catch my enthusiasm for miniatures. The real building Ken and I lived in had been leveled to the ground in an early redevelopment effort in the Bronx, but the spirit of our apartment lived on in miniature in my own California living room.

Maddie and I deposited our purchases on the backseat of my car, and walked across the street to Willie's Bagels. As soon as we were seated, Maddie called her parents, expecting at least one of them to be home on a Saturday morning. Lucky for us, it was her mother, my daughter-in-law, Mary Lou, and the flexible one of the parental unit, who answered. Maddie's side of the conversation was upbeat.

"Guess what, Mom?"

"No, it's not about today. Grandma's taking me to New York!"

"When? Pretty soon. Tuesday, I think." Maddie kicked her skinny legs mightily as she did when she was excited. She looked at me and grinned when I held up three fingers.

"Yeah, we're leaving in three days. Some kind of crafts fair with her friend, Mrs. Mellon. Remember her? Grandma and I are going to help her set up the booth in the hotel."

"I don't know the name of it yet, but it's in New York. Isn't it awesome?"

"Okay, thanks Mom. Love you, too. Here's Grandma. She'll tell you more about it."

I didn't know that much more, but I filled in some details for Mary Lou, whose main concern was my son, Richard, the surgeon, who treated every new idea as a major medical procedure, to be researched, thought about for weeks, and decided upon with great care. Second and third opinions were welcome. His rule of caution was great for his patients, but sometimes tough on his family.

"Richard might be nervous about this," Mary Lou said. "He gets a little tense around the holidays anyway, with all the change of routine."

"Hmm, that's news to me."

Mary Lou laughed. "But I'll take care of it." How well I knew, both that Richard would bristle at his little girl's making a last-minute trip across the country, and that Mary Lou could handle him. "We might need a planning meeting," she added.

"No kidding."

Dinner at my house this evening would be the kick-off meeting for the trip. I had all afternoon to plan it.

I looked up and saw my fiancé, Henry Baker, and his granddaughter, joining us as scheduled, at Lincoln Point's number one bagel shop. The fact that Willie's was the only shop in town with fresh bagels had little to do with its high rating. Family ownership through three generations had paid off for the small business. Henry, tall and lanky (which might also be said of me), with eleven-year-old Taylor in tow, wore his usual broad smile. He kissed me on the cheek and gave Maddie a quick back rub that got her giggling. He might have thought her excited look was for him and Taylor only, and not some *totally* awesome news.

"What's the big news?" he asked her, perhaps more perceptive than I gave him credit for.

"Guess where I'm going?" Maddie asked, in a voice that might have included the other half dozen Willie's patrons. Then, to my great surprise, she sang a few lines from a Frank Sinatra hit that she'd heard many times at her late grandfather's knee. "Start spreading the news…"

What followed were squeals and hugs from the two tweens, while Henry and I got to the business of ordering bagels and drinks. I'd reconnected with Henry at a reunion of alums from Abraham Lincoln High School, our former employer, though we'd met only briefly during our active teaching years. We'd both taken our granddaughters to the reunion, for a confluence of reasons. The four of us bonded over the children's pool hour at the host hotel, and at a boring banquet later. Though they lived ten miles apart—Maddie in Palo Alto and Taylor down the street from me in Lincoln Point—the girls had been BFFs since the day they met. A very handy development for Henry and me.

Today Willie's provided the perfect background for our mid-morning snack—Willie's décor was all New York, on all walls, probably because the bagel-family ancestors had entered the United States by way of Ellis Island. Framed black-and-white photographs of the major bridges leading into the city were interspersed with views of Times Square, the Statue of Liberty, and many other landmarks recognizable even to kids Maddie and Taylor's age.

Maddie could hardly contain herself as she told Henry and Taylor about the upcoming excursion. I'd already done the math (though not my strong suit), so I knew that our time in New York overlapped the Baker family trip to Hawaii, about three thousand miles in the opposite direction. The Bakers—Henry, Taylor, and Taylor's parents, both lawyers—had planned a getaway week on Maui to coincide with a conference. "The legal term is 'boondoggle,'" Henry had joked. They were leaving on Thursday, two days after us. The contrast wasn't lost on me: Henry and his family had been planning the Hawaii trip for a couple of months; Maddie and I had just over two days to get ready for New York.

"I can't believe it's the same week," Taylor said, chewing on a piece of her long blond hair. "Or we could go with you." Maddie and Taylor hugged each other, in a premature bon voyage session common to tweens, and bemoaned the fact that they'd be taking separate vacations.

"It is too bad," Henry said. "I'd always hoped you'd show me your Bronx."

"There's lots of time. What's that expression? 'Maybe next year.' Isn't that what the Yankees say?"

"It's 'Wait till next year,' and I think it started with the Chicago Cubs, but so what?"

"I should never attempt to use a sports metaphor," I admitted. Henry smiled. "I know we'll get there together some time."

I wondered why I wasn't as disappointed as Henry seemed to be. Why did I feel instead a sense of relief that he couldn't join us for our week in New York? My mind went over tricky ground. Maybe I wanted the Bronx and Manhattan to belong to me and Ken alone, not to me and my new fiancé. But that didn't make sense. First, I probably wouldn't get anywhere near the Bronx on this trip; and second, I loved Henry, in a way that I never thought I could again. And I was happily committed to our approaching marriage. Maybe I simply wanted some time alone with my granddaughter, just Maddie and me. And Bebe, and eight million other people, I mused.

"Gerry?" Henry waved his hand to wake me up. "Everything okay? I'll bet you're making up your to-do list right now. If not, you ought to be."

"You got me," I said, and returned to my coffee.

While I'd been analyzing myself, the girls had swapped promises to send postcards and fill requests for souvenirs. A Hawaiian print shirt for Maddie, and an I ♥ NY shirt for Taylor. Not even their favorite chocolate chip cookies kept the girls quiet for very long. How convenient that neither Henry nor I could get a word in edgewise.

THE original plan for this weekend had been that Maddie would stay with me until Sunday evening when her parents would pick her up. But in the light of the New York development, we all thought it best if they came for dinner sooner—tonight, Saturday—instead, and took her home to Palo Alto to get ready. I thought back to the days when that branch of the Porter family lived in Los Angeles, and how much better it was to have them fewer than ten miles away.

There was no question of how Maddie and I would spend Saturday afternoon once we got back from Willie's. We had to review the projects we'd begun for Christmas, figure out what we might need for colder weather, and check out the calendar of exhibits and shows in New York during our week. Fortunately, a SuperKrafts administrator at headquarters was taking care of the logistics of travel and hotel.

After a quick grilled cheese sandwich (Maddie needed lunch even after our hefty bagels-and-cookies snack), we headed for my primary crafts room. Henry and others had wisely pointed out that the rest of my house was a secondary crafts room, with dollhouses and room boxes in various stages of completion scattered throughout my four-bedroom Eichler. The Eichler design, with all rooms built around a courtyard, had always motivated me to at least keep the center atrium clear.

Maddie surveyed the cluttered crafts table and picked up her

contribution to a school raffle, coming up next weekend. I'd
called the organizer as soon as we got home to arrange a pickup for Monday. "I know I was supposed to do this skating scene
myself but I want to make a second one for New York, and I'll
never finish in time unless you help, Grandma."

"No problem."

Maddie had already made a few trees from chenille sticks,
a variation of what we called pipe cleaners in my day. The new
version was softer, but basically the same structure of bendable
wire covered in colored fuzz. She'd carefully wrapped the green
"branches" around the brown "tree trunk," with the larger pieces
on the bottom, and stuck them in a circle on a foam base that
surrounded a plain glass mirror. I thought all that was left was to
dab a bit of white glitter glue on the branches to simulate sparkly
snowflakes.

"I hope it snows," Maddie said, and I figured she meant not
here in Lincoln Point, where it almost never had, but in New
York while we were there. She'd drawn the skating figures, cut
them out, and was ready to stand them up on the ice-cum-mirror.
"I need lots more trees. If you have a gazillion trees, they don't
look so fake."

I'd taught her that little trick—flaws didn't show up as much
when large quantities were involved—and now I had to pay up.
I dug in and made a dozen more trees, squeezing them in between those that Maddie had already stuck into the foam base.
The crowning touch was a string of lights, meant to be a necklace
of tiny plastic bulbs, across the whole circle of trees.

A phone call interrupted our wallowing in admiration of our
newest miniature scene.

"Hey," Bebe said.

"Are you calling to tell me we have to leave tonight?" I asked.

"Ha, ha. No, I just want to confirm our flight this coming
Tuesday, returning the following Tuesday. A car will pick you up
at home, et cetera, et cetera. I'll forward you the email with the
itinerary as soon as I get it. Probably later today. Maybe we can
have lunch tomorrow or Monday and go over some details, like

what our space will be like in the hotel ballroom, et cetera, et cetera. Did I tell you the venue is right near Grand Central Station?" Bebe took a breath. "I'm so excited."

"I couldn't tell." I wondered how Bebe had managed to spread the word so quickly. Jeff, Bebe's brother, had left a message on my phone telling me how great it was that I was going to help his sister and see the amazing holiday sights. Several members of our local crafts group had sent emails with congratulations, expressions of envy, and specious offers to join us, as well as tips on how to arrange the booth.

Now that the inexplicable worry about being accompanied by Henry and Taylor had passed, I was beginning to feel the excitement that only a trip like this could bring. So many passions coming together. Working at a crafts booth in the middle of Manhattan with Maddie at my side, holiday decorations, food, and music everywhere. If the hotel was near Grand Central, then it was just a brisk walk to the New York Public Library and Bryant Park. A modest cab ride to the Met. I could think of no downside.

I mustered even more excitement when I thought of my old East Coast friends with whom I'd stayed in touch. "Your Bronx peeps," my nephew Skip called them, though in fact, none of them still lived in the Bronx. Many had retired and moved to Florida for reasons obvious to those who had weathered a nor'easter; others went north to the outlying counties of upstate New York where they could have a bigger lawn but missed easy access to a subway. At least I could send them all "remember when" postcards. The favored few moved to the more expensive neighborhoods of Manhattan, like my friend and former Bronx neighbor, Cynthia Bishop. Cynthia and I had commuted to college together, taking the IND train downtown to the Washington Square arch. We were seldom lucky enough to get seats and ended up grasping a pole, me with one hand holding my English lit book open, Cynthia trying to annotate her cumbersome biology text.

Though I'd talked to Cynthia only a few times this year, we'd sent notes, electronic and paper, regularly. She'd ended a long career as a nurse in the boroughs' hospitals, and took a post-retirement job with the government, as a consultant evaluating worker's compensation cases. "A lot of paperwork and a lot of driving, but much easier on the back and feet," she'd explained. A few months ago, she'd moved into her aunt's Manhattan apartment, an arrangement suitable to both. I looked forward to seeing them. It was time to make phone contact with the Upper West Side.

I addressed Maddie. "Sweetheart, why don't you check your closet for any clothes you have here that you might want for the trip?"

Maddie skipped away and I dialed my college friend and gave her the good news.

"This Tuesday?" Cynthia asked, her voice rising to emphasize the day of the week. "Gerry, I can't believe this. It's so creepy."

Creepy? I thought she'd be thrilled that I was practically on my way to her apartment and could deliver Christmas presents in person. On the contrary, she seemed to be crying. "I was going to call you today to let you know—Aunt Elsie died yesterday. A heart attack, they said."

My own heart sank. "I'm so sorry, Cynthia. This must be incredibly hard for you. I know how close you were." An understatement, since Aunt Elsie had raised Cynthia when her parents died. "What happened? The last time we talked, you said she was doing well."

Cynthia cleared her throat, still struggling to speak. "That's just it, Gerry. She *was* doing well. I told you, she had hip replacement surgery last month and she still had some pain, but it was under control. She's also been on blood pressure medication for years and they're saying she forgot to take those pills and that precipitated a heart attack. I'm so upset. They determined that she forgot to take her meds, by reason of old age."

"They called it that? Old age?"

"Not in so many words, but that's what they meant. Better than their first consideration, which was, you know, that it was deliberate."

Suicide. I understood why Cynthia wouldn't want to say the word out loud. She'd spent a great deal of her time helping Aunt Elsie enjoy her senior years. Suicide was not an option that was easy for a family to live with. I decided I didn't need to say the word, either. I preferred to remember Aunt Elsie as the strong woman of our youth, a former WAC, at the time the only woman I knew who had worn the uniform of the United States Army.

"I'm so sorry you have to go through this."

"I don't believe them."

"Them?"

"The police, the medical examiner, whoever. They said that when she needed that extra prescription for the pain from the surgery, she lost track and forgot to take her blood pressure pills as well. That's what they decided. As if being ninety-five automatically makes you dumb." Cynthia paused. "I think Aunt Elsie was murdered, Gerry. In fact, the more I think about it, the more I'm sure of it."

"Murdered? What makes you say that? I assume they looked for the pills she supposedly didn't take?"

Cynthia was silent for what seemed a long time. I took that as a "Yes." It turned out to be a "Yes, but."

"There's also some money missing," Cynthia said after a while.

"You mean cash that was around the house?"

A hesitant "Yes."

I guessed it might have been the theft of cash that pushed Cynthia over the edge to a motive for someone to murder her aunt. "How much?" I asked, meaning "enough to kill over?"

"I have no idea. But a lot. I'll explain when I see you. I know you'll figure this all out, Gerry."

I gulped and took a tense breath. "All I can do is promise to be there for you, Cynthia. I can't tell you how sorry I am. Aunt Elsie always treated me like family. I'll do whatever I can to help you through this. "

"That's what I wanted to hear. I know you work with your nephew sometimes and I'm counting on your help."

Uh-oh. So that was it. My nephew. I was sure she meant Skip
Gowen, high-ranking (to me) homicide detective in the Lincoln
Point Police Department. "Cynthia, I can't—"

"Remember that time when we were juniors at Hudson and
you figured out who was finding a free way to get the drinks
from the vending machine in the commuters lounge?"

"Yes, but—"

"And the time you helped the campus police with that serial
mugger near the library?"

"Cynthia, those incidents were simply—"

"Besides, you talk about Skip a lot and I can listen between
the lines. I can tell you've been a big asset to him and his department."

What had I told Cynthia about LPPD cases? Nothing that
would lead her to believe that I was anything like the pseudo-
detective she was making me out to be. "You have it wrong,
Cynthia. I—"

"The police here won't listen to me. Just because Aunt Elsie
was old, they assume she somehow caused her own death. But I
don't buy it. Her mind was as sharp as it ever was. At least I can
be sure you'll care enough to get to the bottom of this. When are
you getting in?"

My head was reeling. I couldn't very well tell Cynthia that I
didn't care enough about Aunt Elsie to investigate on her behalf,
which wasn't true to begin with, but neither could I tell her I'd
investigate her aunt's death. I wondered how she even knew that
I'd helped Skip a few times? That was a mystery in itself. Right
now the only thing I could do was answer her question.

"We get in on Tuesday night. I'm not sure what time."

"Probably about five, local time. That's the usual nonstop
from the West Coast. Why don't you come here for dinner and I
can give you the details of the NYPD's so-called investigation."

"Let's not plan on Tuesday. I'll be with Maddie and the woman I told you about, my friend, Bebe Mellon. For all I know
we might have to check in with the fair organizers or the hotel

people right away. There might even be some prep work to do that evening."

"No way. You have to have dinner."

Besides my reputation of being a wimp when dealing with Cynthia's brand of assertiveness, there was another reason for my inability to refuse her. Cynthia worked for many years as a registered nurse, and when Ken was diagnosed with leukemia, she dropped everything and came to California. She spent three weeks helping set up doctors through her extended network and arranged for services we didn't know existed. Then she stayed on his case from a distance and did everything possible to help us both through a difficult time.

My thoughts turned to my initial commitment to Bebe (who had her own brand of assertiveness) and the fact that SuperKrafts was footing the bill for my stay in New York. Conflicting loyalties—the worst kind of decision. I made one more stab at reasoning with my longtime friend.

"Cynthia, I'll need to work. I'm being paid to do a job." Only a slight exaggeration. I didn't tell her about Maddie's lineup of sights not to be missed. "But of course, I will definitely make time to see you." I hoped I hadn't insulted her.

"Great, Gerry. I can hardly wait. I'll have all the paperwork, police reports, and so on, ready."

Some people were hard to insult. I hung up, unsure of what I'd agreed to do or not do. I wasn't even clear on whether Cynthia knew not to expect me for dinner. She'd had the last word, after all.

The downside had shown itself.

Chapter 3

I LOVED A full house. Saturday evening's group of ten called for an insert to the dining room table, extending it into the living room, almost to my seldom-used hearth. Maddie and her parents; my nephew Skip and June Chinn, his girlfriend and my neighbor; my triple buddy, Beverly Gowen (who was my late husband's sister, Skip's mother, and my best friend) and her new husband, Nick Marcus; Henry; and Taylor sat around the rectangular table. Five of us had a view of my patio, with its pansies, golden mums, and dark pink cyclamen; the other five could admire the three-foot potted ficus tree in my atrium.

Although I'd expressed the need to empty my fridge and freezer, my guests brought salads and desserts, perfect additions to my chicken pot pie. The noise level was high at this dinner, a bon voyage party of sorts, with several conversations flying around the room.

"I still wish Grandpa and me were going with you," Taylor said, with a sweet pout and kids-these-days grammar that I'd seen and heard often.

"Don't worry about your mail and newspapers and stuff, Gerry. I'll take care of them," June offered. "And if there's trash or anything, just let me know and I'll make sure it gets taken away."

"We'll come by, too, in case there's late package delivery or something," Bev said.

"Or to see if there's been a break-in," retired cop Nick added.

"I can't wait to see the Rockettes dressed like toy soldiers and do that falling-like-dominos thing," Maddie said. "I saw it on YouTube."

"I read that a woman had an eight-thousand-dollar necklace ripped off her throat in the subway," my son, Richard, the glass-half-empty guy, warned us. "Do not take the subway."

"And do not miss the Met," Mary Lou advised. "There's a great exhibit of Mary Cassatt paintings on exhibit now. And even if that's too crowded, just browsing their permanent collection is heavenly."

"If she could afford an eight-thousand-dollar necklace, why was she riding the subway?" June asked. "I'd have taken a limo."

"Do not take the subway," Richard repeated, this time holding his fork straight up for emphasis.

"Did you know there are thirty-six dancers in the line, and sometimes they have live animals in the show," Maddie added, to anyone who was listening to her Rockette pitch.

"Make sure you guys don't stray into fringe neighborhoods," Richard predictably advised.

"They get the animals from the zoo in Central Park," Maddie explained, to those who cared.

"I just wish I could be there when the NYPD finds out Gerry Porter thinks they're all her nephews," Skip said.

"What's a fringe neighborhood?" Taylor asked.

"I have to throw in one New York cop joke," Nick said. "Do you know how a New York City race is different from all the others?" He paused for effect. "It's the only one where the starting gun gets return fire." Nick and I were the only ones who laughed, possibly because none of the others present had listened long enough to hear the punch line.

"I hope you have a great time and come back safe," Henry said, summing it all up.

As if it were our birthdays, everyone had come up with little gifts for Maddie and me. Travel-size cosmetic products, bed socks, extra scarves, and fleece-lined gloves. Even with so little notice,

Mary Lou, ever the artist, made three-dimensional bon voyage
cards with good wishes expressed in her lovely handwriting. An
artist's handwriting, when she wanted her messages to be read.
Anyone watching would have thought we were off on a month-
long excursion. If the idea was to make sure we wouldn't forget
them, it was all unnecessary.

JUNE, the tech editor next door who claimed to suffer from
"too much chair time," left before dessert for a session with her
personal trainer. Not that anyone could tell from her tiny, seem-
ingly fat-free body that she needed help. The rest of us moved to
the other end of the living room where my resourceful daughter-
in-law served coffee and what her Palo Alto bakery called "genuine New York cheesecake." I told her I'd bring back samples from
around Manhattan for comparison. I had a certain Seventh Avenue deli in mind, as well as one in Times Square.

"I love New York cheesecake," Maddie said, in keeping with
her love affair with the city, less than one day old and sight un-
seen. No one was surprised when she asked for seconds.

Threads of conversation from the table were left behind, others were picked up. I absorbed lots of travel advice and offers for
help with the inevitable pre-trip errands. At about nine o'clock,
Maddie and Taylor said tearful good-byes, as if they were parting
forever. Henry promised to swing by tomorrow and take care of
whatever I needed.

More good-byes, then only Skip was left. "Let's have it," he
said. "I get the sense that there's something you're not looking
forward to about this trip."

I tried to act surprised at the idea. "What makes you say
that?"

"I'm a detective."

"What else?"

"I've seen how excited you get when you're just going to
San Jose for a miniatures show, or to shop at Shellie's in San
Carlos where you buy all that ridiculously tiny furniture. Now
you're going to work at a humongous show in the Big Apple,

with probably miles of crafts, and I don't see any real enthusiasm. When you think no one's looking, your face is...I don't know, sober."

"I have a lot to do for the trip. Pay bills, get cash, dig out winter clothes—"

Skip ignored my pitiful attempt at defense. "I know you're not afraid to fly, and you have friends in New York, and you'll have the Little Squirt with you—"

"She doesn't like to be called that anymore," I said. Anything to change the subject, but Skip forged ahead.

"So something else is making this a good news/bad news thing. Are you going to miss Henry? Is that it?"

"Right," I said, but too quickly.

"Uh-uh. That's not it." Skip sat back on the couch, took a sip of coffee, and waited. I imagined just such a pose in an LPPD interview room with a suspected felon. He was good at his job: I was as intimidated as if I were a hardened criminal with a bare light bulb over my head.

I drew in a deep breath, then let it out slowly, and told him about Aunt Elsie's death.

"Were you close to Elsie as well as her niece?"

"Not so much lately, but when we were young, she was a big part of my life. She was essentially Cynthia's mother."

Skip screwed up his nose, the way he did when he was twelve and trying to figure out a math problem. "Something else?"

"You *are* a good detective," I said. After another long breath, I told him about Cynthia's concerns. "And she thinks I can help," I added, in a softer voice.

Skip laughed and sat up straight. "I wonder where she got that idea."

"I don't know. Seriously, Skip. I would never tell her about your cases here. She remembers that I was always reading Sherlock Holmes, and she tells these little stories about me from when we were kids."

"Tell me one."

I waved away his request.

He took another cookie, crossed one leg over the other, and resumed his patient, waiting posture. "I'm in no hurry."

"Okay," I said, and reached back to a minor success in Manhattan. "Once, we were shopping together in midtown and I suspected a woman of shoplifting. I told Cynthia I thought the woman had taken clothes into the dressing room, then put her own clothes over the new ones, and walked out onto the retail floor, headed for the door with all the clothes still on."

"Why did you suspect her?"

"Her jacket was tighter across the shoulders than when she went in, and I noticed that it couldn't be buttoned. And, also, from the way she bit her lip and looked around, I knew something was off. I didn't report her or anything, but a few minutes later the alarm went off and store security took her aside."

"And Cynthia thought you were a detective genius. I get it. I think you are, too. Are you planning to look into her aunt's death?"

"I wish I knew."

"I know you. You'll let yourself be dragged into it, whether you want to or not."

I shook my head. "Okay, that's enough." I took the opportunity to retreat to the kitchen for refills on coffee and my homemade ginger cookies that Skip loved.

"Can I give you a little background?" he asked, grabbing another cookie.

"Absolutely."

"There are a lot of people who prey on the elderly, mostly for financial reasons. You've got fraud, gimmicks like giveaways, fake cruises, and sweepstakes or some fantastic investments that will triple their money. All you have to do is—"

"Hand over your life savings."

"Uh-huh. The stereotype is that old people are poorly informed as well as mentally failing. Easy marks."

I nodded. "I know all that. But I'm not about to go into Aunt Elsie's financial records. I barely understand my own."

"But I'll bet you'll be great at helping Cynthia think through the situation. She's very close to it and maybe needs someone more objective to look at things."

"Maybe."

"Elders are the fastest growing age group in the country. Every week we're getting briefed on resources available in town or through the state or federal agencies, like this new ombudsman program the LPPD is pushing. Of course, New York City is a mega-center for this issue. I read an article that said they have something like a hundred thousand older adults victimized each year in their own homes, and most of the cases—like, ninety-five percent—aren't reported until it's too late."

Too late for Aunt Elsie. But I remembered that she'd had Cynthia to protect her. "Wouldn't that apply mostly to those who live alone?" I asked Skip.

"Not necessarily. Sometimes it's relatives who are the guilty parties. Exploiting their older kin. They're too poor or they can't wait to get what they think is coming to them."

"Not in this case. I'm sure of that."

"Then find out if there's been a new so-called friend in Elsie's life recently. Someone she met casually, maybe at a market or a church function, or just while she's out on her daily walk. Older people tend to adopt routines like that, and someone could have been watching. Then that person worms his or her way into Elsie's life. It's easy to get an older person who maybe doesn't have a lot of friends left to trust a stranger."

"But she had Cynthia, who's not only her niece, but worked as a nurse for many years."

"That may not have been enough, no matter how much Cynthia loved her. Elsie may have thought it was important to find friends of her own. A small expression of freedom and independence from her niece. It doesn't mean she didn't love and trust Cynthia, but she was probably a responsible adult at one point, with a job or a household to run—"

"She was in the army," I said.

"Really?" I nodded. "Well, there you go. I guess she could have felt she could do at least some little thing on her own."

"Like finding a friend without ties to Cynthia."

"Exactly."

"She might even have thought she was helping Cynthia, giving her a break," I offered.

Skip nodded. "You got it."

"I should find out who comes in when Cynthia's not there. Like a visiting nurse, or even a person delivering meds."

"You should do that. I mean, if you decided to investigate."

"Right, if." On my way back to the kitchen for more coffee, I stopped at the couch and gave my nephew a big hug.

Before he left, Skip reached into his jacket pocket and pulled out a blue-and-gold patch. He handed it to me. "Take this in case you need it."

I took the item and read the embroidered printing. "An LPPD patch? You just happened to have one in your pocket?"

"I had a feeling that you might need it."

"Why? You think I can't go on a trip without needing police help?"

"Can you blame me? But, I'm giving you this to carry on a long custom. If you find yourself in the office of an NYPD detective for any reason, or happen to run into any one of the thirty-five thousand or so NYPD officers, give this to him."

"Or her?"

"Or her. And ask for one back for me. It's a custom."

"So you said." I took the patch and raised my right hand. "On the off-chance that I meet one of New York's finest, I'll carry out this mission."

Skip laughed, turned to leave, then swiveled back in the next second. "Maybe I should go with you?"

I pushed him out the door. It was ten o'clock and I still had a lot to do. What I tried not to do was rethink my decision to go to New York in the first place.

LEFT to myself, I did two loads of wash and made three batches of ginger cookies, some to leave around town lest my friends forget me, and some to take with us on the plane. Between my tasks, I fielded a few more calls and emails from friends and relatives.

From Bebe: The limo company would pick her up first, me second, and then Maddie in Palo Alto. Could I be ready at four-thirty A.M.? (Of course.)

From Maddie, way past her bedtime: Did it ever rain in New York and, if so, should she take an umbrella? (No, if we needed one, we could buy an umbrella from a street vendor for a couple of dollars. The same was true for a host of other necessities—books, scarves, pretzels, and designer purses. Don't worry, New York has more of everything.)

From Maddie, fifteen minutes later: Was it okay to wear jeans to the Radio City show? (Yes, if you were under forty. I was taking my best pants.)

From various crafters in my miniatures group by email: New York must have ten times the number of miniatures stores as Santa Clara County. Could I pick up a half-scale bathtub (for Karen), a one-inch-scale floor lamp (for Susan), tiny figurines like the Statue of Liberty or the Chrysler Building (for Mabel), and a wood inlay coffee table (for Linda, money no object.) (Of course.)

From Henry: He loved me and would miss me. (Ditto.)

From Maddie, the last call before she climbed into bed, she promised: Could she come over on Monday to finish up some of the scenes she'd been making for Christmas presents? (No, she needed to spend time with her parents and finish packing.)

Another task accomplished was to drag out my large suitcase and my travel checklist. I packed some of the basics for hotel living, then organized the scenes Maddie and I had selected for display and raffles at the show. They'd go in our carry-on luggage with a separate, TSA-approved bag that held indispensable tools for a crafts booth staffer—small scissors, two kinds of tape, four kinds of glue, punches, markers, a ruler, and card stock. I hoped I'd have room for my clothes.

I made a third, or fourth, to-do list for Sunday and Monday and crawled into bed a little before midnight.

I couldn't get Cynthia and Aunt Elsie out of my mind. Was it as short a time ago as this morning that I'd decided to go to New York, called my friend, and learned of Elsie's death? In my semi-awake state, I tried to go back to the time before Maddie and I met Bebe at SuperKrafts. My image was distorted by the presence of thirty-six long-legged dancers falling backwards onto each other, to the tune of "The Parade of the Wooden Soldiers."

SUNDAY passed quickly with cancellations and rescheduling of lunch dates and appointments, and checking off other items on my lists. I put together a folder with slips of paper as reminders of promises I'd made to my Lincoln Point peeps. A kind of New York shopping list, consisting of cryptic notes such as "T-shirts & key chains for all." I considered myself fortunate when calls from everyone in my friends-and-family plan stopped coming in by midnight.

I shouldn't have been surprised by the call from Mary Lou, around nine the next morning.

"Richard is going nuts," she said.

"Anything in particular, or just general angst about his daughter running loose in the evil city—the city he was born in, I might add."

"I'll spare you the whole list, but number one right now is how is his baby going to get to the airport? He's afraid a limo is going to pull up and Maddie will be expected to get in and ride with a strange man with a black hat. I'm surprised that he hasn't booked us on the flight."

I spelled out the logistics for Mary Lou and assured her that both Bebe and I would be in the car when it arrived for Maddie. "Problem solved," I said, wishing my deeper problems could be handled with such expediency. I'd have been happy even figuring out what they were.

"Say, while we're talking, Mom, have you and Henry set a date?"

I admired my daughter-in-law, the insightful artist that she was, but was she also tele-psychic? "Why would you ask that right now?"

"We're afraid Henry is going to follow you to New York and you'll come back married."

"Not a chance," I said, not a little distressed at how vehement I was.

"You're not going to deny us the pleasure of a wedding?"

"Of course not." I tried to sound thrilled at the thought of being the center of attention at the gala everyone seemed to want.

HENRY and I spent most of Monday together, shuffling between our (life-size) houses. My favorite retired shop teacher was now using his skills for his own projects. And mine. He had one last piece of white scalloped trim to add to our (one-inch scale) blue cottage before the dollhouse would be ready for a local school raffle. I watched as he smeared glue on both surfaces, pressed the trim against the roof, and clamped it in place.

I pulled him off his stool and declared a lunch break. I'd made reservations at a new restaurant outside town, one with a European flavor that used cloth table linens. "You have fifteen minutes to change," I said.

EVEN at one in the afternoon, the restaurant was dark, the only light coming from the candles at each table. Henry tilted his menu this way and that, straining to read it against the light reflections.

"I think this place is meant for office trysts," he said, indicating the romantic, flowery décor.

"It's a little more formal than I anticipated."

"I should have worn my tux." Not that he owned one. "Speaking of formal wear"— Henry put down his menu and leaned across to me—"didn't we say we'd set a date this weekend?"

I gulped at the segue. "Now?" I said.

"You wouldn't be stalling, would you?"

I shook my head, but I knew I was. Stalling. I blamed New

York. I had been ready to set a date, until Saturday morning. The upcoming trip was taking me back to my past in so many ways. Back to my youth, to college, to Ken, to Richard's birth. I thought I'd settled all that in my mind. Henry and I were both moving on from long, satisfying marriages that had ended sadly, in illnesses and the deaths of our spouses. Henry was my future. Why wasn't I ready for *that* trip?

"It's just, with the holidays coming up, and now this travel…"

"How about the first weekend of the new year?"

"For what?"

Henry sat back and blew out a breath, the way he did when he was disappointed. Or exasperated. As if he'd hammered a nail at a bad angle and split the wood.

In a second I was aware of my mistake. I mentally slapped my head, the way Maddie did in a similar circumstance. "Henry, I'm sorry. This trip has me so preoccupied. Packing in a hurry has been dreadful. I'm afraid I'm going to get off the plane and realize I forgot something." I congratulated myself on the dodge.

"Well, whatever you forget, you can probably pick it up in Manhattan, with about a hundred choices of size and color. And if it's something back here that you forgot to do, you have a posse at your disposal. We can do it for you, whatever it is. We can lock it up, if that's the problem, or unlock it, or haul it to the dump before it smells. You'll have your phone; Maddie will have her laptop—"

"I get it."

"What else?"

I reiterated my conflict about helping Cynthia. "I'm happy to provide comfort and support any way I can, but I'm afraid she expects more."

"I sure wish I were going with you."

This time we both leaned across the table. Closing the space between us was easy since we were both at the top of the height charts. Now that his face was so near, I kissed him, and let that be my response.

Chapter 4

TUESDAY MORNING. The limo—more correctly, I knew, a sleek black Town Car, though the word "limousine" was in the title of the transportation service—would arrive at four-thirty, practically the middle of the night. I stopped my internal whining when I remembered that Bebe Mellon would have been picked up even earlier. I wondered if I'd be able to handle her pre-dawn enthusiasm.

I showered myself awake, dressed, and added the last few items to my luggage. I zipped one large suitcase, one carry-on full of crafts and fix-it supplies, and a tote that I would insist was simply a large purse and qualified as the personal item allowed by the airlines. I'd followed my usual procedure of wearing two pairs of socks so I could remove the outer pair after I'd walked on the less-than-sanitary linoleum that covered the security area.

I cruised through my house one more time, making sure small appliances were unplugged, and checking the locks on the windows and the patio doors in the living room and my bedroom, even though I knew Henry would be stopping by before he left, to make the same tour, to be followed by Skip while the Bakers were in Hawaii. I paid a visit to Maddie's bedroom, formerly her father's, to be sure there was no device, charger, or old food lurking in a corner. Then, dressed in my most comfortable slacks and jacket, I sat in my atrium and wished I were already in New York. Like many people, I loved the idea of travel but dreaded the hassle of getting there.

Give my regards to Broadway…

I'd nodded off, to be awakened by a version of a favorite song cutting through the crisp morning air. Maddie's doing, of course, and I thought I knew when she'd pulled it off. At one point, she'd asked, "Where's Herald Square, Grandma?"

It had been our little game for a couple of years—she would secretly change the ring tone on my cell, as often as possible, and certainly for holidays and special moments. This day qualified as special, by any criteria. I'd never caught my granddaughter in the act, and the pretense was that I had no idea who periodically reprogrammed my phone.

"Hey, Gerry. Ready to go?" Cynthia's voice on the phone, once I let one of my favorite songs play through.

"The car should be here in ten minutes." I tried to sound awake and excited, but imagined I failed on both counts. Not that Cynthia noticed.

"I can't wait. You have no idea how your coming has consoled me already. I'll pick up something of Aunt Elsie's, like her favorite tray or something, and start to cry"—her tone indicated she was in that state now—"and then I remember that help is on the way."

"I hope—"

"As soon as I knew your itinerary, I made arrangements for Aunt Elsie's service to be on Wednesday, so you could be there. Since no one except you and me thinks there's a problem with her death, there was never a question of having her released. Won't that be perfect?" I could think of many reasons why not. Jet lag for one. "You know how on TV the criminal always shows up at the funeral? Well, this is your chance to pick him out." I almost added a snarky "I'll check the perimeter," but Cynthia's voice had cracked further, and, more important, it was no laughing matter.

Beep. Beep. Another call coming in. Perfect timing, whoever it was. "I have to go, Cynthia. That may be my driver." A small fabrication, since the ID said otherwise.

"Okay. Safe trip," Cynthia said.

I clicked over to Maddie.

"I'm all ready, Grandma! My friend was in a limo for her vacation and she told me the car will have little bottles of water for everyone. I'm really excited."

Really?

OTHER than needing a few more hands to deal with removing shoes, keeping track of my jacket and of my granddaughter and her bright new backpack, plus handing and rehanding over my license and boarding pass, the first part of the journey went smoothly. Maddie loved every minute of the adventure and didn't calm down until we were buckled in our seats and over the Sierra. She gave Bebe and me a good laugh when, looking out the window intensely, she tried to find the boundary between California and Nevada. Until now her flying experience had been restricted to a pathway up and down California—trips to visit Ken and me when she lived in Los Angeles, and then back for Disneyland and reunions with friends after the family moved to Northern California.

About an hour into the flight, she took out her new journal, which she'd picked out herself on Sunday's family shopping trip in Palo Alto. Judging by the journal's size, about eight by ten, with an inch-or-more thickness of lined pages, she expected to have a lot to share at the preteen version of show-and-tell at school. The book was black and spiral-bound; on its cover was a three-by-five black-and-white photograph of the New York City skyline. I watched as she wrote the date on the first page, scribbled a few lines, and then reluctantly fell asleep with her head on my shoulder.

The trip was pleasantly boring, with no delays, emergency water landings, or, I hoped, lost luggage. Maddie and Bebe slept most of the way. I alternated between naps and a mystery novel on a new e-reader Richard and Mary Lou had presented me with at dinner on Saturday.

"We were saving it for Christmas," Mary Lou had said, "but this seemed like a better idea."

"It's fully loaded, but if you don't like a selection, you can just remove it from your device." Richard could always be counted on to point out the worst-case scenarios.

"You'll have hours of reading time," Mary Lou reminded me.

"And hours with Maddie to help me learn its ins-and-outs."

"That, too," Richard responded.

The exciting part came when we arrived at John F. Kennedy International Airport. Smooth, shiny floors, massive flags hanging from beams below an impossibly high ceiling, and throngs of people trailing luggage, speaking many languages—these things were just the beginning. The personal touch came as we descended two floors to Baggage.

"There's supposed to be a car waiting for us," Bebe said. "I'm looking for a sign that says 'Mellon' or"—she waved her arm at a man in a black suit—"there he is. There's the SuperKrafts sign. That's us!" She pointed to the right.

Maddie pointed to the left. "Over there," she said. "The sign says 'Porter.'"

Such a common name, I thought. Until I saw Cynthia running toward us, carrying her hand-written "Porter" sign, like a cheerleader gone rogue. The two sign-bearers, one in a black suit and cap, the other in a classic wool coat, arrived together, converging on the three of us.

"Gerry, you haven't gained an ounce," Cynthia said, bear-hugging me. "And I'll bet you still eat like there's no tomorrow, too."

"Can't help it," I said. A repeat of the same conversation we'd had all our lives together, with Cynthia envying what she called my "skinny genes," and me regretting that my hair hadn't stayed the same rich brown as hers, wishing now that I had a scarf to cover my drab, graying locks.

Cynthia looked at Maddie, whom she hadn't seen since she was a toddler. "And you, almost as tall as your grandmother and me," she said, giving Maddie the same full-strength bear hug. Since Cynthia had gained significantly more than an ounce over the years, Maddie nearly fell back into the cart rack. At the same time, Bebe was conferring with the black-capped man. I had trouble keeping up, and before I remembered my manners, Cynthia (nodding to the black cap) introduced herself to Bebe and suggested we all retrieve our luggage and follow her to her car. Bebe held it together better than I thought she would in the face of this glitch in her plan and her loss of control.

"We have a driver," she said with only a trace of "I'm in charge here" in her tone.

Maddie had taken on the role of announcing every three minutes that carousel number six was rolling and our luggage was probably on it. Fresh from her naps, my granddaughter had more energy than ever. I wondered what she would write in her journal as Bebe and Cynthia volleyed over whose car would be engaged to take us into Manhattan from the airport. The official chauffeur wisely stood aside while the decision was negotiated. I imagined he'd get paid either way.

"You'll all come to my apartment first," said Cynthia, the hostess.

"My corporate driver"—Bebe gestured toward the man, and he gave her a respectful nod—"is here to take us to the hotel," said Bebe, the businesswoman.

"I think I see our luggage. It's on carousel number six," said Maddie, the third focused member of the group.

"We'll have a bite to eat," Cynthia added to her suggestion.

"We have work to do at the hotel," Bebe announced.

The two women, one short and slim (Bebe), the other tall and heavier than she needed to be (Cynthia), continued their polite-sounding argument all the way to the carousel. I felt as though I were in charge of a group of kids, where Maddie was the most mature of them.

I distanced myself as far as possible from the decision-making, but not far enough to avoid hearing phrases like "no offense"

and "with all due respect" from each woman. In the end, we left
JFK in two vehicles—Bebe, miffed, in the chauffeured Town Car,
headed for the hotel with all our luggage, and Maddie and I in
Cynthia's midsized sedan, making our way to the Upper West
Side. I'd agreed to a quick bite at Cynthia's and promised to meet
Bebe back at the hotel no later than nine o'clock, local time.
Bebe had been kind enough not to remind me that I was flying
on SuperKrafts' dime and was expected to work; in return, Cyn-
thia did not pull out the "mourning" card.

WE'D joined rush hour traffic that rivaled anything I'd seen in
Northern or Southern California, the big difference being the
continual honking of taxis, limousines, and, now and then, an ordinary commuter. Maddie busied herself looking for Bebe in the
shiny black Town Car and searching for a glimpse of the Statue of
Liberty, her smartphone camera at the ready.

One pleasant interruption came from Henry. Taylor had been
tracking our flight on her computer and he wanted to be sure
that, indeed, we had landed.

"How's everything there?" I asked.

"The house is burning. Come right home," he said. It took
me a few seconds to catch on. I blamed jet lag. "I'll call Richard
and Mary Lou, so they'll know right away that you're there, and
you can catch your breath." Henry, thoughtful as always. I missed
him, but I was glad he was not here. How convoluted was that?

As she drove, Cynthia talked nonstop about Aunt Elsie, how
she'd wanted to be cremated, how she'd hoped Cynthia would
continue to live in the apartment that her family had lived in for
three generations.

"I'm torn, Gerry. I know how much Aunt Elsie wanted to
keep the co-op in the family, and you know I love living in Manhattan, but I always thought I'd retire to someplace warm. I'm
getting tired of trudging through these winters." I knew Cynthia
had been spending a month or so in Florida in January or Feb-
ruary where several friends from her nursing career lived. She'd

been making the trip for many years. "But, still, it would be hard to leave this home. As you'll see pretty soon, my building is one of the gems of Lincoln Square. Built in the thirties, only nineteen stories."

I heard Maddie's gasp from the backseat, and her exclamation. "Only?"

Cynthia laughed and continued. "I'm on fifteen, and I have beautiful views of Central Park. Each season is magnificent in its own way." Cynthia sounded already nostalgic about the changing seasons though moments ago she'd told us how she could do without the cold one.

"Take some time to figure out the next step," I said. "Isn't that what you told me when Ken died?" Cynthia nodded and dabbed her eyes with a tissue. "You don't have to decide now," I added.

"I know. You'd be amazed at how many offers I've had already from realtors and private buyers."

"You've put it on the market?"

"No, no," Cynthia said. "People here can be like vultures when it comes to choice real estate. Agents especially. They always seem to know when someone's leaving, or…" The word "dying" was left unsaid.

Maddie had kept her "Are we there yet" questions to a minimum, but she tucked her journal and phone into her backpack and clapped when Cynthia pulled up to a beautiful Art Deco building and announced that we were, indeed, "there." She handed her car keys to a uniformed doorman, a middle-aged man with significant girth and a pleasant demeanor. Santa—in a burgundy jacket, without the beard.

"Thanks, Duncan. It's nice to have you back. As usual, your replacements weren't half as competent," Cynthia said, handing him a bill.

"Thank you, Miss Bishop. It's good to be back." I wondered how Duncan could sound so happy to be working while his red face and watery eyes showed how cold he must be.

"I won't need the car for a few days," she said.

"Wow," Maddie said, as we entered the lobby of Cynthia's building. "You have valet parking?" An amenity that clearly impressed her more than the myriad of ornaments on the large tree and the garlands that decorated the spacious lobby entrance.

Cynthia smiled and explained. "I keep my car in a garage down the street. It's not a bad walk, but I figured you're probably not used to this cold weather." Cynthia shivered, as if to emphasize the wisdom of her choice. "Duncan Williams is our regular doorman, and he'll see that my car gets put away till the next time I need it."

"You don't use it, like, all day?" asked my California-born granddaughter.

"No need to, most of the time. I can hop a bus or take the subway, though I don't do that a lot these days. Bad knees. Easier to just hail a cab. Much easier than trying to park anywhere in midtown. I used the car a lot when Aunt Elsie was sick, for doctors' appointments. We could have taken a cab but she was more comfortable with me driving." Cynthia allowed herself a soft chuckle. "Here's my aunt's favorite New York cab one-liner. 'Anytime two or more New Yorkers get into a cab together without arguing, there's been a bank robbery around the corner.'"

Maddie laughed politely though it was clear she didn't have the context to get the reference to stereotypical cantankerous New Yorkers. As we waited in the lobby for the elevator to Cynthia's floor, Maddie's response to the moment was "I wish I lived where there was a doorman. Did you see those gold buttons, Grandma?" Again, more impressive than the gold star at the top of the tree. Had my granddaughter already forgotten her spacious Palo Alto home, with its playroom, three-car garage, and newly added swimming pool?

We took the elevator to the fifteenth floor and entered Cynthia's home. I marveled at the beautiful hardwood floors and lavish carpets in the foyer and in the open-plan dining and living room. The eclectic mix of antique and modern furniture was the hallmark of a home that had seen many generations of one family. A few tasteful Christmas pieces—a small origami Nativity scene on the walnut hutch, a poinsettia plant in front of the marble fireplace—adorned the rooms. I imagined there had been significantly merrier decorations last year and the years before. Cynthia pointed out her typically long, narrow New York City kitchen, and led us on to a large bedroom. At that point the tour took a turn for the worse.

"You can have this room, Gerry. It's normally my room, but I've fixed up Aunt Elsie's room for me this week. This one's much bigger and, you see, you have your own bathroom."

My heart did a flip. Not another bone of contention. I thought I'd made it clear that we'd be staying at the hotel with Bebe. Where I had work to do. Which was why I'd come to New York.

"Cynthia we can't—"

"It's no bother. It was actually good for me to get in there and go through some of Aunt Elsie's things, although I can't handle her clothes and more personal items yet. I'm hoping you'll help me do that. Moral support, you know? I'm storing a lot of stuff in the basement for now. Each tenant has a generous storage area next to the bike room."

"You have a bike room?" Maddie asked, eyes wide. I imagined she pictured a room lined with shiny bikes, at everyone's disposal. She walked over to the terrace doors and looked out. I followed her partway. Her series of "Wow"s hardly did justice to the view. The treetops, the buildings surrounding the park—magnificent. But I had to keep on course with my friend.

"Cynthia, we need to stay at the hotel tonight," I said, as firmly as I could. "SuperKrafts is footing the bill for—"

She held up her hand. "I know, I know, but I want you to see that this room is ready for you if you change your mind. Or if you need a break." She rubbed her hands together. "Now let's have that bite to eat."

Cynthia deftly added a place at the table, waking me up to

the fact that she hadn't planned on Maddie's presence. I gave her credit for not making a fuss over not having me to herself. But the week was just beginning.

BY eight o'clock, local time, seated at an elegant mahogany dining table that must have been Aunt Elsie's, we'd finished the "small bite." Cynthia had served clam chowder, tomato-and-mozzarella salad, and fresh bread (from around the corner, Cynthia explained). In Lincoln Point, Maddie wouldn't go near clam chowder or anything that looked like soup, and she'd never been a big fan of salad, but this evening, in Lincoln Square, a few blocks from Lincoln Center, my granddaughter transformed herself into a sophisticated New Yorker and uttered a tasteful "Mmm, this is delicious" after every sip or bite. I was pleased that Cynthia noticed and seemed flattered. When we dug into our dessert, authentic New York cheesecake, my "Mmm" was louder than Maddie's.

Give my regards to Broadway...

My cell phone indicated Bebe was on duty. Maddie smiled at the ring tone, kicked her legs, and said, "We're here; we're here."

Bebe, on the other end of the ring tone, wasn't so cheery.

"You wouldn't believe what a mess it is here, Gerry. The concierge let me into the ballroom where the fair will be. He stood by me the whole time, of course. New Yorkers, you know. It looks like no one even bothered to make sure the signs for our table were ordered or anything. I wouldn't be surprised if everything was shipped to the wrong hotel."

"It's only Tuesday. The fair doesn't start till Friday. We'll have it ready," I assured her.

"I don't know. All the other tables are ready. At least it looks that way. The SuperKrafts table has a cloth on it. Period."

Cynthia cleared the dishes while I continued the conversation with Bebe. "We can sit down in the morning and call the SuperKrafts office and find out what's going on. We have plenty of time to figure it out. I don't need to be back here until about one-thirty tomorrow afternoon."

Big mistake. Bebe let out an exasperated sound, half breath, half wail. "Back where? To Cynthia's? Gerry—" She sounded like a three-year-old, not even close to the businesswoman image she'd been trying to present.

I carried the phone toward the foyer. "It's a memorial service for her aunt, Bebe." My response was regrettably in kind—sounding like a parent scolding that three-year-old. I took a breath. "You and I will have the whole morning to work. And I'll join you again as soon as the service is over."

"Fine." The tone I was familiar with, when Bebe was in a snit.

My turn for exasperation. Cynthia had come up next to me and put her hand on my shoulder and, though I'd hung up, half whispered, "You'd better go, Gerry. I don't want to cause trouble between you and your friend."

"Everything will be fine," I said, wanting to believe it.

I'D forgotten how long it takes to dress for cold weather. Sweater, jacket, scarf, hat, gloves —all the items that stayed in the back of my closet in Lincoln Point. Cynthia rode down in the elevator with us. As soon as we stepped into the festive lobby, a different doorman greeted us. A young man with carefully sculpted facial hair and intense dark eyes. Presumably the night shift. He'd been pacing the sleek tile floor. There was a chair behind the small desk, but I wondered if doormen were allowed to sit, ever. "Shall I get you a cab?" he asked Cynthia as he readjusted his cap to accommodate his dark curly hair.

"Yes, thanks, Cody. My friends are going to the Lex near Grand Central. We'll wait in here." Maddie chose to join Cody outside. With both of them out of earshot, Cynthia confided to me in a low voice, "December vacation. College boys. They're the standard substitute help." She *tsk-tsk*ed and shook her head. "Not as conscientious usually, but this one, Cody Nugent, is better than most and the board has decided to hire him part-time through the year. We have high standards. I hope he works out." I wondered what it took for a doorman to please Cynthia. I wondered what it took for me to please Cynthia.

We watched Cody in action from the doorway. Maddie, who had a ringside seat, looked on in awe as he stepped out into the street, blew his whistle, and waved his arm. Less than a minute later, a yellow-and-black vehicle pulled over. Cynthia hugged me, waved to Maddie, and headed back upstairs. I stepped out in time to hear a breathy "Wow" from Maddie as she snapped a picture of Cody, our obliging New York knight. I figured that before the week was over, Maddie would be needing more journals: "New York City, Parts One to Seven." I was glad the days of having to stock up on film were over.

Chapter 5

IN SPITE OF the vast expanse of the crowded Lex Hotel lobby, I saw Bebe immediately. She was sitting on an upholstered bench in a center grouping of seats, facing the front entrance, ostensibly reading a newspaper. But, I suspected, like cops and hit men in the movies, she was on stakeout for our arrival. She tossed the newspaper and jumped to her feet when she spied us.

"Gerry, I thought you'd never get here."

"Here we are," I said, opening my arms.

"I wish you'd been with me to see the exhibit hall. I know the bell boy, or bell man, whatever, won't open it for me again tonight." She looked at her watch. "It's after nine."

My watch said two minutes before nine, but I didn't quibble. "Let's ask someone at the desk how early we can get in tomorrow morning."

"I don't want to be a pest."

I swallowed my first thought—*Now you're worried about being a pest?*—and instead said, "That's their job, Bebe. And, look, they're all merry and bright with holiday pins on their jackets. They're just waiting to give us cheerful service."

Bebe shook her head. No dice. "Let's go upstairs. We can call from there. We're on the same floor, the twentieth, but I couldn't get us adjoining rooms." She blew out a disappointed breath. "Too bad, because it would have been so convenient. Like having one big suite for the three of us."

I shivered. I hoped Bebe interpreted the involuntary reaction as my having a chill from the cold breezes that wafted through the lobby every time the door to the outside opened.

THE room Maddie and I would share was not as large as the one Cynthia had offered in her home, but it would do nicely. Instead of a park view, the two windows looked across the busy 42nd Street, where, even at this hour, there was a traffic jam of buses, taxis, cars, and pedestrians.

"Wow," Maddie said, hoisting herself on the heater, the better to see the street below. "This is five floors higher than I've ever been. It looks like I'm watching a miniature scene. Where are all the people going?" I wondered myself, a little sad that I'd forgotten what it was like to be a New Yorker and never run out of things to do, places to go, and the energy to do it all.

Our accommodations included twin beds with a bedside table and lamp between them, a desk and one office-style chair, a small dresser with a television set on top, and a tiny closet with an ironing board and a safe. The décor was old New York, with silvery draperies and framed black-and-white cityscapes on all the walls.

"Just like Willie's," Maddie said, "without the bagels." At that, Bebe, who'd helped us transport our luggage from her room, finally smiled.

Technically, it was only dinner time for our bodies—barely six-thirty in California—but it seemed like midnight, as if the three-hour time-zone change were reversed and our friends who'd stayed in California were ahead of us. It had been a long, stressful day, and all I wanted was to lie on a bed. My toothbrush and toiletries could stay packed till morning if it meant I could get to sleep sooner. Bebe, on the other hand, was on her second or third wind. She sat on one of the beds and indicated that I should sit on the other bed, where my lucky granddaughter was already stretched out behind me, using her backpack for a pillow. Was Bebe really calling a meeting? Now? It seemed she was.

"We have a lot to do, guys," she began. "I can't believe you're not going to be here the whole time, Gerry. That was the idea, that you'd be my helper. I need you by my side, to—"

"But someone died," Maddie said. She who was thought to be sleeping had come awake and to my rescue.

Bebe paused and let out a big sigh. "Okay, you're right," she said, addressing me instead of the little girl who had stopped her in her tracks. "I know you'll help with the heavy lifting, and that you'll be there when I need you, but I want your company, too," she admitted. "You know, for support. This is an important trip for me. It could mean a lot in terms of my career with Super-Krafts."

"Grandma always does her best," said my sweet PR person. I reached behind me and ruffled her hair in gratitude.

"What I don't get is, what makes Cynthia think you can solve a murder, if there was even a murder? Did you tell her that's why you came to New York City?" Bebe asked, a hint of accusation in her tone.

"No, I did not."

"Everyone knows Grandma is good at solving puzzles, like the ones the police back home have. Remember when she helped you with your case?" Maddie asked. "Weren't you glad when she made sure you and your brother didn't go to prison? She does that for everyone."

I wanted to correct her (I'd merely offered a little insight to assist my cop nephew, in a loose, unofficial capacity. Once or twice. Maybe three or four times) and thank her at the same time. Part of me wanted Maddie to go to sleep and not worry her young mind about murder cases; the other part wanted to high-five her and buy her the biggest slice of pizza in Manhattan. Or, simply, "slice," as in "Wanna grab a slice?" as the natives said. I was glad the language, at least, was coming back to me.

"Okay," Bebe said, standing up. "Point taken. Let's get some sleep. I'll see you for breakfast downstairs in the hotel coffee shop. They open at seven. That should be early enough for us to get started."

Once Bebe left, Maddie and I gave a high-five, albeit a weak one, and fell asleep with our clothes on.

I PROBABLY wouldn't have made it to breakfast Wednesday morning without Maddie's help unpacking my clothes. Also, the threat of her snapping my picture for her journal before I made myself presentable was strong motivation to get moving. I grabbed my carry-on duffel; we rushed to the elevator banks and arrived at the coffee shop at seven, with seconds to spare.

"It's four o'clock back home," Maddie said, in case we'd forgotten. "I'm glad I'm up." I hoped she remembered that feeling when it was school time again, and one parent or another had to drag her out of bed.

Bebe was already seated with a cup of coffee and what looked like apple juice, tapping her fingers on the menu. She raised her eyebrows when she looked up and saw us. No good-morning smile. An out-and-out fight would have been better than the silent treatment. I wanted to return to the room and crawl back into bed. Or, better yet, escape to the New York Public Library, only a few blocks away. Anything but face the day and the tug of war I knew would continue between Bebe and Cynthia, and their respective agendas, with me in the middle. They'd each had their own struggles in their youth—Cynthia losing her parents; Bebe also without help after an unfortunate early marriage, struggling to make it in business and watch over her younger brother—and both had emerged stronger, if cantankerous when things didn't go as they'd planned.

"You look great," I said to Bebe. I'd complimented her yesterday on her new professional haircut—short and neat, as opposed to her long, unruly locks of last week. In her last three days in Lincoln Point, she'd fit in a salon appointment and had taken the advice of the stylist as to what was appropriate for a forty-something woman on a business trip to New York. She must have found time to shop also, since she wore a navy business suit and an ivory blouse that looked brand new. I'd thrown on pants and a shirt. "I expected to be doing some dusty work this morning," I said, by way of apologizing for my appearance.

"I suppose you'll change for Cynthia's this afternoon."

"For the memorial service. Yes," I said.

"I'm starving," Maddie said. "I'm getting the buffet special." Maddie led us through the line, piling scrambled eggs, muffin, fruit salad, and turkey sausage onto her plate. Not her usual choice for breakfast, but I figured she considered oatmeal too childish, or too suburban.

We made it through the buffet line and breakfast without too much fuss, left the coffee shop, and headed for the exhibit hall.

The room was set up like every other crafts fair I'd attended—certainly more than a hundred of them over the years, sometimes as a vendor, sometimes as a customer, and several times as the organizer, though only for small shows. The hall that stretched before me was at least twice as big as any showroom I'd ever seen. Row after row of tables lined the space, with an area for workshops, and even a break room for vendors separated from the main hall by an accordion door. A rough survey of the tables yielded a count of between two hundred and twenty-five and two hundred and fifty vendors. Bebe's estimate of three hundred hadn't been far off, especially given my sloppiness with arithmetic. Once the doors had opened, craftspeople and their staff or helpers like Maddie and me, piled in, wheeling dollies, lugging cartons, pushing large carts full of boxes. We all greeted each other like old friends, though I recognized only a few from the larger fairs in California.

Besides miniatures, the show featured ceramics, jewelry, wooden toys, fabric crafts, "And More," as the brochure advertised. I spotted several items that I knew I'd be taking home with me. A handmade silk scarf in Mary Lou's favorite blue-and-lavender Monet-like hues. Hammered metal pendants that would be perfect for Henry's daughter, Kay, and several of my crafter friends. A pair of delicate glass earrings that I pictured on June, Skip's girlfriend. A notebook with handmade paper that would be ideal for my sister-in-law, Bev. An assortment of wooden puzzles that Henry might use as models. I imagined my last stop of this trip would be to Bloomie's for an extra piece of luggage.

"Wow," Maddie said. "This is *sooo* much bigger than our high school fair."

Bebe laughed. "Ya think?"

As a sign that things were starting to go right on this trip, our own SuperKrafts spot was stacked with boxes, two and three high. Some muscular good fairy had come at midnight, I supposed, and delivered the inventory. Another touch that put Bebe in a good mood was the fair's program, listing the vendors. With great pride she showed us the entry for SuperKrafts.

"Look at this," she said, pointing to her name. BARBARA MELLON, LINCOLN POINT, CALIFORNIA, STORE MANAGER. I had to confess to a little thrill at seeing my friend and my hometown in a brochure for a big Manhattan event. "And here's a set of business cards with my name, too. They must have really rushed to have these made up on time." (I distracted Maddie with a tug on her curls before she had a chance to tell Bebe that she herself had whipped up a set of business cards on her computer for her mother's art gallery, in no time. I could almost feel her choking back "It's not that hard.") Bebe placed a stack of her new business cards on the corner of our table and fanned them out in an artistic semicircle.

Maddie pulled our mini-scenes out of my duffel and we arranged them along the front of the table, each under its own plastic dome, with the idea of showcasing what could be made with SuperKrafts products. "Buy from us," was the message, "and you, too, can make this festive winter snow scene with chenille-stick trees." One of the larger boxes we unpacked contained dozens of kits—big sellers at our SuperKrafts store, and, we hoped, at this fair. Each small plastic bag held everything you'd need, except glue or paint if necessary, to create a desk or chair for an office, a purse, a hat, or even a wedding dress for the dollhouse resident. Maddie picked through the kits. She passed on a three-inch cello, an entire bedroom set, and a four-inch hutch. "These need paint," she said. I wondered what she had in mind until she extracted a kit for making an old-fashioned suitcase. "Can I open this?" she asked Bebe.

"Sure. That's a good idea, so people can handle what's in the package."

"I was thinking I could demonstrate," Maddie said. Bebe gave her a questioning look. "You know, I could sit here and make the suitcase or whatever, and if someone wants to buy it already made, they can. Or if they just want to see how easy it is, I can show them. I can make a lot of them or I can keep making and unmaking the same one."

Maddie demonstrated for us by laying out the pieces on card-stock she found in my duffel. (One never knows when one will need to make a tent sign at these events.) She spread out strips of brown leather in two tones, with strategically placed needle holes for the tiny gold brads (also included), a belt and buckle, a rounded handle. She built the small satchel before our eyes, with touches of glue, then wrapped the belt around it. Bebe and I clapped, drawing a wide smile from Maddie and a little attention from surrounding vendors. One them, a young woman, a vendor of her hand-knit goods, seemed especially interested. Maddie chatted her up, telling her the price of the kit, and adding, "If you want, you can even put a little sticker on the side that says Los Angeles or something."

"Can you save me three of those kits?" the woman asked.

It was my turn to snap a picture and I captured Maddie, the successful retailer, and Bebe's first customer of the fair.

AFTER a couple of hours opening boxes (Bebe), arranging our goods (me), chatting with the other workers (Maddie), and browsing at neighboring tables (all of us in turn), we repaired to the break room, which consisted of a row of vending machines, a countertop with a machine and supplies for coffee, tea, and hot chocolate, and the same kind of tables and chairs as in the hall, but without the white cloths. The room already smelled of stale coffee, like every other break room I'd used, at fairs and at Abraham Lincoln High School, where they called it the "teachers' room."

"Grandma, the vending machine has aspirin and bandages," Maddie said, from across the room. "Ours at school doesn't have those." One more slam from my granddaughter at her deprived childhood in an affluent suburb in Northern California.

"Do you need first aid? I don't see any blood," I said, with a fake laugh. Bebe smiled. Mission accomplished.

Give my regards to Broadway . . .

Bebe fixed herself a cup of coffee while I pulled my phone from my purse. Cynthia calling. I admired her restraint in holding off till almost eleven o'clock in the morning.

"I was thinking I should have our doorman send a cab for you, Gerry. Save you the bother."

"Thanks, but I'm sure the doorman here can get me one, and I have the address." I rattled off the address of the West Side Chapel to assure her.

"Okay. Are you on your way?"

"The service is at two, isn't it?"

"Yes, but I thought you'd come here first. I just ran downstairs and got a bunch of fresh salads from the deli. And those big, soft black-and-white cookies that you used to like."

"Mmm, thanks. I still love them. Save one for me, please. But I think it's better if I meet you at the chapel. There's a lot to do here."

"Sure, sure. I was just missing you."

If I hadn't been hired, sort of, to do a job, I'd have taken the next cab to Cynthia's side. But sitting across from me as a reminder of my duties, was also someone who would miss me if I left. Bebe was moving in now, inching her chair toward me, as if she could get close enough to hear the other side of the conversation between Cynthia and me. I was glad there was no one else in the break room.

"I'll try to get to the chapel by one-thirty," I said to Cynthia. "I still have to change my clothes. I'd better hang up if I'm going to make it."

"See you soon, Gerry."

"One-thirty?" Bebe said, when I'd clicked off. "Isn't the service at two? And it's right across town."

"I can't wait to meet everyone, Grandma. I'm ready to help."

It took me a moment to realize Maddie was talking about helping, not with the crafts fair, but with what we lovingly called "A Case," such as her Uncle Skip worked in Lincoln Point.

"I don't think so," I said. "You can stay here and have a nice lunch with Bebe, and then help her with whatever she needs."

Maddie's expression turned grim, not her most attractive look, as if she were a spoiled kid and Santa had left only coal in her stocking. She pulled up a seat and took one more shot.

"What if there's something to do on the computer, like research someone who looks suspicious. Uncle Skip says the criminals always return to the scene of the crime. Isn't that why you're going?"

"The service is not a crime scene, and it's not *at* the scene of the crime."

"You know what I mean. It's where the dead person is. I'll bet Cynthia doesn't know how to use search engines as well I do. And I learned about facial recognition software in computer camp. I might be able to take a picture and then find the person online."

"I'm sorry, sweetheart, but it's just not the place for you."

Maddie folded her arms across her chest. *Great.* Another person mad at me.

While Maddie and I duked it out, Bebe had been busy with her fingers, on her phone. She answered some simple questions from a recording, it seemed, and looked up with a happy grin as she hung up. "Hey, you know what? There's a two o'clock show at Radio City, and there are still some tickets available."

Maddie's sour face slowly brightened into not quite a smile. "Really? The Rockettes?"

Bebe nodded. "The Rockettes. All we have to do is get to the box office by one-thirty."

"Bebe, are you sure you want to—?" I asked.

"Are you kidding? I've always wanted to see them," Bebe said. I looked at her, trying to discern if she was being magnanimous, knowing I wouldn't want to take Maddie to a memorial service. I detected a sparkle that told me she was, in fact, looking forward to an afternoon in an auditorium full of kids, watching a lot of tall women touch their toes to their foreheads. "Really," Bebe added, "I watch them on TV every year, and ever since I was a kid I've wanted to see the Christmas show in person. This is my chance." She gave Maddie an affectionate look. "And I'll have a genuine kid as my cover."

"Can we go? Can we go?" Maddie asked, rotating her head from Bebe to me and back.

"Please, please," Bebe pleaded, mimicking a kid.

"Well, let me think," I said, drawing out the game. They both laughed and I savored the moment. I couldn't believe my luck. I reached to the floor and picked up my purse. "My treat."

Chapter 6

MY CABBIE, a heavily bearded man of indeterminate age, was fully engaged with the Bluetooth device attached to his ear, so I had a few moments virtually alone as the taxi sped (in the midtown-traffic sense) west. The sights and sounds were at once new to me, and at the same time, buried as recollections of my youth and my early years with Ken. Before we turned from Fifth Avenue, I gave a slight nod to the majestic New York Public Library lions, Patience and Fortitude, now decked out in enormous holiday wreaths, and stanchions of my college days. I pulled my turtleneck collar up to cover my mouth, breathed in the warmth, and allowed my mind to swing from snippets of old memories to my current preoccupation: the possible causes of Aunt Elsie's death.

My fondest wish was that Cynthia would accept her aunt's death as accidental, as the police had ruled. Cynthia's doubts notwithstanding, it wasn't that unusual for a ninety-five-year-old woman to miscalculate and take either more or fewer pills than she was supposed to. I recalled with dismay, during my own recent regimen of antibiotics, that I'd had trouble a couple of times remembering whether I'd taken the pill for that hour. I'd resorted to filling in a chart with check marks. Aunt Elsie had decades on me; it wasn't hard to envision her fatal mistake.

Give my regards to Broadway…

Henry calling. I could barely hear him over the noise of the traffic and the strange music playing in the cab. "Are you having lunch?" he asked, right as we were passing a chocolate shop on 39th.

"I'm eating a bag of honey-roasted airplane peanuts, on my way to a chapel in the West Sixties."

"The West Sixties, huh? You sound like a native."

"Once a New Yorker…" I said, dropping the bag of peanuts onto my lap so I could block one ear against the incessant honking outside and the dissonant sounds inside.

"I hope Cynthia isn't going to monopolize your non-work time."

"She's very needy right now."

"We all need you, Gerry. You have something for everybody."

I uttered a weak "Thanks," and felt a blush creep up my neck. "If I'm lucky, I'll think of something to put her mind at ease."

"You could write a note and pretend to find it. The note could be from Aunt Elsie and say that she decided to spare her niece all the work involved in her care, and…you know."

"I don't think so."

"I don't either."

"No matter what Cynthia ends up believing, you can be sure she'll feel guilty. She was supposed to protect her," I said.

"No one's realistic when it comes to loved ones," Henry said.

How true. The cab slowed down in the middle of a block of brick buildings, surprising me. We had arrived at the funeral home. I said good-bye to Henry and pulled out my wallet, preparing to exit. I didn't realize how I'd gotten used to California's open spaces, at least where mortuaries were concerned. Here, instead of the usual landscaping and parking lot surrounding a home, the West Side Chapel was just one in a row of brick-building businesses, down half a flight of stairs from the street, with other offices and apartments above them. The chapel was distinguished by white trim on the doors and windows, heavy gold lettering on the sign above the establishment, and wrought iron trim. Three large planters with green shrubs and tiny pink flowers marked the territory. All in all, a Colonial look. I took a breath and opened the front door.

The lobby was stark, with dark red carpeting and heavy furnishings. A guest book stood on a wooden stand with a small light attached. At the entrance to the chapel itself were men in dark suits, hands folded in front of them, looking like sentinels. They probably were sentinels, I realized, ready to intervene at the first sign of trouble. I looked around. Where were the poster-sized photographs of Aunt Elsie's happy, eventful life? Aunt Elsie with darling little Cynthia on her knee and then later with Cynthia at college graduation? Aunt Elsie on a cruise with her church group or playing dominoes with friends? In her uniform during her service as a WAC in World War II? The last several memorials I'd been to in California were billed as celebrations of life, where friends and relatives gathered to honor the deceased. Not here. I finally remembered that Cynthia had already prepared me for this. "I don't believe in putting up all those happy photos," she'd said. "They make me even more sad. And Aunt Elsie felt the same way. 'No eulogies,' she told me more than once." Happy photos may have signaled sadness for Cynthia and her aunt, but I couldn't imagine anything sadder than the somber mood generated by the heavy fabrics and dark colors of the West Side Chapel.

Cynthia herself was all in black as were the few people I noticed already sitting in the back rows of the chapel, chatting in low tones, waiting for the service to begin. "Gerry," Cynthia whispered, rushing from the other end of the lobby. "You're here." I was here and, luckily, also in a black pants suit. Cynthia linked her arm in mine. "There are people I want you to meet." Her voice was soft, conspiratorial.

We walked, still linked, toward a young woman who looked to be in her early twenties, wearing a short dress that was much more chic than the black outfits Cynthia and I wore. "This is Ashley Goodman. Ashley is a nurse who cared for Aunt Elsie on a regular basis. She works for an agency that provides caregivers at various levels." She paused, then continued in a tone that suggested she was reading from a teleprompter. "Because Ashley is a graduate nurse, she had more responsibility for Aunt Elsie than some of the others. The agency's student nurses aren't allowed to dispense meds, for example."

If Cynthia could have been any more obvious, I didn't know how, unless she held up a sign, like a chauffeur at the airport: SUSPECT #1. But perhaps my perspective was colored by what I knew her to be doing—lining up persons of interest for me to evaluate at the least, interrogate at the worst. I felt nothing would make Cynthia happier than if I took out a notepad and pen as I greeted each guest. But I did no such thing. I was still not ready to plunge in as an investigator in any capacity. Where was my homicide-cop nephew when I needed him? Internally, I was shouting, "Skip! Help!" I allowed Ashley to move on to the guest book and sign in. Maybe I'd do better with the next candidate.

When Cynthia was called away by one of the stiff-lipped sentinels, another young woman came up to me. I figured that, having been seen with the next of kin of the departed, I'd been pegged as a member of the Bishop family.

She offered her hand and we shook lightly. "I'm Candace Sellers, a student nurse with the same agency Ashley works for. I'm sorry for your loss. It's so sad about Ella," she said.

"Elsie," I said, before I could stop myself.

Candace gasped. "Elsie, of course. I'm so sorry. Ella is in Seventeen-D; Elsie was Fifteen-D. I have quite a few patients in that building."

"I guess it's hard to keep them straight," I said. I almost added, "And they all look alike," but this time I caught myself.

She gave me a weak smile and moved on with seeming relief, giving her place to a middle-aged man with a light stubble. These days I couldn't tell if stubbles were a sign of laziness or a fashion statement. On this man, I thought the latter, only because he was dressed for the occasion. Or maybe for the event after this one. "I'm the super of the Bishops' building," he said. "Neal Crouse.

Cynthia said you were Elsie's good friend. She was a wonderful tenant, bought in long before I came on. I'll miss her."

"It seemed sudden, didn't it?"

He gave me an odd look. "She was ninety-something," he said, then—choking back a laugh—"I'm sorry. I don't know what I was thinking. You're right, we really had no warning."

I was the one who should have apologized, asking such a question. I was failing at homicide investigation. Miserably. I wished I could escape to call Skip; even Maddie would be doing better. Cynthia was at my side again, to introduce me to a group of three women who arrived together as Aunt Elsie's "very good friends." A theater group, she told me. I thought I detected a shake of the head from Cynthia, as if to say, "These ladies are not suspects." For their part, the women each greeted me with a form of "You're the one from California who's going to help Cynthia figure out what really happened to our beloved Elsie." All said in soft voices. I hoped my smile spoke volumes; otherwise, I was speechless.

One helpful guest was the day doorman, Duncan. He was in a dark suit, not a velvet-collared uniform this time, but I recognized him immediately. Duncan introduced me to Joel, the deli worker for thirty years, who told me Elsie always had a smile as he prepared her order of crab salad; and to Louie, the baker who saved an almond croissant for her every Sunday morning. Duncan also introduced me to several residents who lived on different floors of the building and the real estate agent who handled most of the property. As I smiled and said how glad I was to meet them all, I couldn't suppress the idea that, if I were to believe Cynthia, any one of them could be responsible for Aunt Elsie's death. Anyone in the building—anyone in Manhattan—could have messed with her pills. A staggering thought.

I'd become trapped in Cynthia's obsession. I reflected on our college days when Cynthia exhibited this same intensity over much smaller matters. Would her professor give her a fair grade even though she'd neglected to send him a thank-you note after he hosted a party for his undergraduate majors? How significant was it that, after a whole day, John (or Derek or Rob) didn't call for a second date? Now I was here wondering: Did the super or the realtor have a reason to want Aunt Elsie out of the building? Was there an offer on that flat with the magnificent Central Park views, easy access to the best in dining, and a short walk to Lincoln Center? Did the theater group ladies want to replace Aunt Elsie, perhaps with a new member, younger and more able to climb the stairs to the balcony? What about Ashley, the pill dispenser, or Candace, the young caregiver who didn't even know Elsie's name? Did either of them misplace the pills and now feel remorseful that she didn't admit it? Was Duncan tired of opening the car door for a frail old woman who took forever, especially when it was near-blizzard conditions? I mentally slapped myself. Why would Elsie be going out in blizzard conditions in the first place? I was overreaching, much the same thing I'd been accusing Cynthia of, through all the years of our friendship.

A well-dressed gentleman hovering around the back of the foyer caught my eye and I walked over to him.

"Were you a friend of the deceased?" I asked, hands folded in front of me, my voice somber, as if I'd just graduated from funeral-director school. The tall, dignified-looking man, who appeared to be at least as old as Aunt Elsie, seemed more despondent than her other friends and acquaintances. He removed his hat, revealing thin gray hair, and half bowed to me. "Sorry to disturb you," he said, though he'd done no such thing. As quickly as he'd doffed his hat, he returned it to his head and slipped out the door.

"That was Philip Chapman, Aunt Elsie's old beau," Cynthia said, coming up beside me. "The word is that he and Aunt Elsie were once engaged, though she never actually told me that. They were both in the theater, mostly off-off-Broadway, but making their way up. Then, when my parents died, Aunt Elsie abandoned him and her career to take care of me."

Quite a load for Cynthia to bear, I thought, no matter how

casually she related a tale I'd never heard before. "No one forced her to do that," I said. Cynthia nodded but said no more.

The gentle sound of a bell signaled us to move into the chapel. Cynthia linked her arm in mine and led me down the dark aisle to the front row. At that moment, I felt so sorry for her, with no immediate family to share her grief. Judging by cards and calls she'd received, I thought she must have a good community of friends, but many of them lived miles away in Florida. Most of her building's residents and neighborhood folks who'd dropped in to sign the guest book had already left to return to their jobs or homes. I felt all the more obliged to keep her company. I wondered what would have happened if my SuperKrafts trip hadn't coincided with Aunt Elsie's death. Would I have flown out to be here just for Cynthia? Would she have asked me to? I remembered that, without my asking, Cynthia had flown to California when I needed help making decisions about Ken's care. She'd anticipated my every need and didn't leave until I was comfortable handling things myself. I decided it didn't matter how my trip to New York came about. I was here, and I would support my friend. Of course, I decided this while Bebe was nowhere in sight.

In the chapel, only one spray of white flowers adorned an otherwise plain wooden podium. The family, that is, Cynthia, had requested that in lieu of flowers, donations be made in Elsie Bishop's name to a charity of the donor's choice. I'd done that, but now wished I'd sent flowers also. The chapel was built to hold many more mourners than we saw today, as might be expected for a weekday service and for an honoree in her nineties.

There was no urn holding Aunt Elsie's ashes; I assumed that Cynthia had already taken custody of them. The officiant made general remarks in a somber voice about the beloved woman who had passed on, and quoted from scripture and from the ancients, on death and dying. There was no opportunity for a testimonial from Cynthia, nor from anyone else. With organ hymns at the beginning, middle, and end of the service, the whole ceremony

lasted less than half an hour. Not even a minute for every year of
Aunt Elsie's life.

OUTSIDE, Cynthia wiped away tears and made her move.
"Let's go back to my house. It's not a bad walk, if you're not
too cold." She smiled and squeezed my arm. "I still have some
black-and-whites."

The black-and-white cookies, or half moons as we called the
imitations on the West Coast, were tempting, especially since my
lunch had consisted of half a bag of airline peanuts. I checked
my watch. "It's almost two-thirty. I should be getting back to the
hotel."

"We've never really been able to talk, Gerry." I knew she
meant that Maddie had been present until this afternoon, when
dozens of people had been around us. "My mind is going ninety
miles an hour. I need you to help me sort things out."

I knew tomorrow, Thursday, would be no better. Bebe would
be doing errands all over town. Her list, as she'd given it to me
in a running commentary over breakfast, included a stop at the
bank, a trip to SuperKrafts' corporate offices on Sixth, and con-
necting with the show coordinator, the hotel events manager, and
all the hotel staff who were involved in the show. Besides that, if
she were going to be on her feet for two days, she might need a
new pair of shoes. That meant Maddie would be with me at least
until midafternoon. This was my last chance to talk to Cynthia
alone until the fair was over and we were almost on our way back
to California. "Let's just have coffee," I suggested. "How about
that little café on the corner?" You had to love New York, with
a café always only a few steps away, even if you'd just exited a
funeral parlor.

Cynthia accepted the compromise with reluctance, as signi-
fied by her heavy sigh. It was that kind of week.

THE thermometer on top of a tall (of course) building flashed
twenty-eight degrees. I could see my breath. Maddie would be

able to explain the phenomenon to me though I doubt she'd ever experienced it before this trip. The sky was overcast and already the lights of Manhattan were popping on, giving the city the mystical quality of the photos on the calendar that hung in my crafts room, one of Cynthia's presents to me every year. I loved the special, wet chill, especially since it was only a few minutes before we were in a toasty café with steaming drinks in front of us. So hardy was I.

The café, another dark room but with better aromas than the West Side Chapel, was empty enough for us to commandeer one whole chair for our jackets, hats, and gloves. Our scarves remained around our necks, however. Most other patrons sat in front of laptops as mercifully soft music wafted through the air. While Cynthia freshened up, I checked my phone for messages. Thanks to the Rockettes, there was no message from Bebe. I imagined she and Maddie would still be in the theater. One call from Henry deserved at least a quick reply.

"I hope you've had some nutrition by now," he said, ever mindful of my well-being.

I looked at the cinnamon coffee cake in front of me. "I'm all set," I said.

We filled each other in on our afternoon activities, his being more fun than mine even if he did spend a couple of hours in a mall buying clothes for tropical weather. We exchanged sweet nothings and hung up.

"Well?" Cynthia said, returning to our table.

I got the feeling I should have been able to whip out my notebook and give my friend-cum-client a full report on the state of The Case, as we called it in Lincoln Point, and my Sherlockian observations in the funeral home. Why not? I took a deep breath and plunged in.

"First, I want to be sure I have all the facts. You said you did find a full bottle of Aunt Elsie's blood pressure pills?"

She waved her hands. "Conveniently sitting right on her nightstand so you couldn't miss it. That doesn't mean anything.

Whoever did this obviously switched bottles, putting the full bottle on the stand before anyone could realize Aunt Elsie had died."

"And you weren't surprised that there was a full bottle? Did you keep track of the number of pills or when she'd need a refill?"

Cynthia bristled. "I did my best, Gerry. I know I should have kept track, but the pharmacy automatically monitors the refills. Plus, more important, she gave no indication of needing that kind of attention from me. In fact, she discouraged it. I tried to give her some independence and at the same time—" Cynthia struggled to maintain control. I wished I could take back my question, which I was sure sounded accusatory. I took her hands in mine, and felt her calm down a bit. I regretted that I'd inadvertently reminded her of what she considered her failing, as a nurse as well as a niece.

I pushed her mug of tea closer to her. "Let's try to just focus on the facts. Otherwise, I'm going to be confused, and we're not going to get anywhere."

"Sorry, sorry. Yes, the police did find an almost full bottle of pills and, no, I can't say that I knew exactly how many pills should have been left in the bottle on any particular day."

I hated to bring up the next question, but I had to be sure. Cynthia had told me the story in bits and pieces. I needed to hear it again. "You said you came in from work and found Aunt Elsie in bed?"

Cynthia heaved a sigh, then nodded. "It was close to five o'clock and I let myself in as usual. I'd called ahead about three. I talked to Aunt Elsie for a minute and then to Ashley, the nurse you just met, about a couple of things she needed to pick up from the pharmacy. Then I told her that I wouldn't need her in the evening since my last appointment canceled on me. She said in that case she'd be leaving soon. So, when I got home, I went into the bedroom to greet Aunt Elsie as usual. I was looking forward to telling her I'd picked up some stuffed chops and that I'd invited the Webers in Fourteen-C to join us. I'd almost gotten through a whole sentence before I saw that she wasn't moving." Cynthia paused to compose herself. "I called to her, felt her pulse, and... she was so cold." Cynthia shivered, as if she were wearing a tank top instead of a sweater and thick scarf. "I couldn't believe I'd made the mistake of sending Ashley home. I called the EMTs right away even though I didn't have any doubt that she'd been gone awhile."

I could imagine Cynthia's distress at leaving her aunt without a helper on the day it mattered most. "And you also said there was cash missing but you don't know how much. Is that correct?"

"Right, but I think it was a substantial amount."

"What makes you say that?"

Cynthia took a deep breath and seemed to be steeling herself for an announcement. "The note she left."

My hand fell to the table and nearly tipped over my mocha. "She left a note?" A nod, yes. "Aunt Elsie left a note, and you're just telling me? You didn't think to tell me before this?" A shrug. I tried to maintain composure, and reined in my voice. So far, no other patrons were paying attention to us and I wanted to keep it that way. "Did you show it to the police?" I whispered. A shake of the head, no. "Why on earth not, Cynthia?"

"It was addressed to me, and it had nothing to do with how she died. Except...well, you'll see."

Cynthia dug into her purse and pulled out a piece of paper, folded to about a quarter of a standard yellow pad. Like the kind TV cops offer for confessions, I mused. I reached for the paper, but Cynthia pulled it back with "You have to promise me you will not tell anyone about this."

"I can't do that, Cynthia." She made a move to return the note to her purse and leave the café. What would be wrong with that? I wondered. I could give her a hug, wish her well, and be on my way back to Bebe and my granddaughter and the real reason I'd come to New York. I could take a trip to the Guggenheim or the Whitney. I could explore the neighborhoods to the south. Greenwich Village, SoHo, Little Italy. I could, but I wouldn't. "Okay," I said. "Let me have it."

"It's not a suicide note, Gerry. Just some last words for me to read whenever she might die. It was in the drawer of her night table."

"Let me see it, please."

The note finally in my hands, I read the large, careful handwriting.

My dearest Cynthia,

I've lived a long life and it's time to say my last good-bye.

You know how much I love you, and have ever since you were a tot! Remember when you first came to live with me? I thought I'd never survive the death of your parents—my brother and his sweet wife. But you came into my home and into my heart and I am forever grateful. Now that you're doing so well, and living back in the family home, I know I can finally let go.

Besides my estate (such a fancy word) I've left you one small present. Well, not so small, really. I've been a rather frugal old lady in the last years and have put aside a box of cash. I'm not sure of the exact amount, but it's more than enough to help you enjoy the rest of your years. It's in our special place.

My wishes for my burial are the same as when we last talked, even though you didn't want to hear about it at the time. Remember me always, dear niece, and know that I am watching over you.

Your loving
Aunt Elsie

I hadn't read anything so poignant in a long time, and I knew that my expression showed the emotion I felt. Cynthia put her hand on mine and slid the note away from me. "I know what you're thinking, Gerry. But, listen to me. I'm telling you, this is not a suicide note."

"How can you be certain? Surely, the possibility crossed your mind."

"No," she said, biting her lip, shaking her head. Determined.

"I was a nurse for more years than I care to count, and I'm still working in the field, as you know. I've seen this happen many, *many* times. Elderly patients nearing death always want to leave a note. Well, not always, but often. They know the end is coming and they just want to put down a few last words for their loved ones. It doesn't mean they're going to facilitate their own end."

"So they just die naturally, some time after they write the letter?"

"Of course," Cynthia said. Then she realized I'd set her up in a way—with all the experience she'd had with this scenario, why couldn't she accept that Aunt Elsie also died naturally, shortly after writing the letter? She frowned and shook her head. I thought she was about to shake her finger at me. "No, no, Gerry. That's not what happened here. Aunt Elsie was as stable as anyone." I doubted that a ninety-five-year-old was even as stable as she herself might have been at eighty, or that her heart was as strong, but I held back the thought and let Cynthia continue. "And what about that missing box of cash?" she asked, in an "aha" tone. "Not that I want it. Or need it. But it shows that someone else was involved in my aunt's death."

I remembered Cynthia's mention of missing cash in our initial phone call. Now I understood why she hadn't wanted to bring it up again right away. The longer I could remain ignorant of Aunt Elsie's note, the longer I'd be likely to believe she hadn't left any sign of an intention to commit suicide. "If someone found the note, and searched for the cash, why wouldn't that person have destroyed the note?" I asked.

"I don't know. Maybe they didn't know about it, but just stumbled on the box. Or maybe Aunt Elsie told the person that I'd be looking for a written farewell letter, and they couldn't take a chance that I wouldn't find one." This time Cynthia did shake her finger at me. "Which is another reason I don't consider this some kind of I'm-ending-it-all thing. She just wanted to be sure she had the chance to write it down, in case she died unexpectedly."

I took a deep, frustrated breath. "I still don't understand why you wouldn't show this note to the police. It seems there's a large amount of money missing. Wouldn't that help get them on your side? You have a real robbery to report."

Bad choice of words. Cynthia flared up, her face turning red as she tried to scream and keep her voice down at the same time. "I reported a *real* murder," she said. "And they didn't believe me."

I put my hand on her arm and we both calmed down enough to breathe evenly. I made one more attempt, treading carefully with my words. "The missing money is a second crime, Cynthia, one they're more used to." As if the police took robbery more seriously than homicide. I was glad Skip was out of earshot, three thousand miles away.

"I can't show them this letter, Gerry. All they'll see is that she wrote her last words and they'll change their verdict from accident to suicide."

There it was. Her great fear. I resigned myself to the fact that there was no stopping my friend while she was on this mission. I decided the expedient thing was for me to play investigator and go over the details of the case with her. Maybe when we laid it all out—who had means, motive, and opportunity, MMO, as I'd learned from my nephew—the light would dawn, and Cynthia could be at peace with her aunt's unassisted, natural passing. I looked across the table. Cynthia had folded her arms across her chest, waiting. I ordered another mocha. It was going to be a long coffee break, and a long road to peace.

Chapter 7

THE CAFÉ MUSIC had shifted to holiday songs, in rhythm with the new direction of our conversation. With a fresh mug of coffee-plus-chocolate in front of me, I was ready to stop challenging Cynthia's theory and give my attention to her concerns. We could settle the matter of Aunt Elsie's death once and for all. I could go back to Bebe and the crafts show I'd come for, and have some fun with Maddie. I could make time for Cynthia and me to go for a long (depending on the temp) stroll in Central Park, the way we did years ago to work out student stress, and she could share beautiful memories of life with her aunt.

I went back to my nephew's homicide mantra—means, motive, and opportunity. Once we'd had a few sips of warm liquid, I put it to Cynthia. "If we take the pill-tampering theory seriously, we need to think of anyone who had the means to replace the real blood pressure pills with a similar-looking placebo and then put the real pills back after Aunt Elsie's heart attack. That person must have had constant access to the apartment, and to Aunt Elsie. How else could someone know when to pull the switches?"

"Like one of the nurses," Cynthia said. "I've thought of that, of course. I hire all the caregivers through an agency. But, you know, I've never been completely happy with them. They're always sending what they call 'equivalent professionals' but really they're subs, not the ones I interviewed. I think part of the problem is that I didn't require full-time care for Aunt Elsie. I'll bet those patients get better service. Maybe you could look into the agency? Maybe it's even illegal for them to send less qualified people than they promised?"

Busywork, I thought, and something Cynthia was much more qualified to do. But I'd do it. Somehow. "I suppose it could have been a pharmacist who provided the placebos, or even anyone who could find something that looked like real pills," I said. I could tell I'd lost Cynthia's attention by getting into details. I needed to keep trying to focus even as I consoled Cynthia. "I'll check out the agency," I told her.

"Great idea, Gerry," Cynthia said, her expression blank.

"And I'll see, for example, if there have been other incidents of older people dying unexpectedly." I realized how foolish I sounded: Was it ever a complete surprise when a nonagenarian died? Besides, I had no idea when I'd be able to fit in time in the library. With no spare time to start with. I could put Maddie and her electronic resources on it, but did I really want to involve her in a project that was so macabre? What if she uncovered some Angel of Death situation involving misguided "mercy killings"? Being so close to her Uncle Skip, who was really her cousin-once-removed, Maddie was no stranger to homicide cases, but we'd always tried to keep her from any direct interaction with the deaths.

"The doorman agency is getting just as bad." Cynthia had reconnected and continued her ramblings. I hoped I hadn't missed anything. "Especially on the night shifts, we get the college kids or someone between jobs or someone's son-in-law. So they should be next under the microscope. I trust Duncan a lot; Cody almost as much, since Aunt Elsie seemed to favor him; and the other on-again, off-again kids hardly at all."

Now I did drag out my notebook and start my list of tasks. A good practice for an investigator, in case I ever did this again. Which I never would. "Let's start again, and tell me all the people who had the opportunity to get to Aunt Elsie and her pills," I said.

The list astonished me. So many people had access to Cynthia and Elsie's home, starting with the doormen, the super, the cleaning staff, and several medical helpers, including the two young women I'd met. Then there were the regular food service workers who knew Aunt Elsie's habits. We couldn't rule out Deli Joel or Pastry Louie or any other takeout staff, who could have played the placebo trick on her. Not that the police or anyone had found the placebos, and there were many other untraceable ways to kill a person, but I didn't want to open things up to that extent, or I'd never get back to the Lex, the crafts show, and my granddaughter. "Aren't all the help, like the doormen and the super, vetted?" I asked.

"Absolutely. The board for the building is very careful. They hire people to do background checks on all the service employees. It's a very sophisticated, high-tech process nowadays."

"Has there been any sign that someone has been in the house that you didn't know about?"

Cynthia frowned, concentrating. "Not that I can think of."

I tapped my pen on my purse-size notepad. Like a detective. "What about that box of cash? The special place she mentioned."

Cynthia looked over her shoulder. "It's a long story, but way back, Aunt Elsie's husband, who died in the war, created a storage area behind the mirror over the dresser. Uncle Mike's theory, according to Aunt Elsie, was that burglars might look in drawers or behind a painting, but they wouldn't think that a mirror stuck to a wall was anything but a mirror. But that's only true for burglars who are in a hurry most of the time; not for someone who has a legitimate reason to be in the apartment often, with all the time in the world to check around."

Intriguing. I had no such "safe place" in my house. A new project for Henry? "What do you usually keep there?"

"Nothing, really. When I was a kid, I knew Aunt Elsie hid presents back there somehow, but it wasn't until later that I found out where the switch is that opens it. I haven't looked in there in a long time, until I read Aunt Elsie's note. And I found it empty."

"How would someone else know to look there?"

"They shouldn't. But, like I said before, that doesn't mean they didn't search every corner and come upon it. Everyone knows old people hide money a lot. The mother of one of my nurse friends had a drawer full of socks and each sock had several one hundred dollar bills in it. There's a reason that sounds like a cliché. They all do it. At least Aunt Elsie and Uncle Mike were creative."

Cynthia smiled at her own depiction of her aunt, and I joined her. A nice respite before I went on. "I'm sure the police questioned all the nurses and other caregivers, right?"

Cynthia heaved a loud sigh. "They did a cursory interview with the main players, like Duncan, the day man, and Ashley, the main nurse. And Neal, our superintendent. Maybe some others. But they all said the same thing, apparently. They knew nothing and didn't see any strangers. Neither Ashley nor anyone else remembered when the full bottle of pills appeared on the night table and they couldn't rule out the possibility that Aunt Elsie forgot to take her meds. I don't blame them. They didn't know her the way I did."

"If the caregivers didn't monitor her meds, what did they do?" I asked.

"In theory, they should have," Cynthia admitted, "but I know Aunt Elsie could be difficult and assert her independence."

To my ear, the nurses sounded more like baby-sitters, there in case of emergency. I refrained from suggesting this to Cynthia, lest she take it as another failure on her part, to be more firm with her aunt regarding what she needed to submit to. So far, the box of cash seemed the best guess as a motive. I put on my Skip hat and thought of other questions. Cynthia shook her head "no" to all of them. She hadn't seen any signs of abuse from a caregiver, hadn't received any letters from supposed long-lost loves needing money. There had been no indication that Aunt Elsie was the victim of a financial scam.

"Could she have promised anyone, like a con artist, a significant amount of money?" I asked.

"Not that I know of."

"You don't sound sure."

"Well, technically, I handle all the finances."

"But?" I prodded.

"I never asked for legal control and I never probed into her situation."

"That means she received checks in her own name? Could she have cashed them herself?"

Cynthia nodded to both questions. "She still got small pensions from her military service, from her various teaching jobs, and also one of Uncle Mike's, who was killed in action. And probably from other sources. I never probed. As modern as Aunt Elsie tried to be, she was old-fashioned in some ways and didn't completely trust banks. I always suspected she kept cash in cubbyholes around the apartment, though I never looked for it. As far as cashing the checks, she would go for walks by herself—with an aide or Duncan on the lookout for her safety—until a short time ago. She could easily have cashed the checks, taken the money home, and hidden it."

It might have sounded as though Aunt Elsie didn't quite trust Cynthia, but I knew from talks with other friends that it wasn't unusual for the elderly to want to keep their own money handy; it seemed to give them a needed sense of security and independence, even if they did love and trust caregiver family members.

"You're thinking that the box she mentioned in her note contained all that cash."

"Which could be very little, or very much."

"There's no other heir, is there?"

"Not another soul."

Aunt Elsie's only niece would get everything: a pricey apartment in a choice neighborhood, and whatever resources were not in the missing box. In any other circumstances, Cynthia Bishop would be the number one suspect.

I quickly erased my friend's name from my mental list, but not before she noticed my face reddening at the thought.

"Something wrong, Gerry?"

"No, no. But I do really need to get going."

"Yes, you have a lot to do. I'll go out with you and put you in a cab."

I was aware that Cynthia's idea of what I had to do was different from mine. After her expert hailing, with holiday bells ringing in front of the café, I climbed into a taxi, grateful for the warmth even though I'd been standing on the sidewalk only a few minutes. I couldn't help feeling conflicted and dishonest. For all my hassling and attempts to reason with her, I hadn't said anything to Cynthia that would dissuade her of the notion that a full-scale investigation was underway.

I'D left the phone on, but muted, while we were in the café. I'd felt a vibration a few times and ignored them all. Now I checked my messages, once again using a cab as my roving phone booth. I returned the messages, starting with Bebe. Might as well get the worst over with.

"Gerry, I can't remember a more fun afternoon," Bebe said. *Phew*, something went right. "We had the best seats and the show was out of this world. Not just glitz, either. Real classy. Maddie and I clapped our hands off. And cried, too. That last tableau… wait, Maddie wants to talk to you."

"Grandma, I'm still writing in my journal. The kids at school won't believe it. You owe Bebe some money because I bought the special program book and got one for Taylor, too. I hope she gets to see the show some time. Wow."

A pause, and another phone hand-off. Bebe again. "Never mind about the money. It wasn't that much, and there was some left over anyway from what you gave me for the tickets. We're waiting to have dinner with you."

"I'm on my way." I hoped I'd get to the hotel before Bebe's good mood slipped away.

While I was ahead, I called Henry.

"I set up a cake-tasting appointment for the Friday after we get back from Hawaii."

Cake tasting? Out of the blue like that, I was stumped. My lucky stars were working, however, and I recovered in time—the cake for our wedding. "Excellent," I said. "I can hardly wait." Never mind that I didn't remember setting a specific date for the wedding itself.

"I know we don't have the date yet," Henry said. I relaxed with the assurance that I hadn't forgotten something so important. "But we did say we'd aim for early in the new year. I figure it's not too soon to start checking things off."

"Good thinking," I said. "I'll call the inn as soon as I'm back." That was about as much wedding talk as I could handle, so I moved on, telling Henry about the "safe" behind the mirror in Cynthia's bedroom.

"Something to think about," he said. "Over the years, Kay has accumulated quite a bit of good jewelry. It would be nice if she didn't have to run to her safe deposit box every time she wanted to wear it." The mention of Henry's daughter reminded me to pick up the hammered metal pendant I'd seen at the show. Not that it was worthy of a safe deposit box, but I had to accept the convoluted way my mind was working this week.

Being an expert now on midtown traffic and layout, I checked the cross street and knew I had time for one more call before we reached the Lex.

"Hey, Aunt Gerry, how's it going in the Big Apple? Did you make NYPD Detective yet?" I laughed, to please my nephew. I gave him an update on Cynthia's current favorite theory and told him about the note (telling a detective outside NYPD jurisdiction did not count as breaking my promise to Cynthia) and the mysterious hiding place for the cash. "Hey, that's a great idea," Skip said, latching on to the "buried treasure." (Uh-oh, if everyone in Lincoln Point started stashing valuables in a cutout behind the bedroom mirror, it would make our burglars' lives that much easier.)

"I'm not sure I want to get Maddie involved," I said, "but I don't see how I can do that research otherwise."

"Make it sound like general demographics. You want to

know the ages of the people in New York, and how many died in each age range. Something like that."

"She'll figure it out."

"I know, but you will have tried. And it will send the message that we're trying hard not to get her focusing on unpleasant things."

It wasn't much, but it would have to do.

WITH all the world-famous restaurants within walking distance, we decided to have dinner in the hotel coffee shop. It suited me fine. What I needed was food as soon as possible—a handful of nuts, a piece of coffee cake, and two mochas since breakfast in this same restaurant was a new low for me—and then a quick elevator ride to my bed. Dinner talk was mostly listening for me. Maddie went on and on about the glittery red-and-green costumes on her new best friends at Radio City Music Hall; Bebe had fallen in love with the stagecraft and costumes, as befitted a crafts store manager. Both had eaten the best deli sandwiches in their lives.

"I love the way the streets are numbered," Maddie said. "You can't get lost here. I wish we had all the streets numbered where we live." Until now, I'd been enamored of Lincoln Point's naming of its buildings and streets after highlights of Honest Abe's life and times. Gettysburg Boulevard, Rutledge Street, Mary Todd Hospital. Even the name of our coffee shop, Seward's Folly, bore traces of our sixteenth president. Charming, but Maddie was right: There was nothing to help with navigation.

I ordered a cheeseburger with extra cheese and fries and a side of coleslaw, provoking stunned looks from Bebe and Maddie. "I'm hungry," I said, by way of explanation. Then I asked the waiter to set aside a slice of cheesecake for me for dessert.

Once our server left, SuperKrafts' Manager Bebe took charge, laying out the next day's work.

"I need to go to Corporate tomorrow. Before then, I have to have a good handle on the inventory, what else we might need, et cetera, et cetera. I'm having a lunch meeting with one of the VPs, but I'm going to leave early because one of the regional buyers asked to meet with me." Bebe couldn't contain a broad smile.

Maddie and I threatened to have our waiter bring us a piece of cake and a candle to celebrate Bebe's burgeoning career, even before the start of the fair. "He doesn't have to know the reason," I said.

"You look like it's your birthday," Maddie said. She who'd had so many fewer birthdays than either of us.

Bebe nixed the idea in a way that said she was serious. "This is New York," she admonished. "People are cool here." As if our little town in Northern California wasn't cool.

"I read that in one of my tour books," Maddie said. "Like, you're not supposed to say anything if you meet a famous person like a movie star, on the street or in a restaurant. You just pretend they're like everybody else."

"They *are* like everybody else," I said. "Just because they're famous, it doesn't make them more special than we are." I got strange looks and no agreement from my dinner companions.

I'D eaten so much, I felt I was waddling from the table to the lobby of the hotel and then across the miles of gray carpet to the bank of elevators. "Let's go right up to the ballroom," Bebe said. "It's open till ten and I'm afraid if you go to your room, you'll fall into bed and I won't see you again till morning." She was probably right.

Many other vendors had the same idea, taking advantage of the extended setup hours. Some crafters had just arrived in New York from all parts of the country; thus, we were the smart ones who could answer questions. Where's the nearest rest room? Is there coffee service somewhere? Where's the trash container? Does the hotel have a gift shop? We knew all the answers. We could even recommend places to eat and give estimates of the taxi fares, although only to points west.

Bebe took notes on what inventory we had, what she thought we could use more of, what might need a touch-up of glue or paint. She fussed over whether Maddie's skating scene should be to the right or the left of SuperKrafts' new punch machine, making its debut at the show, and I moved the scene back and forth at her will. The new machines came with a variety of cut-out designs and shapes—hearts, circles, trees, flowers, "And More," which seemed to be the theme of the show. I thought of my home crafts group and the two camps they fell into: those who had every gadget and attachment available, and those who thought using such tools was cheating. I liked to think that my granddaughter and I were the happy medium.

Maddie was quick to connect with a girl her age who'd just driven in from New Jersey with her dad and her crafty mother. Maddie and her new dark-haired friend, Crystal, shared crafts tips. Maddie showed me a cute party hat that she'd made from a small lunch bag and colored paper given to her by Crystal. Not exactly mini, but a nice idea for a party favor. In return, Maddie shared some of the rainbow-colored rubber bands she'd brought to make her latest bracelets. Another maxi item, using a loom that most adults would call a plastic pegboard, but crafts were crafts, and better than many activities I'd seen preteens engage in. Before long, Maddie was wearing a green-and-gold party hat and Crystal sported several narrow rubber-band bracelets. Eleven-year-olds bonded so easily. Why didn't it remain so?

I had only one message from Cynthia, to thank me for being at Aunt Elsie's service and for all the help I'd been so far. The call would have been perfect, if she hadn't ruined it with her double-whammy sign-off. "I'll be looking forward to your first report, Gerry. Oh, and remember, I'm hoping you can stop by and help, or just be with me, as I go through Aunt Elsie's clothes. I know you're busy with the fair over the weekend, but maybe Friday, or early next week?"

Early next week for me consisted of one day, Monday, before we flew out on Tuesday. I deleted the message and turned my attention back to my job.

I helped Bebe throw a plastic cover over our table and headed for the exit, when I saw the strangest sight: Maddie was sitting off to the side reading a newspaper. The girl really was following through on being the quintessential New Yorker. I couldn't wait to see what happened to these new habits and new food preferences once we landed in our home state.

"Anything interesting?" I asked, approaching her.

"A man fell off the platform onto the tracks in front of a subway train, or he might have been pushed. But he survived because he dove into the space between the rails when the train rode over him."

"That's quite a feat," I said, marveling at how the man could have flattened himself to fit into the roadbed.

"And another guy died accidentally in his apartment when he fell from a stepladder and hit his head. He lived in Midtown South and was a medical student at a midtown college. We're in midtown, right, Grandma?"

I nodded. I couldn't help noting that Maddie's two articles had overtones of crime or death. Was Maddie looking for another Case?

AS different as the setting was, with car horns blaring even at eleven o'clock at night, Maddie and I kept to our usual good-night time. The end-of-the-day ritual had morphed from mostly reading and a little chatting when she was a toddler, to a bit of reading and a lot of chatting lately. Tonight, there was no reading. Maddie started the chat.

"Where's the Bronx exactly, Grandma?"

"About a half hour away, more or less."

"That's where my dad was born, right?"

We'd had a version of this conversation a number of times, even back in California, but it was bedtime, and I played along. "That's right."

"And where you lived with Grandpa."

"That's right, too. Do you want me to show you on a map?"

"Can we go there? I know you told me they tore down the building, but still I'd like to see where it was."

"If we have time," I said, confident that we wouldn't. There was too much to see in Manhattan, even without Cynthia's agen-

da for us. Earlier today, my cab had passed the spot where our
favorite Times Square deli used to be. It was now a tween clothing store.

Through the years, I'd followed the ups and downs of life on
the four-mile-long Bronx Grand Concourse in a sketchy way,
until everyone I knew there had moved and I no longer had a
contact to keep me up to date. I didn't need to go there; I didn't
need anything to recall my days with Ken. They would always be
with me, just as Henry would always have memories of Virginia.
Two lucky people, getting together to make more memories.

While I'd been absorbed otherwise, Maddie had moved on
to her next topic.

"How many suspects do you have for Aunt Elsie's Case,
Grandma?"

"I thought you were going to tell me more about Radio
City Music Hall and your souvenir shopping. Did you buy some
T-shirts?"

"A few. They were really cheap. This guy was selling them
out of crates right on the sidewalk. I got one for Taylor with a
big heart on the front, just like she asked for, and one that says
THE CITY NEVER SLEEPS for Uncle Skip, 'cause he's always at your
house late at night. I'll show them to you tomorrow." She yawned,
but I knew she wasn't finished yet. "Grandma, remember when
I asked you if I should pack an umbrella and you said, no, there'd
be tons of them?" It seemed like years ago, but I nodded, yes.
"You were right. One of the guys had a crate of umbrellas! And
I think they were, like, three for ten dollars. Why would anyone
want three umbrellas? This is really the 'And More' city, isn't it?"

I nodded, and leaned over to kiss her. "You're right about
that, sweetheart. Have a good sleep."

Too soon. "Now tell me how many suspects. Then I'll do
some math."

"Okay." I was a pushover when it came to humoring my
granddaughter. I made a rough count, based on the number of
guests I'd met at the memorial service.

"Nine," I said.

Maddie bit her lip and focused for a minute. "That means you've eliminated eight million, three hundred and nine thousand, nine hundred and ninety-one people." She fell back onto her pillow, seeming tired from the arithmetic. "Want to know how I know that?"

"Uh-huh."

"I found out there are eight million, three hundred and ten thousand people in New York City, so I subtracted nine and that's what I got." Maddie seemed pleased with herself, so I congratulated her, even after she admitted that the starting census figure was based on a two-year-old estimate. "Wouldn't it be great if I could figure out Miss Bishop's Case," she said. Tired as I was, I thought of the research project I promised Cynthia, to find out if there was a rash of deaths of elderly people in the neighborhood. Did I want to involve Maddie in a real case? "I really wish I could help," she added.

It was now or never. "Actually, you can."

Chapter 8

THURSDAY MORNING I felt much more in sync with East Coast time. As I expected, by nine A.M. Bebe was on her way to the SuperKrafts corporate offices with her neatly written inventory list and her best professional outfit, as close to a three-piece suit as a girl could get. She'd stopped by our room and received the appropriate supportive approval.

It was just me and Maddie in our Big Apple hotel room and not much to do for the show until further notice from Supervisor Bebe. But once I'd told Maddie I could use her help on a computer search project for Cynthia, our plans for sightseeing in Manhattan took second place.

"I thought you wanted to see the Statue of Liberty," I reminded her.

"I did, but remember that book Grandpa read to me when I was little? It was all about the Statue of Liberty and how you can see it from all over the city if you're up high enough. We can just go up on the roof of the hotel."

"I doubt it."

"Plus, there's so much online about New York," Maddie said. "You almost don't need to leave your computer. There's a whole website for subway pranks." She laughed as if she herself had pulled them off. "Too bad Dad insisted on us never taking the subway. Last week a mariachi band went through the cars, just for fun, and cheered everyone up. People were dancing, even. Then another time a team of performers went through pretending to be panhandlers, but funny. Like, one dressed up like a Wall Street guy and he was yelling about not being able to pay off his really expensive car. A Fraro, I think."

"A Ferrari, probably. Would you really rather stay in and work on your computer than do any of the things you checked off in your tour book? How about the Children's Museum?"

"Maybe later. Just for right now, Grandma, I want to do this research. I've been looking up all the obituaries of old people that lived nearby. Manhattan is only a little more than two miles wide, so that's the radius I'm using. Besides it's nice and warm in the room."

"Do we need to buy you some warmer clothes? You know there's an entire shopping mall below us, part of Grand Central Station. Maybe we can pick up an extra sweater to wear under your jacket?"

"Nah, I have enough clothes." She looked at me as though she'd do anything to get rid of me. "You're supposed to call the agencies like the one Cynthia uses for nurses, right?"

"Right." I got the point, and decided to give Maddie a little more work time before forcing a good time on her. I knew I couldn't call all the agencies in Manhattan, or even in a two-mile radius. In fact, it seemed unlikely that a care worker could afford to live in this part of Manhattan. I guessed they were commuters from less pricey neighborhoods, and therefore we should be looking everywhere else. An impossible task.

I pushed aside the fact that my eleven-year-old granddaughter was collecting statistics on New York citizens between eighty-five and one hundred years old, who died in the last three months while patients of healthcare workers. It was my fault that Maddie wasn't on a ferry ride to the Statue of Liberty, or at a children's museum, which is where her father envisioned her, I was sure.

Rring. Rring. No New York tune this time; just the plain old landline of the hotel room. I picked up the cumbersome black receiver.

"Mrs. Porter, I'm so glad I caught you. I thought you might be sightseeing by now." So did I, but the gravelly-voiced woman didn't need to hear that. "This is Jackie Cromwell, the organizer of the miniatures part of the fair. I'm afraid we have a problem. We could really use your help."

"What can I do for you?" I asked, as if I had nothing else going on.

"We've had a rash of thefts in the exhibit hall. Several vendors are reporting things missing, even though we have as much security as we ever have at these events. Usually this doesn't happen until the show starts and people start coming in off the streets."

"I'm sorry to hear that."

"Lots of expensive things are being taken this time, not just the usual little doilies or mini-plates of food that are piled on the tables and can easily be swept into a purse. For example, the Langland Editions people are missing an heirloom-quality miniature tea cart. It's made of inlaid wood, with gold accents, worth almost two thousand dollars. Another missing item is a small porcelain pitcher from Japan that's worth several hundred dollars. And at least three jewelers have reported the loss of hand-blown glass pendants."

"That's most unfortunate. What can I do for you?" I asked again, this time emphasizing the *I*. I held my breath, but it didn't do any good as far as keeping what I feared at bay.

"I met Bebe Mellon at a vendor meeting yesterday, where we were talking about this, and she tells me you work as an auxiliary to the police department in your hometown in California. That's just the kind of expertise we need to supplement our own security staff. Would you be able to come to the office on the second floor of the hotel and work with Ronnie O'Brien, our head of show security? Maybe you could look at some footage we have from the last couple of days."

I started to formulate a correction of Bebe's description of me as other than the relative of a homicide detective, a designation probably shared by many others connected to the show, but thought better of it. If nothing else, here was a chance to do something for Bebe, whom I'd come to serve. "Of course," I said. "I'd be glad to help." I went on to explain that I was with my eleven-year-old granddaughter and would have to bring her with me. No problem, it seemed. I didn't mention that if anyone would see something significant on the screen, it would be Maddie.

WITH our new schedule in place, an excited Maddie and I rode down to the second-floor security office. At the sight of the banks of monitors stretched across the gray-paneled room, she uttered her approximately one-hundredth New York "Wow." A greeting from Ronnie O'Brien, NYPD, Retired, interrupted her counting of the screens at twelve.

"Hey," he said, extending his beefy hand to Maddie first. "You like all this? Maybe you can come to work for us some day." Maddie's nod and "Uh-huh" were too enthusiastic for my taste. I'd spent most of her life trying to dissuade her from a career in crime, on either side of the law. Ronnie, as we were asked to call him, set us up in front of our own monitor. "We've gone over these videos already, but Jackie—that's Ms. Cromwell— thinks that a new pair of experienced eyes might spot something we didn't." Ronnie's tone said he doubted it, especially if the eyes were those of a little girl and her grandmother. I was ready to agree and move on to our next project, but Maddie had made herself comfortable and I had promised to do whatever she wanted today. Never mind that I pictured us walking around the Egyptian Temple of Dendur at the Met, not a dark room that was Security central for a hotel.

Ronnie left and we turned to the task of watching people come and go on video, through the main turnstile entrance on 42nd Street, in and out of the elevators on all floors, and in and out of the ballroom where the show was set up.

"Everyone wears a coat in New York," Maddie said. "Not, like, a heavy jacket or a down vest. A real coat. There's one lady in a coat with a collar that's as big as a cape over her shoulders. My mom would love it. And even some men wear coats. I wish my dad had a coat."

"Maybe we can buy him one for Christmas." A thought that made me realize that the countdown for that was quickly heading to single digits.

Maddie laughed. "Dad wears the same jacket he wore when I was little."

"And that was so long ago."

"Uh-huh," Maddie said, not missing a beat, not seeing the humor.

"Did you find anything that will help with the thefts?"

"Not yet, but this is fun, Grandma. You can see what people do when they don't know someone's watching."

Worse than a cop or a criminal. A voyeur. "I think it's better not to know," I said.

Maddie smiled and I knew she disagreed with me.

WE sat at a small marble-top table in the bustling food court on the lower level of Grand Central Station. Elbow to elbow with other diners, most looking like office workers, Maddie and I shared a lunch of tomato-and-mozzarella panini, sea-salt chips, gourmet pickles, fruit cups, and cheesecake, from four different vendors. My young partner and I discussed our cases.

"I think I know what's happening with the robberies, Grandma. But I need to watch more video in the security office," Maddie said.

"Do you actually have a lead, or do you just want to look in on people and their private lives?"

"It's not exactly private, Grandma. They're in the hallways or the ballroom or the lobby. It's not like they're taking a shower or anything." I took her answer as evidence that she had no real lead but didn't want to abandon such a fun project. Too bad it was past the era of washing little mouths out with soap. Or had that been only for bad language?

"Still, we said we'd leave the video monitoring and work on Cynthia's project after lunch," I reminded the offender. She was quick to agree—a Case was a Case, after all.

On the way out, we bought cookies to go at another vendor stand. Maddie stuffed them in her backpack as we made still another food purchase, small cups of gelato at the last little shop, at the doorway to 42nd Street. "I wish the food courts at home were like this," Maddie said.

BACK in our room, Maddie worked on her laptop, and I used her phone to call the first agency on the list. While I was on hold to watered-down holiday music, I thought of what we were missing in the city that never sleeps. I pictured Maddie making journal entries at a play or concert or walking with me in one of the many parks. Even a wobbly, top-heavy, red tour bus would have been preferable to being holed up in a hotel room bent over a computer. An older-sounding woman picked up the agency phone, breaking into the on-hold music and my musings.

"Alliance Caregivers," she announced. "Helping you overcome challenges."

I cleared my throat, wondering how she knew about my current challenges, and turned away from Maddie, to pave the way for the yarn I was about to spin. "I'm looking into hiring a caregiver for my elderly father. One of my friends likes your agency and recommended that I call you."

"We're here for you," she assured me.

"But I've also heard that there was a problem with a recent patient." I chided myself for the lameness of my opening salvo.

"Oh? What kind of problem?"

"My friend says that one of your patients, an elderly woman, died when she inadvertently stopped taking her blood pressure medication." I tried not to sound accusatory. Or too much like a fiction writer.

I heard a heavy sigh on the other end of the line. "Well, to be perfectly honest, we did have a similar situation last year, but the relative who'd hired us had insisted that the patient did not need help with pills."

Cynthia? It sounded true to her form. But the timing didn't match. "Wasn't there a similar case more recently, maybe a week or so ago?" Now I was winging it, and, I was positive, revealing myself for the amateur investigator I was.

"No, no, you've been getting bad info. The only case I can think of involves the Fairhaven Agency, where one of their patients fell from a balcony, possibly due to a drug reaction."

"It seems I've been misinformed."

"It certainly does. Now, can we schedule an appointment for you and your father?"

I'd forgotten my lie for a moment—that I was calling about my elderly father (who'd passed away before the agency was in business probably). I found myself perspiring, worried that the woman was tracing my call and alerting a federal investigatory bureau, perhaps putting my number on a list. "I'll think about it and get back to you." I hung up with haste, hoping that Richard, the registered owner of Maddie's smartphone, wouldn't get solicitations from Alliance.

Strike one. Strike two, if I counted the Fairhaven Agency with its death by falling.

My calling plan seemed doomed. I realized that no one was going to give me useful information under these conditions. I seemed to be a better strategist in a small town. I reached over to Maddie, sitting on her bed with her laptop, and patted her shoulder. "Come on, sweetheart," I said. "Let's grab our coats and get out of here. We're taking a break."

"Where to?" Maddie asked, her brows knitted, her fingers still dancing over the keyboard. "I'm trying a new search engine."

How to grab her attention? "We're going to look at some creatures that have been dead for millions of years," I said. "Not only that, but no one knows exactly how they died."

Maddie's eyes lit up. "I almost forgot. The dinosaur museum is here. Let's go!" She grabbed her jacket and frowned when her journal didn't fit properly inside her backpack. Until she realized that what took up room was a bag of cookies. Her smile returned and we were on our way.

Fifteen minutes later, we were bundled up in a taxi, protected against twenty-degree weather, heading across town to the Upper West Side. This time we'd visit, not Cynthia, but a *T. rex* at the American Museum of Natural History. Surely the dino tour was a journey more fit for Maddie's report to her class, and to her father.

DURING our educational afternoon, I declined two phone calls, one from Cynthia and one from Bebe. Instead of answering, I walked the enormous halls with Maddie for a while, marveling at the mammoth creatures composed of fossilized bones, then retreated to a bench while Maddie roamed among the rest of the dinosaurs. She made several trips to and from my seat to write in her journal and report to me on her findings—the *Deinonychus* (seven feet long, with sharp claws); the *Velociraptor* (sharp teeth and sickle-shaped claws); and, her favorite, the *Triceratops*, one of the last dinosaurs standing. This was what I had pictured—Maddie bent over, not her computer, but documentation for the fossilized imprint of the carcass of a prehistoric creature.

"This *Triceratops* has an injury on its skull, Grandma," she told me on this latest visit to my bench. "Can you imagine? It's partially healed and they think it was in a fight with another dinosaur sixty-five million years ago." She let out one of her "Wow" sounds. "I wish Dad was here. He would be totally amazed. Did he come here? Is that why he's an orthopedic surgeon? Fixing bones and stuff?"

I'd have loved to have told Maddie that her orthopedist father was inspired on a visit here by the exhibits in the hall of reptiles and amphibians, but the truth came out. "When we lived here, your dad was a little too young to appreciate science. Remember, we moved to California before his fourth birthday."

"I wish you'd stayed in New York," she said.

Give my regards to Broadway...

My phone saved me from having to comment on that complicated topic. This time I took the call, from Henry, who was in the San Francisco airport on his way to Hawaii. I relaxed and smiled, remaining seated while Maddie left for another tour of ancient claws and hipbones.

"I figure we'll be about seventy degrees away from each other in terms of temperature," he said. "Did you bring enough heavy clothing?"

I assured him we were keeping warm and described the sauropods Maddie had lately informed me about.

"I can't believe you're not working one of your cases. According to your email, you have two now, right? Your friend's aunt's death and the thefts at the show?"

"Yes, as if I needed another pull on my time."

"Well, good for you, taking a break today." Anyone listening to Henry might have thought I was a career homicide detective on vacation instead of a simple retired English teacher and grandmother who was a miniatures enthusiast. Or maybe that was how I'd sounded in my last email to him.

I accepted his praise, but confessed the reason for our respite from police work. "We're at a stalemate." I explained the lack of any leads in Aunt Elsie's death, and likewise from the security footage of the exhibit hall. "Not that any of these facts have dissuaded Cynthia or Bebe from prodding me on. Cynthia's as determined as ever to prove that her aunt's death was not an accident, and Bebe is convinced I'll be able to catch a thief."

"I can hear the tension in your voice. Maybe you should get on a plane and meet us on Maui. We can relax on the beach together."

"Thanks for the laugh. I'm sorry to dump on you. I have to figure out how to meet my responsibilities to Bebe and her managers and at the same time honor Cynthia's special needs."

"If anyone can do it..."

My "Thanks" was simple, but heartfelt.

"What do *you* think happened to Cynthia's aunt?" he asked.

Henry's question took me by surprise. I hadn't considered my own position on the matter. I'd simply gone along with Cynthia's conviction. I'd challenged her mostly because I didn't want to become involved in a potential murder investigation in a city where I didn't even know where the nearest police station was, let alone have a nephew on the force. I'd tried exercising Skip's system of Means-Motive-Opportunity, but I hadn't allowed myself to ask hard questions or look carefully at the circumstances of Aunt Elsie's death—the appearance of a full bottle of pills at just the right time; the disappearance of a secretly placed box, probably containing a significant amount of cash; the number of people who had access to Aunt Elsie and her home. I hadn't even followed up with interviews of alleged suspects, like the nurse, Ashley, and the almost-nurse, Candace, and the super, Neal, whom I'd met at the memorial service. Or the deli and bakery workers. Or the doormen—Duncan, Cody, and any other temporary workers. Or Aunt Elsie's old beau, Philip. "I'm not sure what I think," I told Henry.

"You can never be sure. What's your best guess?"

"I don't have enough information." More stalling.

"Then get it. Think of Skip and what his interview with Cynthia would be like, and go for it. Then get Cynthia to put you in touch with all the people you told me about, who were at the service. Once you've done all that, you'll have everything you need for an informed opinion, and you might even decide how to help Cynthia present a case to the police."

"As Maddie would say, 'Wow.' While you're on a roll, Henry, what about the missing little treasures?"

"I did give that some thought, and remembered a time I went to a woodworking show while I still taught shop at the high school. A couple of crooks worked in pairs. One guy dropped something or created some kind of disturbance, and the other whisked away a valuable piece. They focused on small items like an inlaid toothpick holder or camping knife with a fancy wood handle. I'm sure it's a common trick—one distracts; the other grabs."

"I can't wait to tell Maddie. No wonder I love you."

"Aww."

My call-waiting buzzed. Cynthia again, as if she knew I was "there" but avoiding her. I declined again, and took some time signing off with Henry and greeting Maddie, who had returned to my bench with new excitement. She held out her smartphone. "Look, Grandma, there's a museum app with a game about accidental poisoning. They give you cases and hints and you have to solve them. Like, sometimes the reason for the poison is from the air or water, or sometimes it's from food. Or it could be from a toxic plant."

"What does this have to do with dinosaurs?"

"It's to show you how scientists work, Grandma. Detectives solve problems like scientists. Uncle Skip says that a lot. You have to think logically, like my science teacher says, too. Ask questions, make a hypothesis, test it, and draw a conclusion. Like, first they thought the *Stegosaurus* had two brains, but they did some research and found out the one it had was enough, even though it was smaller than they expected."

I had a not-so-pleasant flashback to learning the scientific method and participating in science fairs in school, perhaps when I was Maddie's age. But it was already too late by then. Baking soda volcanoes and batteries made with pennies didn't work for me, either 'physically or interest-wise. Now, thanks to my fiancé and my eleven-year-old granddaughter, when I did call Cynthia back, it was with a new attitude. No more tiptoeing around. I was going to approach the problem like a scientist.

"We have to talk," I said to Cynthia. "I need to ask you some questions and get honest answers."

"You mean, sort of forget we're friends?"

"Sort of. Some of the questions might be hard."

"I'm ready," she said, as if I were going to hook her up to a lie detector. "Where are you?"

"About ten blocks away, where the dinosaurs live."

Cynthia laughed, a nice sound. "That's easy then. Just come to my place."

"I guess the break's over, huh, Grandma?"

We headed for the magnificent lobby of columns and flags, said good-bye to the plant-eating *Barosaurus* rearing up over the banners, and picked up our coats. "I guess it is."

Chapter 9

I DIDN'T WANT Maddie present while I questioned Cynthia. I called Bebe to get her okay, then handed Maddie over to her at the hotel and returned to the Upper West Side. Two more jerky cab rides. I almost wished I'd had enough time to take the subway. The in-cab video service, with looping news reports and talk shows playing on the screen in front of me, did nothing to make the ride smoother. Neither Maddie nor Cynthia was thrilled with the new arrangement. As if I were having a good time.

"Sure," Bebe had said when I called with the request. "I can always use Maddie's help." The unspoken implication was "since her grandmother is too busy to be useful to me."

Maddie's reaction was too fraught with emotion to be recalled verbatim, but I know that phrases like "You don't love me" and "I never have any fun" were thrown around, and I thought I heard "You said it would snow." As if I'd make a promise like that. As if I had control of the weather. Or of anything else this week.

"This is not your most attractive moment," I told her.

She got it immediately and gave me her most sheepish look. To further establish peace, I told her Henry's idea—that there might be two people, partners in crime, working the exhibit hall thefts. I got the positive reaction I wanted when I suggested she review the security videos with that in mind.

Cynthia wasn't in a great mood to begin with, either. She'd missed my message about needing more than thirty minutes, because of the round-trip taxi logistics to and from our hotel to deposit Maddie. It was nearly three-thirty and almost dark by the time Duncan opened the door of my cab in front of Cynthia's building.

"Evening, ma'am," he said, gracious as always, though it had to be near the end of his shift. In fact, the second of two New York doormen that I knew by name, Cody, was waiting inside the building to call the elevator for me.

"Aren't you early for your shift?" I asked him.

"I'd like to claim that I'm conscientious, but really I'm planning to leave early. This will be my first evening off in over two weeks. Big date, so I made a deal with the graveyard guy. He's going to replace me in a couple of hours." Cody responded to my confused look with further explanation. "Midnight to eight in the morning? The graveyard shift?"

I nodded, understanding at last. It occurred to me that I should arrange to meet the graveyard guy. Who had a better opportunity to sneak around the building without interruption? I wondered what precautions were in place to ensure that no one, even one with a key, could enter an apartment in the middle of the night. My small, unattached home in the suburbs had its advantages.

"And what's the graveyard shift's name?" I asked Cody, all casual, as if I were writing checks for holiday bonuses.

"Paul. We call him Pastor Paul, because he's a seminarian."

Really? A man of God? It wasn't impossible that he could be a closet killer, but I doubted it. I had to draw the line somewhere. I gave myself a painless mental slap. In about an hour I'd gone from a slacker to an overzealous sleuth. I erased Paul's name from my suspect list as quickly as I'd added him moments before.

CYNTHIA and I sat at her dining room table, a lovely, flower-patterned tea set in front of us. The cookies—our now traditional black-and-whites—on a matching china plate seemed to be giving me sardonic grins. The hot, fruity drink seemed to calm us down, however, and after a few minutes of deep breathing and reconnecting, we took on her problem in earnest.

"Let's start with what was new in Aunt Elsie's life lately," I said.

"I can't think of a thing," Cynthia said. "Until she became ill and lethargic that last week or so, she had her routine. Daily walks, church, her theater group. I'm the one who was busier than usual. My case load nearly doubled this fall and I was often gone from dawn to dusk, driving to New Jersey, spending the day with clients on Long Island or up in Yonkers, all over."

"So you needed more helpers for Aunt Elsie? Maybe people who were new to you and her?"

"That's right, but they were all bonded, from the same agency. You met the principal caregivers at the memorial service. Ashley and Candace. I doubt that anyone who was here once or twice could have done this. It had to be someone with long term access, don't you think?" I agreed with a nod, since my mouth was busy with the chocolate half of the black-and-white. "Have you talked to Ashley and Candace since the service?"

"No," I admitted.

"Don't you think you should?"

I felt my face flush. I needed to gain control of this exchange, to take Cynthia up on her suggestion, and Skip's, that I should forget we were friends. I braced myself and prepared to use my stern-teacher voice, the voice I used about once a month in the classroom, whether I needed to or not. "I will talk to them, but I'm not a detective, Cynthia. I have no clout, no insider information, and no way to obtain it in this city. You'll have to set it up. You can start by giving the agency a call and asking them to send the women by. You can say there are a few loose ends to settle for insurance or tax purposes. I'll figure out a way to talk to the doormen and the super."

"Okay."

Could it be this easy? Maybe Cynthia had been waiting for me to take charge all along. "Let's get started. While you call

Ashley and Candace's agency, I'll call down to Duncan and see if I can catch him before he leaves."

Cynthia looked at her watch. "He'll be going off shift soon. You should just go down there now."

I took a last sip of tea and pushed away from the table. Cynthia was back in charge. That didn't take long. Henry would not be happy.

IN the lobby, Duncan was preparing to relinquish his position to Cody. As I approached the men, I heard talk that signaled the transfer of duties.

"Watch out for Nine-A, he seemed a little out of it today and might need help getting to his flat," Duncan advised. "You can forget about the entire third floor. Looks like they've all taken off for a long weekend."

"I saw Nine-A get in a cab with Nine-B. I'll be on the lookout for them. Don't worry. Did you fix the problem with Eight-A?" Cody asked.

Duncan nodded. "All set."

I was amused at how the doormen referred among themselves to the building's occupants. Not surprising; however, both men had called Cynthia "Miss Bishop" in her presence. It seemed they were bilingual.

"Excuse me," I said. "Could I speak with you for a few minutes, Duncan? I know you're almost on your way home and I won't take long."

"Sure. What's on your mind?"

I half expected him to add "Friend of Fifteen-D" at the end of his question. "My granddaughter is writing a report for her class about her trip to the big city. She's lived in California suburbs all her life, and is fascinated by the idea of doormen. I think she's calling that chapter 'The Eyes and Ears of Manhattan's Buildings.'" Duncan grinned and didn't correct my (Maddie's) impression. "Since you've had such a long career in this magnificent building, it would be very helpful to have your view of things."

"Sure," Duncan said. "She's such a cutie, your granddaughter." He looked around. "Where is she?"

Uh-oh. I cleared my throat and thought of one of Skip's mantras. *When lying during an interview, stick to the truth as much as possible.* I decided to give it a try for a change. "She's been pressed into service over at the Lex, which is where we're staying. We're getting ready for a big crafts show there and she's the talented one." All one hundred percent true.

"Oh yeah, I've seen the banners for the show on the lampposts along 42nd. Didn't know you were involved."

I explained how Maddie and I came to be in Manhattan in the first place, leaving out the part about the incident in 15-D.

"I'll cover," Cody said, apparently not offended that he wasn't considered a spokesperson for the building.

"I might have some questions for you, too," I said to Cody.

"Cool," he responded, and straightened his ill-fitting jacket.

Duncan led me to a pocket door that blended in so well with the ivory-colored wall and light wood of the lobby that I wouldn't have noticed it if he hadn't slid it open for me. We entered an area that was clearly a break room for the staff, with lockers, a vending machine, and a sofa that looked like a castoff from an upstairs apartment. Another door led, I assumed, to the employee bathroom. Duncan unfolded a metal chair from a row of them, and directed me to sit on the sofa. I sat, sank almost to the floor, and immediately wished I'd been offered a folding chair. The door slid back a few inches and Cody stuck his head in.

"Would you mind if I just picked up my cap?" he asked. "I left it in my locker."

"No problem," Duncan said, and Cody came and left, cap in hand, in a matter of seconds. "Cody's a good kid, majoring in art. Don't ask me what he's going to do with that." I made a note to ask my daughter-in-law if she'd mind doing a little long-distance mentoring. "A lot of the part-timers, mostly college kids, aren't invested as much. They usually don't bother to get to know the residents. But I have to say, Cody makes an effort. Not like some of the others."

I sympathized with "the way the world is going" and prepared my notepad and pen, trying to look like an interested, dedicated surrogate reporter. "If you don't mind, Duncan, we'd love to have a description of what you do."

Duncan sat back and seemed to puff out his chest a bit. "We do more than open doors and say cheery 'Good mornings,'" he said, letting go with a hearty laugh that reinforced his Santa image. I tried to mimic the laugh, hoping it would establish a bond of trust between us. "Our first priority is the security of the building. That means screening all visitors, whether they're workmen, deliverymen, or guests of the residents, and keeping a log." I wrote "check log" on my pad, acknowledging to myself the slim chance that a stranger intent on doing evil to one of the residents would sign in. "You'd be surprised at what our residents expect of us. We can't know everything, but we try to respond to questions about the weather, or sports, or what time the concert starts. One of the things we get asked most by people off the street is 'Are there any units for sale in this building?' and 'How much?'" Duncan grinned. "I base my answer to that one on how rich they look."

"I never would have guessed," I said. "I'll bet people tell you things they wouldn't tell anyone else."

"I have stories," he said. "Like what I'd like to do when someone snaps their fingers at me. But probably not for your granddaughter's report. Let me just explain the serious side a little more. We have staff to do the actual maintenance and repair work, but it's up to us to monitor the needs of the facility, as well as the neatness of the lobby, elevators, hallways, and even the flowerbeds outside. We help with packages, of course, take care of pets—sometimes for long periods while the owners are away."

I stopped writing. "You actually go in and feed the pets?" I hoped Duncan didn't grasp the underlying question, which was "Do doormen have keys and free access to all units?"

Duncan nodded. "You bet. Or, we can be asked to simply keep an eye on a resident's car while it's double-parked and they just want to run upstairs for a minute. I should say that the residents of this building are very generous with tips on these occasions, even though most of these services fall under the normal doorman's job description." Now who had an underlying meaning to his statement? I was glad I'd thought to take my purse downstairs with me, and was already estimating the worth of Duncan's interview. "Then there are those times that are more delicate," Duncan continued, "like when a guy might be entertaining someone, if you know what I mean. That's what we call a 'you-didn't-see-nothin' tip.'" Duncan's laugh was a notch higher at that revelation. "Not that that ever happened with your friends upstairs on Fifteen, but Aunt Elsie—we all called her that, by the way, affectionately, of course—her old boyfriend did show up a lot lately and I got the distinct impression from the large bills he gave me that he'd prefer the niece didn't know, if you get my meaning."

I nodded to show that I grasped the meaning in Duncan's last comment. I was beyond thrilled and relieved that Duncan had opened that door, so to speak, in television lawyer talk, and we could now talk about Aunt Elsie and let Maddie's report needs slide. "You mean Aunt Elsie's friend, Philip Chapman? Has he been here? I thought that relationship ended decades ago."

"That's what I understood also. Not that we spread gossip, but when my old retired buddies come back to visit, we naturally reminisce and share a bit of history. After a long absence, old Phil has been coming around lately. I don't know whether the younger Miss Bishop likes him or not. As I say, from the size of his tips, I gathered he wanted to keep it between him and Aunt Elsie and the lamppost, and that's what I did. It's not like they were underage." Another big laugh. "And something else, though I don't want to get him in trouble, a couple of times he walked out with a package he didn't come in with."

I felt my own tip to Duncan mounting in size. "You don't

say." It was all I could do not to ask the size, color, shape, and weight of the packages.

"Nothing big, like furniture, mind you, but a bag or a briefcase he didn't have when he got out of the cab. He seems like a nice enough guy, though, so I figure it's possible Aunt Elsie was cleaning out and maybe passing some things on, could be some sentimental things, like photos or gifts from their early days."

"That sounds reasonable." And worth looking into, I added to my notes.

Duncan checked his watch. "Hey, I gotta go or the missus will be on my back. We like an early dinner and some TV, you know? Then I'm back here at eight tomorrow. Dressed and ready, you tell your little granddaughter."

I assured Duncan that he'd been very helpful. I handed him the largest bill I had in my wallet. His smile of thanks seemed to signify that I could have a sit-down with him again some time. When he slid the door open, he nearly knocked Cody, ostensibly straightening a dark green plastic garland, off balance.

"Have a nice chat?" Cody asked as he called the elevator for me.

"Very nice," I said. I had the feeling that Cody hadn't missed much. "I just thought of one other thing, though," I said, in a move that Skip would have called "too *Columbo*." "Do all of the doormen have keys to the apartments, or just the day shift?"

"They're on a board in there," Cody said, pointing to the room I'd just exited. "But they're locked up, too. You need a key for the keys." He laughed. "Funny, huh?"

I didn't think so, but before I could follow up, the elevator doors opened. Cody touched his cap and walked away.

WHEN I got back to her apartment, Cynthia was waiting, still at her dining room table, her laptop open in front of her. Once again I was struck by the spectacular view of Central Park behind her. I wondered if I'd ever get used to it as Cynthia seemed to have. Would I have been able to work on my dollhouses? Prepare

materials for my tutoring at the library? Would I have managed
to turn my back on the windows at all? Another question: Would
my little rose garden in Lincoln Point, California, ever again seem
like the perfect view outside my kitchen window?

Cynthia had been busy while I was lounging on a second-
hand couch. She'd contacted the agency that supplied Aunt Elsie's home care.

"The girls can come over tomorrow morning," she said. It
took a moment to realize she meant Ashley and Candace, Aunt
Elsie's nurses.

"It was that easy to set it up?"

"They do a lot of business in this neighborhood, and they
know word gets around, both plus and minus, so they want to
please."

"I'll be here right after breakfast, but I'll have to be back at
the hotel for the afternoon workshops."

I took Cynthia's grunt to mean "I understand." What she said
aloud was "I left a message with Neal Crouse, our super, to call
you."

"Thanks," I said. I considered grunting, but passed on the
idea.

I'd had the whole fifteen-floor elevator ride to consider
whether I'd tell Cynthia about the alleged return of Aunt Elsie's
old boyfriend. I was curious whether there was a tip threshold
such that Duncan would look the other way as Philip neglected
to sign the log book.

I took a seat at the table, my back to the windows so I could
concentrate. "Did you get anything interesting or useful from
Duncan?" Cynthia asked.

"Definitely interesting to me," I said, deciding on the spot
that sharing and openness with her was the best course from now
on. "Supposedly, Philip Chapman has been stopping by to visit
Aunt Elsie."

"I knew that," Cynthia said. I sat back. Apparently, open and
complete sharing wasn't one of Cynthia's resolutions. "For one

thing, the man has been smoking the same pipe tobacco since World War Two. After he'd leave, Aunt Elsie would spray the rooms with the same rose-scented air freshener every time, but I'm a little smarter than that." I nodded agreement. "A few times I thought of telling her she didn't have to hide anything from me, but what was the point? I'm pretty sure she knew I knew; it was like a little game. I'm not sure why she thought I'd mind, since there was never any real animosity between Philip and me, just this unspoken competition for her affection. But that ended long ago. At least it did for me."

"You didn't think to tell me all this when he showed up at her memorial service?" I asked, in a surprisingly (to me) calm tone.

"I was trying to keep your focus on possible suspects. Old Philip certainly had no motive to kill the love of his life. He's a harmless old man who never let go of his first love."

Selective sharing, I thought. Which gave me permission to keep from Cynthia the small matter of Philip's takeout from the apartment. If her assessment of him as a harmless old man was correct, he probably didn't steal the Bishops' money. And if he was poorer than he looked, and Aunt Elsie decided to give it to him, that could stay their little secret. For now.

"Did he have a career in acting after Aunt Elsie quit?" I asked, revealing my ignorance of New York theater. Other than watching the Tony Awards every other year or so, I'd been out of touch with that part of my cultural history. Maybe Philip Chapman had won Tonys the years I wasn't tuned in.

Cynthia cleared up that thought. "He lost ambition after that. I heard he made a lot of money in real estate and became a patron of the arts. He produces now and then, I think, but he never acted again. I never understood why Aunt Elsie and he couldn't have worked something out. I was only a kid, but lots of people, couples and singles, raise a kid while following a career."

I put my hand on Cynthia's arm, almost feeling the heaviness of the load she'd been carrying. "Did you and Aunt Elsie ever talk about the breakup? It may not have had anything to do with your coming to live with her."

Cynthia raised her eyebrows. I could tell by her look that she'd never considered that possibility. "I don't know what you mean."

"Things look different to kids. Everything is simple. They see *A*, then *B*, and figure *A* must have caused *B*. You were six years old, right?" Cynthia nodded. "For all you know, they were about to break up for any of the usual reasons couples decide they're not right for each other. But you had just come to live with Aunt Elsie, and it looked to you as if your arrival sent him away."

Cynthia shook her head and made an unpleasant chuckling sound. "One big coincidence, huh?"

"Think about it. Hasn't that ever happened to you at work, for example? Maybe you dropped a patient for reasons of distance or time, and the person thought it was because he'd said something that displeased you. Or maybe that patient developed a pimple on his forehead just before you terminated your arrangement and he blamed the pimple."

"How did you know?" Cynthia laughed again. "Thank you, Gerry."

I relaxed in my chair, an unfamiliar sense of accomplishment taking over. Maybe we'd made a little progress in one arena. If I couldn't clear up the matter of Aunt Elsie's death, I could try to remove a load of guilt from Cynthia over ruining her aunt's life. I resolved to come back to this topic before my trip was over.

"I still think it's worth my having a chat with Philip, by the way."

"I don't know why you would."

"Aunt Elsie might have shared something with him that she wouldn't necessarily tell you."

"Like what? We talked a lot, shared everything."

She didn't share the real reason for the breakup between two budding actors, I mused. "No one shares everything, Cynthia." I had an image of Henry, and how I might need to be more open about my reasons for not wanting him in New York this time. "Aunt Elsie may have had a fear or a suspicion of some kind," I continued. "She wouldn't want to worry you, but she might have shared it with Philip. Now, since we're considering that she may have been murdered, that becomes important."

"I suppose it's possible he knows something," Cynthia admitted.

Or that he has something, something that would fit in a small bag or briefcase. "Do you know how to get in touch with him?" I asked.

Cynthia reached in the drawer of the hutch behind her and surprised me by pulling out a cell phone. "Aunt Elsie's," she said. "I insisted she have one. It's not too smart or anything, but it's lightweight and she could keep it with her at all times."

"In case her alert bracelet and security system both failed," I said, slipping in a reminder of how well Cynthia took care of her aunt.

"You can't be too secure," she said. She scrolled through a list of numbers, stopped at Philip Chapman's, and read it off. Techie that I was, I entered the number directly into my own contact list. Maddie would be so proud.

Maddie! Bebe! I'd forgotten that they'd be waiting for me, tapping their feet by now. "I have to go," I said, nearly knocking over the teapot in my haste. "If I don't show up for dinner, my life won't be worth much." I grabbed my coat and accessories before Cynthia could dissuade me.

"Do you want me to ride down with you?"

I shook my head. "I'm on good terms with the doormen."

Chapter 10

I SHARED the elevator to the lobby with an older couple, Gwen and Frank, the Windoms from 16-A, as they identified themselves. "You're Cynthia's friend," Gwen said. "It's so nice of you to be here for her, all the way from California." I looked down at my feet. Had I inadvertently worn my flip-flops? Or had Duncan spread the word about a West Coast visitor? Should I think of the Windoms as suspects? Maybe there was a thing called elevator rage in Manhattan, to match road rage on the freeways at home. Before I made a fool of myself, I smiled and told them how nice it was to meet Cynthia's neighbors.

In the cab, en route between the Upper West Side and the Lex, we crossed Park Avenue with its legendary median strip that I never tired of. Today my driver, another cabbie occupied with his long-distance Bluetooth passenger, took the road through Central Park, crossing Park at 59th. I loved the sight of the rows of Christmas trees with multicolored lights that were featured along the avenue this month. I knew they'd be replaced by the appropriate flowers for the other seasons and I had an unmistakable urge to come back for each motif.

As I waited to connect on my cell with Skip, I noticed how well put-together New Yorkers looked. Though they were wearing as many winter accessories as I was, somehow their scarves, hats, and gloves seemed to be fashion statements, while mine made me feel like I was engulfed in enough padding for a Mrs. Santa tryout. When I met them, face to face, on the street, I wanted to apologize, imagining myself shouting, "I know my accessories don't match, and they're all low-end, but I need to keep warm and this is all I have."

"Hey, Aunt Gerry," Skip said, from a sunny place. "Need help with an interrogation?"

"Funny, but not really. I wish you were here."

"Are you making any progress?"

I gave Skip a status report for the two situations I'd gotten myself involved in, and asked for some tips. "This is not like helping you with a case in Lincoln Point. Here there's an unlimited number of suspects."

Skip laughed. "You're saying I have it easy?"

"I didn't mean that exactly. It's just that with the entire population of Manhattan to think about, it's hard to see any progress." I looked out the window at the streams of people on the streets—heading home from work, doing last-minute shopping, picking up dinner in one of the dozens of establishments, from delis and restaurants to fragrant food wagons on the street corners. Falafel here, chestnuts there, pretzels everywhere. Even small children seemed to be able to keep up with the pace. Had I been like that once? Probably. But not even my life in the Bronx had been as fast-forward-moving as twenty-first-century midtown Manhattan, especially during holiday season.

"I've been doing a little research for you," Skip said, adding more music to my ears, matching the carols coming from the cab's radio. "I'm sure Maddie's on it, but I've been digging, too, and haven't seen evidence of anything like an epidemic of mercy killings or suspicious deaths among the elderly in that area. My gut feeling is that if your friend's aunt was murdered, it was a crime of opportunity. He or she saw some money or the possibility of money, like the box you told me about with something of value, and went for it."

"That means I don't have to consider every single person who had even a nodding acquaintance with Elsie's care, or delivered a package for her birthday last summer."

'Yup."

"And I probably do have a limited pool of suspects right here, people who were a regular part of her life, saw her often."

"That's my feeling."

"Good enough for me," I said, with a mental thumbs-up.

"Another thing. I reached out to a cop I met at a conference several years ago. We've kept in touch and met up at other conferences, and yada yada. Great guy. He's retired now, but still connected to friends in the NYPD, and is willing to sit down with you if and when you think you have something. He told me he's waiting for his inspector interview 'cause he's the kind of guy who'll go nuts just hanging around. Anyway, his name is Barry Arnold. Everyone calls him Buzz. He's famous for quoting Yogi Berra at key moments. If nothing else, you can shoot back some Shakespeare. I'll send you an email with his contact information."

"That's fantastic, Skip. Thank you so much."

"No problem, especially since I'm sitting in your kitchen right now and I found the stash of cookies."

"Is everything okay there?"

"Oh, sure. I just happened to be in the neighborhood." A visit to June, I realized. "You could use a better hiding place for the sweets, however," Skip said. "Oh, and, remember, 'If you come to a fork in the road, take it.'"

"'Tis neither here nor there,'" I responded.

"Don't tell me that's Shakespeare?"

"*Othello.*"

"I'd love to be there when you pull that on Buzz."

I hung up with renewed hope that the upcoming interviews with the aides and friends (except for the killer) of Elsie Bishop would be useful in determining how she died. And I now had a friend on the NYPD. How much better could it get?

I STILL felt a little jet-lagged and tired enough to grab a few minutes of sleep. If a cab could be a phone booth, why not a bed?

We were traveling slowly enough in midtown rush hour traffic. I scrunched down a bit, got comfortable, head back, legs stretched out as far as possible, volume turned to zero on the video display in front of me, then...

Crunch!

A flat tire? In the middle of crowded Lexington Avenue? From the quick stop and words from the cabbie, words that were directed to an SUV driver and not fit for Maddie's journal, I guessed no, not a flat, but a fender-bender. At a rate lower than the speedometer could register, I'd hardly felt the jolt, which was less violent than what I remembered from operating the bumper cars on the boardwalk at Coney Island.

"You okay back there?" my driver asked, opening the door to exit and examine the damage. He sounded more like a man who hoped to avoid the inconvenience of an injured passenger than one who was concerned for my wellbeing.

"I'm fine," I said, as he slammed the door. A light changed somewhere and traffic started to flow, but without us.

On my first cab rides of this trip, I'd been worried that something like this would happen, given the way the drivers careened in and out of lanes, slammed on their brakes, and sped to a red light, stopping within inches of cars around them. But after a few trips, I'd gotten used to cabbies using every bit of space to move forward on the street. It turned out I'd been right to worry. Someone would be scraping yellow paint from the left front fender of the gray SUV that had just gotten a taste of my cab's front. And there went my clean record of taxi-riding.

My cabbie and the SUV driver pulled over and met where a white line would have been if there had been lane markers on the street. They each inspected the two vehicles and shrugged their shoulders.

"We oughta just exchange info and go," the SUV driver suggested.

"Yeah, yeah," my cabbie answered. He pulled a long, narrow strip of metal from the front grill of his vehicle, bent it in half, and tossed it through his open window onto the passenger seat of the cab. Minor blemish.

"Hey, hey," I heard from a voice in the distance. "Stop right there."

"Uh-oh, here comes the transit cop," the SUV driver noted.

"So what? He's not a real cop, anyway. Let's move."

And move we did, half onto a curb and down to the nearest street where it was legal to turn left. The transit non-cop, on foot, lost out. Or gave up.

New York City law and order, in action.

For the rest of the trip, I held onto the strap attached to the doorframe. There would be no napping in this cab.

As we approached the Lex, I couldn't wait to leave the NYC transit system and detective work behind for a while and get back to miniatures.

I'D called ahead and arranged to meet Maddie and Bebe at the hotel's restaurant, overlooking busy, loud, 42nd Street. As soon as I felt my granddaughter's arms around me, I put aside thoughts of evil nurses' aides and old boyfriends and not-so-petty thefts, and enjoyed her red curls tickling my chin. In a year or so, I figured, we'd be eye-to-eye, two tall, thin Porter women.

I got it over with and told Bebe as soon as we were seated that I wouldn't be available in the morning. There was little to do until the show opened on Saturday, anyway. Whereas, on the other side of town (a scary cab ride away), there were caregivers to attend to, interviews to be conducted. If she decided at the end of the trip that the help I'd given her wasn't worth SuperKrafts' paying my way, then so be it. I'd refund the money.

"I figured you wouldn't be around the whole day. I'm giving one of the Friday afternoon workshops, before the show opens, and I already covered by asking Maddie to be my assistant."

"This won't go on much longer, Bebe—"

"Neither will this trip."

I sat back, resigned to whatever Bebe might throw my way.

Manhattan in Miniature 119

Not even my brief relaying of the taxi mishap was enough to gain her sympathy or understanding. I was almost sorry I'd played down the incident for Maddie's sake. It was my fault, after all, that I'd let my friend's agenda interfere with Bebe's big moment. I swallowed her sarcasm and picked up the poster-size menu. "Look, Maddie, they have mac and cheese."

"Yeah, and they make it with smoky gouda," she said. I expected her standard turned-up nose at a strange foodstuff, but not in Manhattan. "I like to try new things," she told our waitress. I cleared my throat and held back my surprise. "And a refillable strawberry shake," she added. That, at least, was the old Maddie.

Bebe was singularly quiet after placing her order of the salmon special.

"Tell me about the workshop," I said.

Bebe took a sip of water; Maddie responded to my question. "We're going to do a Christmas room in a box that's wired, so the lamps work. SuperKrafts is providing the box and all the materials. Well, it's not free exactly, because there is a fee for the workshop, but we'll have everything you need. At the end, everyone will take away a living room with a fully decorated tree and a flickering fire."

"What a great promoter you are," I said. "What's your assignment?"

"First, I'm going to help the people in the class wrap tiny presents for under the tree, and also I'm going to show them how to put up wallpaper. It's a big class." She turned to Bebe. "Fifteen people have signed up, right? Bebe will do all the lighting and other stuff."

Bebe, was it? When had Maddie gone from "Mrs. Mellon" to "Bebe"? Was it a sign of her burgeoning maturity, or was Bebe getting chummier with her only hope of assistance at the fair? Either way, Maddie seemed excited to have been drafted into service and that was all that mattered. She'd already seen the Rockettes and the dinosaurs; and I hoped to fit in some Fifth Avenue holiday windows with her before we headed home. I tried not to feel guilty that she might miss *The Nutcracker* at Lincoln Center, Saint Patrick's Cathedral, the Cloisters to the north, and all of lower Manhattan to the south. There would be other trips. And so far, I'd heard no complaints from her about anything other than being left out of all the details of Aunt Elsie's case, and being deprived of snow.

"Any errands I can do?" I asked Bebe.

She didn't give in a bit to my guilt-ridden offer, but gave me a look that said "too late." We dug into our newly arrived dinners. I wanted to ask Maddie if she'd had a chance to review the security footage, with Henry's partners-in-crime theory in mind, but I wasn't sure if Bebe would count that in my favor or against me. It was she who'd offered my assistance to the exhibit organizers, after all, just not that of an eleven-year-old. I thought of reiterating my experience as a New York City traffic-incident statistic, until I remembered that, one, there was no need to add negativity to the meal; and two, I wasn't really a statistic, since my event never made it to the record.

I looked at my watch. Only eight o'clock and the awkward dinner was over. "We still have time to see some sights." I said. "We can go to the top of the Empire State Building, look at all the windows along Fifth to Central Park South—"

"Or check out the exhibit hall," Bebe said.

I thought she was being a little obsessive since we'd gone over our table arrangements many times, but this was not the time to argue.

"Great idea," I said. "Let's visit our table."

"I'll look at the security video again first," Maddie said. "I haven't done anything since Uncle Henry had that new idea."

Bebe mumbled something that might have been positive, about assisting the show organizers, but it was hard to tell.

THE massive hall was abuzz, but not in a good way. People were crowded around vendor table 126, in a row near the entrance, where a jeweler was near tears over the loss of a dozen pairs of handmade earrings. "They were in a plastic bag, ready to be separated into little boxes," the distraught, middle-aged woman choked out.

"How awful. We have to do something about security," said a trim older woman. "Who can afford these losses?"

"It's not as though they were diamonds or emeralds," the current robbery victim admitted. "A lot of hammered silver, a little Venetian glass. But it was hours and hours of work, and a big part of my inventory."

Murmurs of agreement and sympathy poured out from the crowd. I saw men check their pockets and women peer into their purses—no doubt worrying about a more hands-on thief. The most interesting thing to me was that so many vendors had left their stations to see what the fuss was about, to comfort the offended one, to rant about the poor security and complain about this "sign of the times." After a couple of minutes, I felt Maddie tugging at my arm.

"It's a distraction, Grandma." I nodded; she tugged again. "I mean like Uncle Henry said."

Of course. The kind of distraction one partner creates while the other does his business in another part of the hall. Who said the distraction had to be as big as fireworks or a bomb threat; it could be simply the theft of less valuable items from a vendor likely to make a fuss and draw attention away from the real target. "I get it," I said, as we both turned to see who was *not* paying attention to the current crisis at table 126. Many tables, including ours, located in the center aisle, were empty of staff.

"Over there, Grandma." Maddie pointed surreptitiously to the back of the hall, keeping her index finger at waist level. A woman in a calf-length gray coat with a large collar had bent to pick up something from the floor. She stuffed whatever it was into an oversized flowery tote, and walked toward the back door, a few yards away. An innocent action? Or a theft in progress?

The lone security guard on duty, Armstrong, according to his nameplate, was at table 126 with the rest of us. As every thief knew better than I did, security personnel could be distracted also. Before I knew it, Maddie left my side and ran toward the table she'd been targeting in the back.

My heart caught, as if she were her father, barely three years old, and had slipped out of my grasp in the crush of a Christmas crowd. I'd stood in a Herald Square department store and screamed his name. Richard had made his way through the throng, eager to give Santa his wish list. For the longest minutes of my life, I couldn't find him and his little blue jacket, until an alert elf picked him up and held him above the crowd. Richard squirmed in the air, annoyed that he'd been stopped on his way to the bright red throne. If he ever wondered why we switched to private Santa parties with willing neighbors, even after we moved to the tamer California malls, he never asked.

Now I hurried after his daughter. Only when she stopped at the end of the rows of tables did I slow down, my breath calming. I was relieved to see that the woman she was chasing after had already pushed through the back door. The last thing I wanted was for her to see Maddie in pursuit. I imagined my sweet granddaughter a hostage in the hands of a thief with nothing to lose. Instead, Maddie was standing at the end of the rows of tables, looking around. I let out a long, deep breath and hugged her to me, until she broke away, concerned. I felt my own annoyance at being reminded that not all my New York memories were pleasant.

"What's the matter, Grandma?"

"Nothing, sweetheart. I'm just out of breath from rushing."

That seemed to satisfy her, and she picked up where she'd left off. "I can't figure out which table the lady was at, Grandma," she said.

"What's up back here?" Ronnie O'Brien, the security officer had joined us. I refrained from mimicking Bebe and reminding him, "too little, too late."

Maddie was quick to give our friend a report on what she'd seen, how it fit with what Henry had suggested, and explaining

that we needed to watch the videos right away. "I think something was stolen from one of these tables on the end."

"We'll take care of that," he said. "You've been a great help."

"But I—"

Ronnie bent his large frame down to address Maddie more
directly. "You run along and have some fun, honey. Let us do
our job, okay? I'm sure you don't want to spend your time doing
boring police work."

If he only knew. Maddie wasn't happy about the brush-off. But
there was no question that the bulky guard could have picked
her up with one arm and carried her out of the hall on his hip, if
he'd been so inclined, possibly even hoisted her in the air as her
father had once been thwarted by a determined elf. I intervened
before that could happen. "Thanks, Ronnie. Let us know if we
can be of any more help. We'll be at our table"—I indicated a
space two rows over and toward the middle—"and let us know
if you need us."

Maddie pouted until we were out of Ronnie's earshot, then
let out her frustration. "It's not fair, Grandma. I'm the one who
saw the lady. I'll bet he doesn't even believe me."

"We don't really know if the lady was doing anything wrong,
sweetheart. She might have dropped her hairbrush or her keys."

"Uh-uh, it was bigger than that."

"A book, then, or an e-reader," I said, hoping to impress her
with my up-to-date knowledge of what might be in a lady's tote.
Anything but dealing with a Cynthia sound-alike with a mission.
Never mind that my brand new e-reader was still in my suitcase,
unused since our flight.

"We have to look at the footage, Grandma. I'll bet we'll see
that she bumped the table first, and then ran off with something.
And it happened right when everyone was around that other
table where probably her partner was working to get our attention away from her."

She had a point. "If that's true, then the security people will
figure it out. Now, let's help Bebe before she crosses us off her list

altogether. We don't want her to be sorry she invited us." Though we may already have crossed that bridge.

"There's nothing to do at our table. She's just moving things around, but really it's all set." I knew Maddie was right. Bebe was using up her nervous energy on busywork.

As predicted, Bebe was fussing at our table, making new tags for the basketful of one-inch plastic baby dolls she'd moved to the back. "I didn't like those little round tags," she said. "I'm making bigger ones. And I don't want to leave the basket at the front edge. They'll be too easy to steal."

I ran my hand over the neatly lined up boxes with full sets of furniture for every room, in a one-twelfth scale (one inch for every one foot of real space) dollhouse. New this year was a set for a game room, complete with a seven-inch pool table and a card table and chairs, as well as tiny balls, decks of cards, and hand-painted cue sticks. "Is anything missing from our table?" I asked.

Bebe raised her eyebrows and heaved a sigh. "Not yet, but we don't want to encourage anyone, now, do we?"

I was getting tired of Bebe's tone, condescending at best, demanding at worst. But I held my tongue. I reminded myself that it was Bebe's trip and that I'd failed to stay by her side, which is what she'd hoped for, whether or not it was necessary for the success of SuperKrafts at the fair. I resolved to show up for her workshop tomorrow and to be in attendance at our table full-time on Saturday and Sunday. "Of course I don't want to encourage a thief," I said, with all the sweetness I could muster. Meanwhile, I pondered on what it meant that our inventory was still intact. That we had inferior goods? Nothing worth stealing? Should we be embarrassed or relieved that the Lex thieves hadn't targeted our offerings?

"What a relief," Bebe said, settling the issue. "Everything seems to be in place. I don't need one more thing to go wrong."

I couldn't think of any glitches in Bebe's plans so far, other than me. Her meeting with Corporate had gone well; all the inventory had arrived in plenty of time; we had a prime spot toward the middle of the hall where the aisles were wider. Bebe did not have a cold as she'd anticipated, nor had she had fallen and broken her ankle—another worst-case scenario she'd hypothesized when she'd tripped on an outdoor mat at the entrance to the hotel. Apparently, I was the only thing that had gone wrong.

"Can we go upstairs now, Grandma?" Maddie asked.

Not a plea I heard very often from my granddaughter and I worried that she might be coming down with something. I felt a pang of guilt that I'd abandoned her so often during this trip. Maybe Bebe's sour mood was contagious. Maddie moped along with me to the elevator, leaving Bebe to chat with neighboring vendors. I knew Maddie was disappointed that a fun part of the security job was now out of her hands, and I hoped that was all that was wrong.

"Are you going to bed already?" I asked when we entered our room.

"Uh-huh. I'm kinda tired."

"No chat?"

"Maybe tomorrow."

My phone pinged that I had an email message. From Philip Chapman. I'd been surprised that Aunt Elsie had an email address for him, though I'd read that almost sixty percent of people over sixty-five were online, and that number increased with educational level, income, and the size of their resident cities. The older couple fit that profile exactly. Philip had agreed electronically to an early lunch tomorrow at the café in the Lex, giving me a legitimate out, once I finished with the nurses at Cynthia's apartment.

Maddie, already in her bed, rolled over on her side, which I took as a sign that the day was over for her. I switched off the light on her side of the room, determined to make tomorrow fun enough to be worthy of a nighttime chat.

Chapter 11

I FELT I could officially be called a commuter, making numerous trips to and from my home at the Lex and my temp job on the Upper West Side. Plus, I had a taxi accident under my belt, even though I had no battle wounds to show anyone. At nine in the morning, I was surprised to have Cody, not Duncan, open the cab door for me in front of Cynthia's building.

"Double shift," he explained. "Duncan's not feeling well and, you know, you can never have enough money, right?" Spoken like a struggling student.

"What about your classes?" I asked. I remembered that Cody was an art student, but wasn't clear on the particulars. Art history? Painting? Drawing? Ken, my architect husband, had taken a number of classes in art, but laughed at the idea that he was an artist.

"No problem. It's mostly studio work at this point," he said.

I swept my arm toward Fifth Avenue and the museum mile. "It must be exciting for an artist to live in the middle of all this."

He frowned. "Yeah, or be a doorman in the middle of all this."

Cody's reaction stopped me. What was the protocol? To tell him he didn't have to be a doorman all his life and risk insulting the profession as well as the absent Duncan? I went into teacher mode. "I'm sure you're a hard worker, Cody, and will have whatever success you want." Clearly I was out of practice on the advice and follow-your-dreams front.

Cody turned to assist other residents who were leaving the

building at this time, and needing doors opened and taxis called. I was on my own to get to the lobby and call the elevator. Quite a hardship. I wondered how long it would take me to adjust to my regular life in Lincoln Point. I suspected that with all that had gone on this week, I'd be ready to open my own doors and carry my own packages. To prepare, I gave the button for the elevator a good, hard push and smiled with satisfaction when the doors opened.

ASHLEY Goodman and Candace Sellers, who'd arrived before me, had taken seats in Cynthia's living room. She had arranged chairs around a low table, which held a coffee and tea service and a platter with the latest in pastry. "Cronuts," I said, with a smile of approval for the flaky half croissant, half cream-filled donut.

"Yeah, old news now," Candace said. "When they first came out, the bakery near my building sold so many they put a limit on how many each person could buy in the morning. Before nine, they'd only sell two to a person. Now you can buy a dozen or however many you want."

I hadn't realized that cronuts were already part of history. Lincoln Point's Willie's Bagel Shop had just recently added them to the "And More" section of their menu, after all the different flavors of bagels and cream cheese.

Cynthia disappeared with "You girls have a good talk. Enjoy the cronuts." I appreciated that Cynthia took my advice and allowed me to question the women without her interference.

"I really don't know why we're here," Ashley said, smoothing her skirt over her thighs, where the fabric ended. I hoped she had a long coat; temperatures had fallen to single digits overnight. "The police already talked to us and we told them we really didn't know anything."

"Are they still looking for a way to blame us?" Candace asked.

Uh-oh. The last thing I wanted was to antagonize anyone who could be helpful to me. I bit into a flaky cronut. To give the image of casualness, I told myself, not to simply indulge myself.

I didn't want my subjects running out the door, afraid I was accusing them of neglect. Or worse. Not before I got as much out of them as possible. "I'm sure you've been asked these questions at least once, and I'm sorry to put you through it all again. But I'm new here, in a way, and I'm trying to ease my friend's mind." Ashley nodded and smoothed her skirt once more. Candace focused on her pastry. "Did either of you notice anything different about Aunt Elsie lately?" I asked. "Did she mention new friends, for example, or did she indicate that anything was missing?"

"I thought so," Candace said, in an "aha" tone. "This is about something missing from the apartment, right? What is it? A family heirloom platter? A piece of jewelry? It happens all the time. An old person misplaces something, and right away, it's the caregiver who took it." Candace blew out an annoyed breath. "Everyone knows you can't trust the caregiver."

Ashley frowned at Candace, then looked at me. "Candace is a little edgy, but she's right, you know. It could be a cheap pen missing from about twenty of them in a holder, and they think the nurse stole it. The same with food, or reading glasses, or a packet of tissues... you name it."

"And there are so many people who have access to these apartments," Candace said, throwing up her hands. "The doormen, for instance. What about the doormen? Did you talk to them? They come and go as they please."

I doubted things were that lax, but I felt there was something to the nurses' story, about patients using them as scapegoats for a failing memory. I hoped they weren't too put out about what they perceived as a lack of respect for them in the Bishop household. "Have there been any visitors while you've been here?" I asked, moving suspicion elsewhere.

"Just her old boyfriend," Ashley said.

"Talk about old," Candace added. "And he has this British thing about him, drinks only a certain kind of tea." Candace picked up her own cup, emphasizing an extended pinkie. "But I'll bet he's just from across the bridge in Queens."

"I think it's kinda sweet how he came and they sat and talked," Ashley said. "He never brought anything, though. No candy or flowers or anything. It was if he didn't want to leave a trace of himself. Hair and fibers, you know." Ashley put her hand to her mouth. "Oh, no. Sorry. I didn't mean anything by that."

Candace broke in. "But he always gave us a tip, and you got the feeling that it was hush money. Like he was saying 'Don't tell anyone I was here.'"

Echoing what Duncan called the "you-didn't-see-nothin'" tip." I imagined the elegant-looking Philip Chapman stopping at his ATM on the way over, getting bills for the doormen, the caregivers, anyone who might otherwise report his whereabouts to Cynthia. He could have saved a lot of money if he'd just told Cynthia he'd reconnected with her aunt, something she'd obviously figured out anyway.

I'd given up on getting a juicy tidbit from either Ashley or Candace, but I did feel their perspective would be valuable. "I'd love to know from both of you—what's your professional opinion on how Aunt Elsie died? Do you think her heart attack came on because she forgot to take her pills?"

There was a long pause before Ashley answered. "No, not really, I guess. She never forgot anything else, like having her tea at a certain time. Or how many cookies to put on the plate."

"Or the list of chores we should do. Or even how many ounces of water she'd had that day," Candace added.

"All due respect," Candace began—alerting me that the opposite was coming—"the niece, Cynthia, is a little off." She touched her head to indicate a more specific meaning of "off." "First, she didn't want to set up a regular care schedule, so we're, like, practically on call."

Ashley, a few years older, perhaps closing in on thirty, came to Cynthia's defense. "I think that's because she works odd hours herself, and likes to be able to call up and say, "Come now," you know, or "You can go now.""

"Yeah, but, who else does that? I don't even know why the

agency lets her be so demanding, except she used to be a nurse, back in the Dark Ages."

I ignored the opportunity of giving the young women a history lesson. "Ashley, you were the last one to be with Aunt Elsie. When you left her that day, did she seem okay to you? Cynthia called around three o'clock, to say you could leave, right? And she seemed fine?"

Ashley nearly dropped her teacup. "Yes, of course. I would have said something if I'd noticed anything wrong. I've been doing this job for more than four years and I have a good sense of whether a person can or can not be left alone." Ashley's hands shook; it took both of them to finally lower her cup to her saucer.

"Is something wrong?" I asked.

"I think we should tell her the truth," she said to Candace. Ashley's face paled, and probably mine did as well. I looked back and forth at the women.

"What are you not telling me?" I asked, using my teacher voice once again, but afraid of the answer.

Candace's body stiffened, then seemed to collapse in resignation. "I was the one who was there, not Ashley," Candace said. "But it doesn't change anything we told Cynthia."

"Or the police," Ashley added quickly.

Of course it did, I realized as soon as I got my breath. It changed a lot. "Why would you lie about something like that?" I tried to address both women, unsure who was more to blame for what I considered a huge impediment to any investigation.

Ashley, still somewhat shaken, closed her eyes. "I didn't think I'd have to go through this again."

"Ashley had...an important meeting to get ready for," Candace said.

Another lie. I shook my head. "Ashley had a big date and you thought there was no need to bother with telling about that little change?" I hadn't spent a long career with adolescents for nothing. And these women may have been adults legally, but they weren't much farther ahead in maturity.

"I wanted to go home and get ready and Aunt Elsie was sleeping peacefully. I asked Candace to cover and left when she got here, right after lunch." Ashley was making an attempt to keep her composure but she wasn't doing very well.

"Cynthia told me she called here at three and talked to you." Like the young women, I tried to keep my voice down, lest I inadvertently summon Cynthia before, if ever, we were ready to share this news.

"She doesn't know us apart. We're just the caregivers," Candace said, her antagonistic tone making a comeback.

Ashley shrugged. "It was cell to landline," she said. "The connection is never that good. It's not that hard to fool someone."

"Especially with a short conversation," Candace said. "It's not like she even asks if the changes she wants are okay with us."

I wondered if Cynthia had any clue how she came across to people who were essentially her employees. I was sure she didn't intentionally take advantage of those she hired to care for her aunt. She was a busy woman doing her best to keep everything going smoothly, I rationalized, and these women misinterpreted her efficiency for a lack of respect for them.

"Are we in trouble here?" Ashley asked.

How was I supposed to answer that question? As Cynthia would? Skip? A judge? A lawyer? I was none of those. I opted out of the decision.

"You'll have to ask the NYPD," I said. "Good luck with that."

I RUSHED out of Cynthia's apartment with a cursory peck on her cheek and a quick "Talk to you later. I don't want to be late for Philip." I knew it took her by surprise that I didn't stay and chat about my meeting with Ashley and Candace, but I wasn't prepared to share, and, also, I really did have to hurry to the other side of town. And what if I had to call my own taxi?

I'd scheduled a meeting with Philip Chapman (from Queens?) in the restaurant of the Lex. Settled back in my familiar taxi-cum-office (hailed by Cody), racing past Columbus Circle this time, I mentally replayed what I'd heard from Ashley and Candace and reflected again on Candace's comment—were the women really interchangeable to Cynthia? Maybe they were right about not being treated as individuals with their own personal lives. I remembered meeting Candace at the memorial service and accusing her in my mind of thinking all old people looked alike. Was Cynthia guilty of the same slight with respect to twenty-somethings? Was I? Was it dawning on me only now how different the two women were? Ashley was thin, with cascading blond hair and a gentle manner; Candace was on the chunky side with short, tight curls and an edge to her approach.

I tried to focus on the impact of the women's lie, on what it meant in terms of Aunt Elsie's death, and how it tainted everything else they'd reported. I felt a call to Skip coming on as soon as I could get to it. For now, as the taxi approached the Lex, I switched my thoughts to my other, non-Cynthia-based life, and made a quick call to Maddie.

"How's everything, sweetheart?" I asked.

"It's all cool, Grandma. Bebe's brother, Mr. Slattery, called from home and wished her luck, which made her happy, and Crystal came around to where the workshop will be and helped for a while because her mom isn't giving a class this afternoon, and—"

"That sounds great," I said, hating to interrupt all the good news, but a Lex doorman had extended his hand, to help me out of the taxi, and to receive his tip. Multi-tasking in Manhattan. No wonder no one ever slept.

I ENTERED the Lex lobby, still ruminating over what I wanted to learn from Philip. Would I be bold enough to ask about his long-ago relationship with Aunt Elsie? Their breakup? Their reunion? That would be beyond rude, I mused, and I resolved to watch my tongue. Time would tell.

With his formal attire (that is, a suit and leather shoes instead of jeans and high-tops), Philip was easy to spot though I'd seen him only briefly at Aunt Elsie's memorial service. He stood to greet me, holding his rich gray scarf close to his body as he reseated himself. To keep it out of his water glass, I presumed. Yes, definitely an elegant man. I had a flashback of my own making as I pictured the gracious Elsie Bishop and the dashing Philip Chapman as the talk of the town a few decades ago.

"Mrs. Porter. Elsie told me so much about you and how you were such a good friend to her niece." His voice boomed, as I should have expected from a tall man, and one trained in the theater.

"They were both very generous to me," I said, unsure of whether he'd want to know that I'd heard a lot about him, too. "It's very kind of you to meet me on such short notice."

"I wasn't surprised to get your call. I imagine you want to know more about me. Why Elsie and I broke up, how we got back together, how I'm doing now, having lost her again."

I'd heard the myth about people in the theater loving the limelight, but were they all this willing to talk about their private lives? Philip Chapman, the mourner, had been replaced by Philip Chapman, the attentive, eager interviewee. Since I hadn't referred to myself as anything but Cynthia's friend, and neither had he, I decided I didn't need to give him a laundry list of all the things I was *not*. A cop, first of all. A reporter for either a top-rated newspaper or a beauty-parlor magazine. A reviewer digging up his old performances for an updated profile. A scout for a new production featuring the elderly. An official investigator of any kind. Philip gave me an expectant look, ready to pour out his story. Who was I to question his motives? "I'm listening" was all I could get out.

He settled back. "Elsie and I met during auditions for a special production of *Much Ado About Nothing*. We were very young, hardly into our twenties." He smiled. "We got the parts."

"Claudio and Hero?" I asked, remembering the sweet young lovers who had eyes only for each other.

Philip chuckled. "Oh, no. Quite the opposite, in fact. We were Benedick and Beatrice."

The bickering lovers, constantly antagonizing each other? I called up a quote I'd used many times in my "Shakespeare's insults" lectures. "I had rather hear my dog bark at a crow than a man swear he loves me," I rattled off, as Beatrice.

Philip responded as Benedick. "God keep your ladyship still in that mind!"— then lapsed into more contemporary language— "Thus men will be spared a scratched-up face."

We shared a laugh as only two fans of the Bard could. Philip came back to the present first. "I'm afraid Elsie and I shared worse barbs off-stage. It was one of those stormy relationships that was destined to destroy both of us if we'd continued. Not to be pretentious, but think Richard Burton and Elizabeth Taylor."

"Good company," I said, though it was hard to picture the distinguished gentleman in front of me in a battle of wits or any other nasty contest with a lady like Elsie Bishop, distinguished in her own way.

Philip's story wandered down many side roads that had nothing to do with my main goals for the interview. I had to admit, I encouraged him as he went back in time, willingly disclosing his favorite roles (himself as Hamlet, Elsie as Ophelia); his position on settings and costumes (historically accurate, please, no "modernization"); memorable reviews (thumbs up on his Othello, thumbs down on his Touchstone in *As You Like It*); his opinion of theater in general (the greatest of all art forms, an immediate sharing among the players and the audience of what it is to be human). The last quote sounded familiar, but I didn't challenge Philip on its origin.

When our waitress returned for the third time, we ordered from the breakfast menu—tea, fruit, and the closest we could get to crumpets: English muffins. I'd have to wait a little longer for a taste of the world's best deli sandwiches enjoyed by Maddie and Bebe earlier in the week.

"We had a good run, Elsie and I," Philip continued. "But in

the end, our paths diverged. I realized I'd never be the actor I'd dreamed of becoming, so I decided to pursue a profession where I could make a lot of money and support those who had the talent."

"You went into real estate, I understand."

Philip nodded. "And it worked. I've led a very comfortable life. Elsie, on the other hand, had become politicized, and felt very strongly about serving her country in wartime. She joined the WACs soon after they were formed, and eventually married a soldier. I always thought it was fate, a sign from the universe, really, that we were never meant to be together. We had different values and would just have gotten in each other's way. I understand she wasn't back in civilian life very long when Cynthia's parents died."

"So you didn't break up over Elsie's raising Cynthia?"

"Heavens, no. We broke up long before. Why would you think that?"

I wouldn't, but I couldn't wait to tell Cynthia it was official: She had one fewer burden to carry around.

I looked at my watch and saw that I had barely enough time to cross the lobby and call an elevator for the workshop floor where Bebe would be holding forth. I charged the meager lunch to my room and, with a second peck on someone's cheek today, said good-bye to Philip Chapman. He was flustered, caught almost mid-sentence in a story of how he and Elsie reconnected only a few months ago when she showed up with her theater group at a play he co-produced.

"Don't you want to know about our recent visits?" Philip asked.

"Another time," I said. I'd thought about querying him on items he might have carried away from Elsie's apartment, but I'd have bet a lot that whatever they were, Elsie wanted him to have them. Old photos, a program or two, a souvenir that meant something only to them. I couldn't give a reason, but I felt that Philip was innocent in the matter of Elsie's death, and might have known less than I did about it. I had no official excuse to miss Bebe's workshop. Philip and I made a quick, mutual promise to keep in touch, and I was off. I wondered if I'd ever see him again. I wished I'd known him while I was teaching Shakespeare. He would have made a delightful guest lecturer. And besides me, at least a couple of my teenage students might have appreciated his Shakespearean voice. I could hear him and see his dramatic gestures, as if we were both in my classroom now: "There was a star danced, and under that was I born."

Beatrice and *Much Ado about Nothing* were a long way from Yogi Berra.

Chapter 12

I TRIED TO sneak onto the Lex's mezzanine floor where workshops were just beginning. My entrance would have gone unnoticed except that Maddie ran over to me, bumping into the coffee cart, and Bebe took the opportunity to announce my presence to the assembled class.

"And this is my esteemed assistant, Gerry Porter, also from Lincoln Point, California. Gerry has led more workshops and crafts fairs than I can count." She beamed a smile at me, probably one of relief that I hadn't abandoned her again. "You've already met her equally talented granddaughter, Maddie. Welcome, Gerry." To my chagrin, the class applauded. There went my chance to think more about the two interviews that had filled my morning; or to call Skip and ask a hypothetical question about twenty-somethings lying to the police. My best guess as to why Bebe made such a fuss: she wanted to ensure that I couldn't sneak out.

I muttered a "Thank you" and donned the special apron Maddie had handed me during her bear hug. SuperKrafts had provided its instructors with red aprons with their logo and IT's A SMALL WORLD embroidered in yellow across the front. In spite of Bebe's unwelcome fuss, my comfort in being among miniaturists was complete, geography notwithstanding. I was pleased and proud to see Maddie distributing materials to the assembled attendees. Each one received a wooden room box and a basket of supplies which, if all went well, would be elements of a lovely holiday scene by the end of class this afternoon.

Two other miniatures workshops were taking place simultaneously, the temporary classrooms separated only by felt-covered
partitions about four feet high, much like the bullpen arrangement that Skip and the other LPPD detectives worked in. If I
were clever I could multi-task and listen in on the other two—
how to make an old-fashioned schoolroom with distressed-wood
pieces; and building a seascape that featured a sea-battered wall,
rocks and shells of assorted sizes, and a tiny but wide-eyed gull.
According to the program tacked to the wall of the mezzanine,
other workshops were being held around the corner in jewelry
making, quill wrapping, woodworking, and shell art. In spite of
the temptation to learn a new crafts technique, I was resolved to
give Bebe and our class my full attention.

A young Goth-looking woman with a serious camera around
her neck wandered the area taking photographs. I hoped Bebe
would be one of her subjects, then highlighted in a SuperKrafts
newsletter report of the fair, or, better yet, in a miniatures magazine. She'd earned it. Since becoming manager of the Lincoln
Point SuperKrafts store, Bebe, herself an expert ceramicist, had
been a great friend to miniaturists and other crafters, joining my
longtime crafts group and greatly expanding the miniatures inventory in the store.

My main job, besides being there to support Bebe, was to
patrol the tables and give assistance where needed. I stopped in
front of one crafter who was lucky enough to have Maddie tutoring her in the use of tacky glue. I arrived in time to watch Maddie run her finger around the bottom of a newly glued ottoman,
made from a leather button, in the holiday living room scene.
Her finger came up with a sticky white streak.

"You might want to try using less glue," she advised in a
sweet voice. "Or you can use something like an expired student
ID or library card to spread it evenly." I smiled at her example.
It wouldn't be long before she'd be recommending a credit card
instead.

The crafter, a middle-aged woman, picked up the container

of glue and pointed to the text. "But it says here not to worry if some glue spills over. It will dry clear."

"That's true," Maddie said. "But it will still show if you look close enough. It just won't be white like now, but it will be bumpy and hard." She shook her long, red curls in disapproval. "You should be able to inspect a miniature closely and have it look perfect. You don't want it to be cute just from a distance, do you?"

"Good point," the woman said.

I fantasized announcing to the room. "That's my grand-daughter." Perhaps they could tell. I moved on and helped Bebe untangle a string of tiny lights to be placed around the windows of one student's room box. We both touted the merits of gluing a postcard or photo of the outdoors behind the window frame, to mimic the "real" outside of the room.

A midafternoon coffee break with, of course, cronuts, brought everyone together to discuss their projects. We admired tiny, yet elaborate bows on mini-presents; coffee table center-pieces; and lush draperies made of bits of fabric—"from the hem of my daughter's prom dress," one crafter explained, with regard to her blue taffeta scraps. It was also nice to hear words like "out-standing class" and "even more than I expected" and "wonderful instructors" from our students. Bebe, Maddie, and I said "thank you" and blushed appreciatively at the praise.

Things took a different turn when Maddie came up to me, hardly able to contain her excitement. "I think I see her," she whispered. When I gave her a quizzical look, she explained. "The thief. I think that's her over by the coffee table. She must be tak-ing one of the other workshops."

"I thought we were going to leave that to Ronnie, the secu-rity officer," I said. Silly Grandma.

"I saw him this morning, Grandma, while you were at Ms. Bishop's, and I asked him, and he said there's nothing on that new video, just a lady who bent over to pick up something and you can't tell really which table she's at. He said he asked a couple of vendors at the end of the rows and they said nothing was taken."

"Why don't we just trust him and let it go, sweetheart?"

"But I talked to two of them and they said Mr. O'Brien never asked them any questions. I think he made it up."

"How do you know who the vendors are?"

"The same way he does, I guess. The program tells you where each dealer is." Maddie dug in her apron pocket and pulled out a show program with its layout diagram. Considering that the show hadn't even officially started yet, I was surprised at how worn the paper was. Maddie had been busy.

"I see," I said, until I could think of a better response. "How did you find the dealers?"

Maddie gave an impatient shrug. "Their names are on the program, like I showed you, so I called them on the hotel phone."

I needed to hear more, but not right now. Bebe was calling the class together for the second half of the workshop. "We'll talk about this later," I told Maddie, while in my head, my main job had switched from keeping Bebe company to keeping Maddie safe. What if there really was a ring of thieves in the hotel? What would be the fate of a seventy-five-pound girl with no street smarts? I got through the rest of the class by keeping no farther away than arm's length from my granddaughter. Fortunately, everyone was so deeply into her project, no one noticed, and, at last, the session drew to a close.

The biggest surprise in workshops like this one was to see how, given nearly identical materials, crafters could come up with a wide variety of décors. The finished rooms on the mezzanine today called up different eras—a few flowery Victorians offering a peek into a holiday living room of old; a nineteen-fifties farmhouse; a sleek, well-lit contemporary loft; and even one "Goth" version of the holidays, perhaps inspired by our roaming photographer, which was all black, except for a tiny tree with a blinking silver star at the top. I heard many renditions of *oohs* and *aahs* at all of them. Not a single boo. At the end of the session, Bebe led a discussion of the fate of the boxes while Maddie took pictures with her phone. I saw the little room boxes going far and wide: to a grandmother, a school raffle, a library display window, a hospital waiting room, and, according to the last response, underground: "This is my first. I'm going to hide it," she said.

Give my regards to Broadway...

No sooner had I unmuted my phone, than it rang. I buried it in my sweater pocket and took it to a corner of the mezzanine to answer. I left Maddie to help Bebe clean up, watching her while I switched gears to Cynthia's call. The best thing about miniatures was the extent to which they took you out of the real world, the world with enormous dimensions, where a dab of glue would never be able to hold down a footstool or keep a drapery in place. And where an old lady isn't safe in her bed and young professionals think nothing of lying to a police detective.

Cynthia's voice came through, calling me back to that life-size, problem-filled world. "I didn't want to bother you before four o'clock when the workshop ended." Looking over the railing of the mezzanine, I could see the large array of clocks of the world in the lobby. Four-oh-five in New York. When it came to time allotment this week, Cynthia had perfect pitch. She went on, "But I'm eager to hear what you got out of the interviews this morning. Did you learn anything from Ashley or Candace or Philip?" Her voice trailed off, becoming less and less hopeful as she realized I was not breaking in with exciting leads.

Finally, I gave her a short answer. "I'm sorry, but there's nothing much to report." How much easier to deal with Cynthia when she wasn't staring me in the face. "I have to go right now. But I promise to call with details," I said, amazingly glib for someone who hadn't yet decided how much to tell her.

"This evening?" she asked.

"It might be late," I said, remembering that I'd promised Maddie and Bebe an uninterrupted evening doing whatever they wanted.

"No matter. I'll be up. I haven't been sleeping much since…
you know."

I assured her I did know, and sympathized. I hung up with
"I'll talk to you soon." It wasn't Cynthia's fault that I felt guilty
not rushing over to the apartment of a friend who couldn't sleep.

I joined my show partners by the elevators.

"They were a very neat group," Bebe said, meaning, I supposed, that the class members were nice to work with, or that
necessary cleanup had been minimal, or both. In a quick meeting
while we waited to go to our rooms, I learned that Bebe had her
mind set on attending the special cocktail hour for vendors and
staff this evening, in less than two hours.

"It's kid-friendly," she assured us. "They'll even have a puppet show."

Maddie, whose first choice was a horse-and-carriage ride
through Central Park, screwed up her nose at the puppet idea,
but I nudged her before she could remind Bebe that she wasn't
five years old anymore. "What's your favorite thing to do, Grandma?" she asked.

What did it say about me that I had to think long and hard,
and the best thing I came up with was, "Whatever you two want
is fine with me."

I ALMOST didn't recognize the Lex lobby at six o'clock. Enormous hanging shades of a sheer gray fabric had been lowered
from the ceiling to mark off a large section of the carpeted area,
while still giving a feeling of openness. Untethered at the bottom,
the super-shades fluttered in the ambient air. Off to the side, a
narrow corridor where guests could check in remained available,
but the rest of the lobby had been turned into a night club. Or
whatever one called places where cocktails and loud music were
offered these days. Tall tables had been brought in, as well as high
stools, and the rest of the furniture was arranged in conversational
units. Not that anyone could converse over the din of the music,
which was part holiday, part rap.

Bebe had packed with the party in mind, appearing in a little black dress and sandals with heels that added four inches to her height. I was glad at least I'd brought a somewhat fancy blouse, but quickly removed the sparkly wreath pin I'd attached to my chest. Christmas pins were passé, I figured, since the only other woman wearing one was my senior by at least fifteen years. I felt less underdressed as I looked around and saw a few other guests in casual attire. Even in New York City, it seemed, the dress code for evening wear had evolved to "whatever."

"I don't see the puppets," Maddie said. I figured she cared only because she wanted to steer clear of them and not wander into their territory by accident.

"I guess I misread the flyer," Bebe said. "Maybe they're part of the entertainment at the show tomorrow."

"Good," Maddie said. She looked charming in black tights, a shiny black top, and a short, deep green fluffy skirt. Her mother, the artist, had packed well. I wished I'd had her pack for me, too. Maddie had already found Crystal and was dismayed that I wouldn't approve of their going off in a corner to play smart-phone games. For tonight, she was going to have to hang out with her grandmother. I was relieved that Crystal's mother agreed that it was a bad idea to let the girls loose in this environment, thieves or no thieves.

To my surprise, Bebe from Lincoln Point mingled easily with vendors from Manhattan and beyond, throwing her head back and laughing at inaudible stories with the best of them. I was happy for her. She deserved to have something go smoothly, in spite of me, her unreliable friend. She navigated toward me a few times and gave me a commentary on the connections she was making. I learned that "The guy with the goatee is second in command over on Sixth"; and that "Number One doesn't plan to show up"; and, best of all, "The guy who's really watching me, I mean, performance-wise, is the younger one in the Italian suit." As if I'd be able to tell.

I did my best to keep Maddie close and still appear sociable to the people who stopped to chat. I laughed as I realized I'd met a butcher and a baker (both of miniature food) and a candlestick maker (of the life-size variety). I also noticed the green voicemail icon on my phone with the name Crouse. It took me a minute to remember the super at Cynthia's building, Neal Crouse. I'd have to call him back during a quieter moment.

By seven-thirty, I'd had all the small talk and hors d'oeuvres I could stand and wanted to get out in the fresh air, no matter how cold. Either that or climb into bed. Maddie and I headed over to where Bebe was just breaking off with "the woman who might come out for an on-site in our store next spring," she told me later.

"Are you ready to leave?" I yelled in her ear.

"This is such a great party," she yelled back. Then she leaned into me and whispered in my ear. "Let's bail."

Less than a half hour later, we'd repaired to our rooms to change and were now fully covered in our warmest knits, and headed out a side door, beyond the waving shades. As far as I could tell from the noise, the party was still in full swing.

IT might not have been the smartest plan, to launch ourselves into the cold night air for our Central Park excursion, but Maddie was excited enough about a horse-and-carriage ride to make up for the discomfort I felt, and probably Bebe, too. It helped a little that for only a few extra dollars, we could each have a flannel blanket.

"Most people bring their own for the trip," the driver said, "but I always keep a few handy on cold nights like this." We tipped him for his thoughtfulness.

We'd opted for the four-mile trip, a ninety-minute tour through and around the entire park. Our driver spent a few minutes first introducing us to our horse, Samuel, a cross-draft horse and native of Amish country, he explained. Maddie gleefully accepted the suggestion that she might want to feed Samuel a carrot. "Wow," she said.

Our journey began at the south end of the park. I enjoyed a moment of nostalgia as Samuel clopped by open areas where Ken and I and a squirming baby Richard had sat on the grass for free performances by the world's greatest actors and musicians. Our driver was an enthusiastic young man who called out the names of the monuments, statues, bronzes, and war memorials in a faux old-fashioned accent to go along with our mode of transportation.

"Wow," Maddie said again and again, though I doubted she had much prior knowledge of the many generals, politicians, statesmen, and artists memorialized in the park. She jumped at the mention of Hans Christian Andersen. "I know him!" she cried as she spied the Ugly Duckling at the feet of the seated storyteller. Bebe and I had a similar, though more subdued reaction, as befitting a Garden of Peace, as we passed Strawberry Fields. As we turned near 85th Street, Maddie pointed to the stately museum, now dark, and said, "There's where the dinosaurs live." I could tell that Bebe believed her, at least for a moment. I know I did.

ON the way back to the Lex in our engine-driven cab, every bit as bumpy as a horse and carriage, we passed the huge, lit-to-the-gills Rockefeller Center tree, still attracting crowds at nearly eleven at night. Carriage rides were offered until after two in the morning, so I guessed this was peak time for New Yorkers and tourists. I tried to calculate the number of hours the streets of Lincoln Point would have been rolled up by now, but lost track because of the time zone shift.

Bebe looked happier than I'd seen her in a long time. Maybe ever. "What a night," she said. "I watch the tree lighting every year on TV, and now here I am." She drew a deep breath. "In the Big Apple itself. And the cocktail party and the carriage ride. Everything. I can't thank you enough, Gerry."

I'd had nothing to do with the cocktail party, and, as I recalled, Bebe had insisted on paying for the carriage ride, so I wasn't sure why I deserved such an outpouring of gratitude. "And Jackie Cromwell told me you and Maddie were a great help to Security yesterday." Was this where I admitted that we'd been relieved of our duties by the officials of the show? I decided to bask instead in Bebe's grateful mood, well-placed or not.

"No problem," I said.

Our cab came to a jerky halt in front of the Lex and we tumbled out. "What's the weather going to be like tomorrow?" Maddie asked the doorman who helped us over the curb. "Are we ever going to get snow?"

"Maybe tonight," he said.

"You always say that," Maddie said.

I thought I saw a red blush creep up the doorman's face. Or it might have been the cold.

"I TOOK pictures of all the boxes at the workshop," Maddie informed me at bedtime.

"I saw that."

"I took a shot of all of them because I didn't want anyone to feel bad."

"That was very thoughtful of you."

"I hate it when our swim coach only takes pictures of the fast kids and not the slow ones."

I agreed, but, not wanting to cast aspersions on her coach, I kept it to myself, allowing only a small burst of pride that my granddaughter, a top-ranking swimmer among the tweens of Palo Alto, was so sensitive.

"I'm sure Bebe will be happy to have those photos," I said. "Can you make copies for her?" As if I didn't know the answer.

Maddie gave a nod that bordered on sleepy. She'd adjusted well to falling asleep to the sounds of honking cars, screaming fire engines, loud sirens from police cars and ambulances, rumbling trucks and buses, and what seemed like random garbage pick-ups. Mary Lou's surprised response when I reported this had been "When she's at home, she thinks my book club's too loud. Maybe

I'll hire some guys to jackhammer outside while we're discussing Jane Austen."

"I can make Bebe an album when we get home," the infinitely flexible Maddie told me now. I thought we were finished for the night, until I heard her last pitch. "I'm glad the show opens tomorrow for real, and all the dealers will be in their places in the hall. Like on the program."

Uh-oh. "Is that because you want to shop for presents?" A fond wish. One I'd gladly have underwritten with a generous allowance add-on.

"Uh-uh. I want to find out if anything is missing from their tables."

"Why don't you believe Mr. O'Brien, sweetheart? He's trained for this kind of thing."

She shrugged, and I recognized the gesture her "uncle" Skip made when he had a hunch he couldn't quite back up yet or when he didn't quite trust a decision of management. "I just think they're not bothering to investigate. Maybe they think the stuff isn't worth much. Not like at a diamond show or something. I might look around tomorrow."

"What do you mean 'look around'?"

"Nothing." She yawned. "I'm tired, Grandma."

I doubted it.

ANOTHER late night. It was about time I learned to call them normal. In Lincoln Point, this would be about the time Skip might drop in. I'd serve him my ginger cookies; we'd talk (or not) about a case he was working or how things were going with June. Now that I thought of it, it was only nine o'clock where Skip lived. I took out my cell phone and called him.

"My car almost auto-piloted to your house," he said. "No matter what time zone, you're up late."

"I was just thinking that. Sorry I can't offer you cookies." I looked over at Maddie, only a few feet away. She wasn't stirring, but still I kept my voice low so I wouldn't disturb her.

"I still have a few left. What's new?"

"I'm so glad you asked." I told Skip what had been on my mind since this morning—the Ashley/Candace issue.

"I know I've told you this," he said. "You have no legal obligation to mention what you learned to the police, unless of course, the NYPD knocks on your door and asks that specific question. First of all, you can't be sure the ladies are telling you the truth now."

"I know you've said that before, but I still feel—"

"You know what to do if you actually see a crime, right?"

"Yes, yes. Call nine-one-one; observe and make mental notes; look for weapons; get physical characteristics; et cetera, et cetera." I rattled off most of the list Skip had forced everyone in the family to memorize.

"Right, and remember, as far as your young nurses' story, it could have been a third person entirely, some friend of a friend of theirs, who actually took Ashley's place. You just don't know."

"I never thought of that. But doesn't this change what the police might have done by way of investigating Elsie's death?"

"I doubt it. The girls could have played it down, which is what they should have done in the first place, if they were smart. Instead of lying, they could have made it sound routine, one person covering for another at a job for an agency where they both worked. No big deal."

"So the only thing the lie accomplished was to get back at Cynthia for giving short notice more often than they would like."

"That's how it looks to me. In any case, my advice to you is 'fuhgeddaboudit,' as they say where you are. What else is going on?"

"Nothing's snapping into place," I admitted, after a somewhat lengthy briefing (an oxymoron? I wondered irrelevantly) on Aunt Elsie's community of helpers and friends. "No one seems to fit the bill. Alibis don't mean anything, because, if Cynthia is right, Aunt Elsie's murder was carried out over a relatively long period of time. The closest we can get to a time line is that, if we believe whichever nurse was with her, Aunt Elsie was alive and well at three in the afternoon, but not so at five. But that doesn't mean that's when the pill bottles were switched, because no one seems to have noticed what was real and what was placebo in the first place." I took a breath before adding one more complaint. "Also, I'm talking to people in artificial settings or at specific times, not just getting to know them in their own milieu."

"Welcome to my world," Skip said. No sympathy there. No tips either, except to urge me to try and relax and not stress over what might be a futile exercise. Hard as it would be for me and especially Cynthia, I might have to accept that there simply was no case.

"And the robberies in the exhibit hall?" he asked.

"I think there's some merit to Maddie's claim that the security people don't seem to care, but we've been politely ordered away in any case." I checked Maddie again, hoping those words wouldn't trigger a thought and wake her up. All was well.

"Better not to aggravate a guy in uniform. Don't you guys build in a certain amount of loss for shows like that? You must expect the occasional misplacing of an item or breakage or even theft?"

I refused to acknowledge thievery among crafters, but I did agree that it wasn't wise to antagonize the security force. I felt much better about the anomaly in Ashley and Candace's story, both in terms of my responsibility and the effect it might have had on the NYPD investigation, but I still needed a little more TLC.

I called Henry in Hawaii and kept our conversation light, to match the ukulele music I could hear in the background. I told him about the workshops and one in particular that I wished I could have attended. "The class learned how to use a table saw and got a good start on a marquetry blanket chest."

"You should have told me you were interested in that. I can help."

"I hoped you'd say that." In fact, I'd hoped to rope him into teaching the mitering technique to my crafters' group, but I didn't need to bring that up during a luau.

I realized I'd promised to call Cynthia and tell her about my meetings with Ashley and Candace and Philip. I'd also wanted to return the call to Neal Crouse. But I was in their time zone now, and it was too late. I heard a soft footstep outside our door and saw a newspaper make its way onto the small square of tile in the entry. No one could accuse the Lex of being late with the morning paper. I'd been out of touch with news since we landed, except for Maddie's summary during her brief turn as a fan of journalism. I treated myself to a look at the headlines—nothing uplifting—and then flipped to the regional roundup. Updates on Maddie's choices of news items a couple of days ago caught my eye: the man who'd saved himself by lying between the rails while the subway train rolled over him was now thought to have been pushed onto the tracks; the med student who was assumed to have died accidentally from a fall from a ladder had been ruled the victim of foul play. Police were investigating both incidents.

I could have searched for good news in the national section, but went to bed instead.

Chapter 13

ONLY A WEEK AGO, Maddie and I had been browsing through SuperKrafts in Lincoln Point, California, without a thought of traveling across the country. Now we'd been in Manhattan for three days—three days that seemed like three weeks in some ways—and, at last, our reason for being here was upon us. Saturday morning, and the show was on.

Upbeat songs about ringing bells, roasting chestnuts, and Santa and his reindeer blasted through the Lex's exhibit hall as the spirit of giving, that is, buying and selling, descended on our fair. Alluring handcrafted objects, from the very large (a ten-inch lion carved out of ishpingo wood) to the very small (a one-quarter-inch cheese grater) beckoned from every table. There was something for everyone on a Christmas list, whether it was a (life-size) hand-sewn leather purse or a pair of fuzzy deerskin slippers. Potential customers handled glazed pottery with care or threw scarves in many colors and textures around their necks to test the effect. People had poured into the area as soon as the huge double doors opened. They wandered the crowded aisles, chatted with each other and with vendors, asked for and shared tips. "How did you do that?" was the most often-heard question. Maddie's camera clicking was the most often-heard sound.

I thought of how much my crafter friends back home would love to be here, and took out my list with their requests. Linda Reed, a perfectionist who rolled her eyes at the idea of a miniatures kit or anything not made from scratch had given me a (verbal) blank check to bring her something from the fair. "Use your own judgment, Gerry, but remember my standards," she'd written in an email before I left. I had my eye on an exquisite miniature cherry mahogany chess table for a scene she was putting together for her son, and a hand-crocheted Christmas-themed afghan, three inches square, for her never-ending Christmas collection. It was always fun to shop with someone else's money, though I'd decided that the afghan would be my Christmas present to her.

In another moment of questionable timing, my phone rang as soon as I stepped behind our table to join Bebe and Maddie. The two of them, in their special aprons, looked like expectant Girl Scouts ready to sell the cookies they'd baked. Maddie was due to spend a shift at the coat check counter with Crystal and her dad. He'd volunteered to staff the service in support of the fair and of his crafter wife, a jeweler with lovely pieces fashioned from gemstones—lapis, tiger's eye, hematite, carnelian, malachite, something for everyone. I motioned to Bebe that I'd be right back and stepped to the side aisle to take the call from Cynthia.

"I tried to stay awake for your call last night, but I fell asleep," she said, with only the slightest touch of rebuke.

I considered explaining to Cynthia that my friend, my grand-daughter, and I were having such a great time, what with a cock-tail party last evening, followed by a ride around the park, under a warm blanket, holding our mugs of hot chocolate, that I forgot my investigative duties. Better left unsaid. "It was a busy night," I said instead. "But I do have something important to report."

She gasped. "You have a suspect?" I was sorry I'd been so dramatic.

"Quite the opposite," I said, and gave her the World War Two and postwar time line of events, most of which had taken place before Cynthia was born, according to Philip Chapman. Cynthia was silent for so long, I thought I'd lost the connection.

"This is going to take a while to process, Gerry. Apparently I've lived with a lie all these years, and even though in a way it was a lie of my own making, it's very much etched in my brain."

"What gave you the false idea in the first place?"

"I've been going over that, asking myself that question, ever since you brought up the possibility. I think it was because when her friends would visit—by that time, Elsie was widowed—they'd tease her, and say she should look up Philip again, that he still carried a torch for her. I was only about six. So, not only was I oblivious of history, thinking she'd just broken up with him, unaware that it had been more than ten years earlier, but also I thought I'd be in the way of her renewing the romance."

I sympathized with her. I figured she still needed time to accept her rewritten history, especially when she hung up without asking whether I'd contacted her building superintendent, who was on our suspect list. Lucky for me, she didn't ask anything specific about Ashley or Candace, and I was happy to follow Skip's advice and not bring it up.

I stood on the sidelines for a few minutes after my call from Cynthia, watching the busy vendors and customers, catching a glimpse halfway across the hall of Bebe and Maddie, smiling, showing off SuperKrafts merchandise as well as the mini-scenes we'd brought. As much as I wished I could comfort Cynthia right now, it was time for me to plunge in and do what Bebe brought me here for. Neal Crouse wasn't going anywhere, and I needed some mini-therapy. If I were being honest, I would have explored the theory that I was putting off that interview because Superintendent Crouse was the last on the list of possible suspects in the alleged murder of Aunt Elsie. If I got nothing from him, I was at a dead end and, thus, a failure. Did I really want to be a failure here? Wasn't New York the city where people were supposed to "make it"? Stalling, my tactic of choice lately, seemed silly. I called Neal Crouse and gave him the same line I'd given to Duncan.

"It would mean so much to my granddaughter if we could have your input for her school assignment."

"I have a lot going on right now. The board is after me for some paperwork; the tenants want their pound of flesh. What else is new? But if you can come to my building some time, I'd be glad to help out," he said.

"No problem. I'm looking forward to talking with you."

"Right," he said and clicked off before we set a specific time.
I decided I could email him later this evening. For now, it was
"Minis, here I come."

Back in the middle of the hall, I arrived at our table just as
Crystal came to claim Maddie for coat check duty. Her dark hair
was pulled into braids, giving me a clue as to why Maddie wanted
her own hair in braids this morning. Was it really that long ago
that I'd check with my girlfriends, Cynthia included, to help decide on the outfit I'd wear before we headed off to the subway
from the Bronx to Manhattan?

"Flats or heels?" I might have asked.

"Flats," she'd say. "Jacket or coat?"

"Jacket."

The current tween, Maddie Porter, had been describing her
newest responsibility: assistant coat check girl. "We get to put
coats and scarves on hangers, give the customer a ticket, and put
the coat in the right slot," Maddie explained.

"And we stuff gloves or earmuffs in the pockets and put packages and shopping bags on the shelves above the coat," Crystal
added. The little girl from New Jersey was still starry-eyed over
having a friend from California help with her big responsibility
in her mom's show.

"That's not all," Maddie said of her new assignment. "We're
going to be lunch runners, too."

"Any vendor who wants lunch delivered from the coffee
shop downstairs just has to fill out a form," said the Jersey girl.

"Lucky you," I said. They skipped off and I began my shift.

Sales at the SuperKrafts table had been good all morning,
Bebe told me. Maddie's idea of demonstrations using our kits to
draw people to the table had been a big hit. Samples were laid
out before me: a suitcase, a hatbox, a mint green baby sweater,
and a man's dress shirt. Several people asked when the young
miniaturist would be back. After lunch, was the answer. Bebe was
thrilled that she'd collected a pile of business cards from indepen-

dent miniatures stores all over the country, wanting to do business with SuperKrafts. The show was a hit, and I'd done nothing to spoil it. *Whew.*

I'd just finished a sandwich and tea brought to me by my granddaughter, the Lunch Runner, when a middle-aged couple came by the table. He had short, cropped hair, a squarish face, and a comfortably worn-in sports jacket; she was in black pants and an attractive blue paisley top. Pleasant smiles, intelligent eyes.

"Geraldine Porter?" the man asked me.

It worried me how quickly my senses kicked in. Or maybe it was the way he said my name, with a ring of authority and a touch of intimidation, but not deliberate. Was it simple instinct? Experience? Or luck? I held out my hand. "Welcome, NYPD," I said. "Glad to meet you, Buzz Arnold."

His loud, sincere laugh drew attention from Bebe and beyond. "You guessed."

My nephew had come through.

THE restaurant overlooking 42nd was now home to me, much as the taxis of Manhattan were my phone booths, and the black-and-whites sold everywhere, and which I ordered now, my comfort food. At this morning's breakfast, Maddie hadn't even flinched or said, "Wow," when she pointed out a man walking west toward the NYPL, his arms raised high. He carried a large, square, decorated cake, holding it as high as possible above the heads of the crowd of people. The frosting was visible to anyone tall enough to see, or sitting at a window up from street level. No one gave him a second glance.

"Buzz is a friend of Skip's," I'd told Bebe—not exactly full disclosure—and asked permission to take my break. All of my breaks at once, in fact, so I could have coffee with Buzz and his wife, Rosalie. Maddie, the busy working girl, was already back from coat checking and lunch running, so Bebe had been fine with the shift change.

"Last time I was in this hotel, it was to see if I could bump into some pro baseball players in New York for the all-star game," Buzz said. He looked around as if a second baseman, perhaps, was still wandering the lobby outfield.

"The Lex seems to be the hub for all the sports teams that come to New York," Rosalie said. "We paid a visit when the tennis open players were in town, too." She patted her husband's arm. "I'll go anywhere not to fix lunch myself."

I told her that if she were a vendor at our crafts fair, she could have it delivered by a very special little runner.

"I've heard about her, too," Buzz said.

"What else has Skip told you about his relatives?"

"He really didn't say everything he said," Buzz answered.

Rosalie patted his arm again. "Yogi Berra," she explained, but I'd been schooled enough by now to recognize a Yogism. Too bad I didn't have a Shakespearism handy.

We all fell silent as our waitress delivered coffee all around, my black-and-whites, and a platter of small pastries unlike those our local donut shop served, and better than cronuts. Éclairs, fruit tarts, custard cups, and petit fours decorated with holly. Buzz was quick to pick up a tart and pop it in his mouth, thereby giving me permission to sample a red velvet petit four, and fast becoming my second-favorite cop in the world.

Buzz gave me a recap on Aunt Elsie that was as accurate as if he'd been by my side for three days. Or having his own e-correspondence or phone conversations with Skip. He'd "done some digging" himself, as he put it, and confirmed the idea of a suspect who was one of only a small group of people who were around Aunt Elsie on a regular basis. "This is nothing official, mind you," he said. "I'm retired. Waiting for my interview and endless paperwork to be a special consultant to the District Attorney's office."

"Cynthia thinks the NYPD lost interest too quickly," I said, thinking how much more forcefully she would have expressed it. "Thanks for looking into it," I said.

"Thank *you* very much," Rosalie said. "Anything to keep him busy."

Buzz put his arm around his wife, reminding me of my own gentle man now in Hawaii. "You have to realize, attention to what we call 'gray murder' is kinda new." When Rosalie and I, both graying, reacted with raised eyebrows, Buzz held up his hand and continued. "I didn't invent the term. But there's a much better understanding now that we didn't have before." He made short work of eliminating a custard cup with a sweet-smelling maple drizzle. "There's a long way to go. We need more interventions by social workers, shrinks, the whole shebang. Trouble is"—he looked at me—"your friend's aunt didn't fit the profile of the usual elderly victim. She didn't live alone; she had all the services she could possibly want; she wasn't poor, but she wasn't so rich that she'd be a target. And, I'm sorry to say this, but she was past the average life expectancy of her neighborhood."

I gulped. "There's data on life expectancies by neighborhood?"

"He reads all this stuff," Rosalie said. "He loves statistics. Should have been a math professor, I tell him."

Buzz turned to me. "Let me ask you this. If you had a badge, what would you do now to help your friend?"

I laughed. "Skip asks me that a lot." Buzz waited while I mentally ran through the possibilities and the MMOs one more time. I'd already determined that collecting alibis was useless, as was looking for a weapon, unless there was a pill bottle somewhere labeled PLACEBOS FOR ELSIE BISHOP. For motive, the only one who profited from Aunt Elsie's death was Cynthia, and even if I were inclined to suspect her, I'd have to wonder why she was demanding an investigation that would lead to her. If someone wanted the apartment, why take a circuitous route? Cynthia was ambivalent about selling; why not kill *her* to be sure the apartment would be available after her aunt's natural death, which couldn't have been that far off. I scratched the horrible thought that the apartment-hungry killer had Cynthia in mind as a second victim. I retained a clinical approach long enough to evaluate that as a poor plan on his or her part, and finally thought of something I might pursue if I were a cop.

"I'd search the apartments of all the suspects for the box that's missing from Elsie Bishop's hiding spot," I said.

Buzz sat back, and shook his head. "You think that's something they'd keep around? Especially after the woman died?"

My shoulders slumped. "I guess not."

"Now you see the problem even a cop has?"

I wanted to explain to Buzz that I already had great admiration for cops, and sympathy for them, trying to do a difficult job. I decided he knew that.

"Work back," he said. "Back from the box."

I was stymied for a minute, then woke up. "The note she left for Cynthia," I said.

"Exactly."

"I apologize for Buzz. I've seen him in this mode before," Rosalie said. "Now that he's not going to work every day, that's what he does." I could tell by her expression and tone that she wasn't as aggravated by her husband's detective persona as her words indicated. She continued, "It's like you're his recruit, and instead of telling you what to do, he's training you. As if you were about to apply to the police academy. He's like that with me all the time."

"I'm glad to be in good company," I said, and to Buzz, "I need to see samples of everyone's handwriting."

"Now we're talking. In a way that needs no probable cause or warrant. Just your wiles."

"Wow," I said, channeling Maddie.

"Here's what I'll do. If you bring me something, like a handwriting match, or a reason to think a certain person of interest wrote that farewell note, I'll work my magic with my friends who are not retired or waiting around to take a test he knows he'll pass and—"

Rosalie again, with a gentle hand on his arm. "I think she gets it, dear."

I felt an exhilaration that had eluded me all week. "Deal." Now all I had to do was get handwriting samples from people I hardly knew.

———

IF IT hadn't been such a good day of sales and publicity for SuperKrafts, Bebe might not have been in such a good mood, and it might have been harder to convince her to join Cynthia, Maddie, and me for dinner on the Upper West Side. Her first response was a predictable resistance. "I don't see why Cynthia can't come over here. There are plenty of good restaurants on the East Side."

"Maddie and I will already be on the West Side. And the building superintendent is doing us a favor by talking to Maddie, so I want to accommodate him."

Bebe smiled in a knowing way. "Oh, right, this is for Maddie's school report," she said, in a tone that left no doubt that my subterfuge hadn't worked on her. I hoped it would work better on Neal Crouse.

At four-thirty, the last door prize was called in the exhibit hall. The dealers from an independent store called Knit Your Browse had submitted a variegated-yarn cowl kit, now claimed by a young woman with so many packages she could hardly juggle them all. Everyone clapped.

At five, the organizers pulled the plug on Rudolph and the music stopped. There was a flurry of activity in the hall—last-minute purchases, exchanges of information and old-fashioned business cards, retrieving of coats and hats—with the security detail helping to usher people toward the exits. "Come back tomorrow," Maddie said whenever she thought anyone was listening. "We'll be here from eleven to four." Most vendors older than Maddie looked tired from a day of intense interaction, standing over and hawking their wares, and handling cartons of inventory. They pulled out sheets of fabric or plastic to cover their tables, as we did, in an attempt to protect the goods from dust, or accidental bumps from the cleaning crew. Or thieves.

"That's not going to help," Maddie said of the flimsy barrier to theft.

"It's a good thing it's not your problem," I said.

She made a sound that lent itself to many interpretations.

Chapter 14

MY IN-CAB ACTIVITIES had been somewhat curtailed as a result of my fender-bender. Slight as it was, the memory of the earlier jolt had made me tense enough to clutch the strap with one hand, making it harder to deal with the keypad on my phone at the same time. I made sure Maddie's seat belt was tighter than ever and pulled on the belt until she squealed and acknowledged that one had to be prepared for a quick stop. Even so, on the way to Cynthia's building, I fit in a call to her with an update on the afternoon's events, slipping in a word about how well the fair was going and how pleased Bebe was about the successful first day for SuperKrafts. The idea was to plant a reminder of my first duty in New York City for one more day, and also to help my two friends get off to a good start at dinner. Not surprisingly, Cynthia was more enthusiastic about my meeting with a retired NYPD detective, his offer of help, and my new goal of collecting handwriting samples.

"That's fantastic, Gerry. Remember, we considered that Aunt Elsie might have had help, but we never pursued it. Now, the more I think about it, I'm almost sure someone else wrote that letter at her direction and that's why she didn't spell out where the secret place is. Who is this cop, by the way?"

"Barry someone. I have his card somewhere." I sneaked a look at Maddie, whose eyebrows went up. I'd deal with her later. "We're almost exiting the cab so I can't talk now," I told Cynthia. "Can you make a reservation for us in your neighborhood? Bebe will be joining us. We probably won't take more than an hour, if that long, interviewing your super."

"Okay. Table for four at seven-thirty. I know just the place, but it is Saturday night, so we'll see."

"And could you also call Bebe when the reservation is set up, and give her the address?"

Cynthia obliged me by taking Bebe's cell number in case she wasn't in her room. So far, so good. Détente at dinner was achievable.

I clicked off, ready to face Maddie, who had aborted her conversation with our driver about how much she loved Manhattan to tune into my side of the phone call.

"You told me Uncle Skip's friend's name is Buzz."

"That's his nickname. His real name is Barry."

"Still. His last name is Arnold and you didn't tell Ms. Bishop that. I guess you don't want her to try to call him on her own."

"Who made you so smart?" I asked, tickling her into submission.

I'd prepped Maddie for the interview without telling her that Mr. Crouse was a murder suspect. That is, a sort-of suspect in an alleged, but officially not, murder. I wanted her to approach the interview assuming the purpose really was to acquire information for her class trip report. "Do you have your questions ready for Mr. Crouse?" I asked.

"Yup. The first one is, did you kill Aunt Elsie?"

"Maddie!" What was Manhattan doing to my formerly sweet granddaughter? More important, would her father notice? Richard called her daily but I didn't know the details of their conversations. I figured Maddie was smart enough to emphasize the innocuous aspects of our days.

"I'm just kidding, Grandma. I wrote some questions on my laptop. It's faster to type when someone is talking to you. Writing by hand is *sooo* slow. And then sometimes I can't even read it."

"We'll discuss that another time. What questions do you have?"

"I have, like, what does a super do all day? Do you know everyone in the building? Did you have to go to school to learn the job? How do you apply for the job? Things like that."

I relaxed, paid our driver, and greeted the young doorman who helped us out. I'd never seen him before and pegged him for another college kid or part-timer who was fortunate enough to get the weekend shift. I remembered Cynthia's telling me that sometimes there was both an indoor and an outdoor doorman who alternated turf, particularly on days of inclement weather. RILEY was on this man's name tag and I assumed that was his first name, following the pattern of DUNCAN and CODY on their tags. I wondered if I should have him sign Maddie's journal to get a handwriting sample, but couldn't think of a way to make that pretext credible.

"Watch this, Grandma," Maddie whispered to me and looked up at the new doorman. "When is it going to snow?" she asked.

"Maybe tonight," he said, and Maddie laughed.

IT seemed strange to be entering Cynthia's building and not riding up to the fifteenth floor. Neal Crouse had left a message at the lobby desk that we should be led to his ground-floor apartment as soon as we arrived. I'd never walked past the elevators and had therefore missed the door marked SUPER. Neal was waiting for us, dressed in sports clothes, something between the coveralls I'd expected and the sharp suit I'd seen him in at Aunt Elsie's memorial service. His apartment was more than a cut above what I remembered of the super's quarters in my childhood home in the Bronx. This apartment was at street level, well-lit, and nicely furnished. A bachelor pad, I guessed, from the overall décor and underequipped kitchen. By contrast, our old Soupy, as we kids called him, lived in two rooms in the basement, both of which resembled a workshop more than a living room or bedroom. I remembered how my friends and I would bang on his battered metal door in the winter, chanting, "More heat, more heat." In the summer, it would be "Cooler, Soupy, cooler."

Now a much younger, more dapper Soupy stroked his neat stubble and invited us to sit at his shiny dinette set. "Help yourselves to cookies. I also have coffee and hot chocolate." Neal was more hospitable than I'd anticipated from his tone on the phone, delivering the drinks in record time. Maybe Maddie's presence softened him. She had that way about her.

"Mr. Crouse, thanks for meeting us," she said, getting down to business, opening her laptop. I wondered if the sales of pens and steno pads, as well as cameras and film, had gone down in the last few years. "First, I need to know your duties as a building superintendent in New York City."

"You can call me Neal, honey." He laughed as he took a seat at the table. "So, duties? How about, I'm on call twenty-four/ seven? What other job requires you to live right there, or not more than two hundred feet away? It cuts into your social life, let me tell you." He paused, maybe sensing that his social life was not pertinent to Maddie's needs for her report. He cleared his throat and started again. "Duties. We have a board and a manager and we're all supposed to agree on what the duties are. One guy wants it to be very specific so he can measure performance, and the other guy is worried that if it's too specific and you ask me to do something, I can always say, 'Sorry, not in my job description.' As if I can't be trusted. So I'm in the middle, which can be a good thing but mostly is not. Am I management or am I labor? Know what I mean?"

"Uh-huh." Maddie nodded as if she understood perfectly, and, in fact, had been there herself.

"What they do is, they write in a few things like the licenses we're supposed to have—heating, air-conditioning, fire safety, mechanical know-how, that kind of thing—and then they add 'Plus other tasks as necessary.'" Maddie's fingers flew over the keyboard but I doubted she captured the political implications of Neal's speech. I hoped he'd slow down, and he did. "Hey, I'll bet you don't need all that. You can just write that I have to know all the systems in the building. Like this morning, I fixed a garbage disposal in Four-B, put in a new wall socket in Twelve-C, and helped a cable guy with an installation for Eleven-E. I fix what's broken, find what's lost, and keep smiling. Those are my duties." He laughed. "Don't get me started."

Too late, Neal.

"Did you take classes?" Maddie asked. Good question. I doubted Soupy had much by way of schooling after he left his old country.

But Neal nodded. "Oh, yeah. All the usual classes to be certified in electrical, mechanical, like I said. Plus, a few years ago the city started mandating classes on communication." Another Neal laugh filled the room. "They called them 'Interpersonal Relations.'" He tapped Maddie's computer. "That means how to manage all the millions of maintenance contractors and get along with all the residents."

"This sounds a lot like what Duncan described," I said, genuinely confused about the difference in duties between a superintendent and a doorman. Neal didn't open doors, and Duncan hadn't taken classes in air-conditioning, but that was about it as far as I could tell. They both handled maintenance, it seemed, and both were responsible for the good working order of the building.

Neal smiled broadly, an assurance that I hadn't just insulted him. "Duncan says I'm a doorman without a uniform. I say he's a super without a license." Neal laughed at his own characterization. "Duncan's a good guy. Cody, too, though he's an artist, so he's not as handy. Cody's friendly with all the residents and is not above doing little favors for them. Which is another thing the board frowns on."

Oops. That rule seemed backwards. I thought I'd never learn to live in New York City again, where a funeral home was likely to be nestled between a barber shop and an ethnic restaurant; a uniformed officer at the scene of a traffic accident is not a real cop; and tipping was the preferred method of ensuring a decent living for so many workers. Maddie expressed my latest question

well. "Why wouldn't the board want you to do a favor for someone who lives here?"

"It doesn't look good," Neal said. "Like playing favorites. Or
it might make the super look bad." Neal wagged his finger in a
no-no fashion for emphasis. "I have a couple of friends with lousy
doormen, like the doorman will tell the tenant he'll give the
super a message about a plumbing problem, but he never gives
it to him, and so the tenant thinks the super fell down on the
job."

"Why would a doorman do that?" Maddie asked.

"They figure if they undermine the super, they get bigger
tips. Duncan and Cody don't do that. They're cool. If they do
favors, like Cody does, and Duncan does, too, but not so much,
nobody takes it wrong. But I'm good to them, too. I don't play
games. Like, I know a super who hides toothpicks in the lobby,
and if the doorman doesn't get it on the shift sweep, he writes
him up."

Maddie's eyes widened, and I was sure at that moment she
saw her parents and teachers in a new, lenient light. She might
even have contemplated keeping her room cleaner. I was aware
of time passing and didn't want to impose further on Neal. I
was pleased that he'd been forthcoming with all the interactions
among a building's employees even though I'd gotten nowhere as
far as what Cynthia expected of me. I started to collect my things,
preparing to leave, when Maddie intervened.

"I have only one more question, Mr. Crouse. What do you
think might have happened to the old Mrs. Bishop?"

I dropped my gloves and gasped. "Maddie! This is not what
we talked about." I was upset, but that didn't stop me from listening carefully.

"It's okay," Neal said. "I know you guys must be curious. It's
only natural. And I have my opinions which I'll be glad to share,
same as I did with the NYPD." Without the advantage of listening in on my talks with Skip and the confirmation from Buzz,
Neal went off in a dozen different directions: Elsie could have

been the victim of foul play—from the neighbor in Fifteen-E
who wanted to expand into Elsie's unit, or from a con artist she
might have met on a social network site, or from someone claiming he was a long-lost relative, or from anyone who snuck in off
the street when Duncan was on break.

I thought we'd better leave before Maddie asked him where
he was every day of the last several weeks. I looked at my watch.
"We've taken enough of your time," I said. We thanked Neal
Crouse and headed out to the lobby, my hand ready to clamp
Maddie's mouth closed at the first sound of speech.

IN the lobby, Cody was now on duty. I wondered if the doorman
schedule was always so flexible. "Hey, you two," he said. "Back
again." Maddie explained that she needed more pages for her report. "I know how that goes," he said. "You know how to make
the font size and margins bigger to give you more pages, right?"
She nodded and smiled as they shared a student-to-student moment. Never mind that I and most teachers had been onto that
trick since the early days of book reports and term papers, no
matter what the tools for preparing them.

Cody pointed me toward the lobby phone to call up to Cynthia, and in a few minutes the three of us were almost out the
door. "By the way," I said to Cody. "The young man who was
here earlier said that Neal had left a message to take us to his
apartment."

"Yeah, probably," Cody said.

"Would he have written the message or texted it?"

Cody laughed, a *pshaw* sound. "Text? Old Crouse? I don't
think so." I doubted Neal Crouse was over forty. Cody didn't
know from old supers in the Bronx of yesteryear.

"Would the note still be here?" I asked.

"Over on the desk, I suppose," Cody said, now confused.

"I wonder if we could have it? It would make such a nice
addition to Maddie's journal. A souvenir of the time we spent
in this wonderful building." I gave out a satisfied sigh, my hand

ready to clamp Maddie's mouth if she uttered the beginnings of disagreement.

Cody lifted his cap enough to scratch his head. "Uh, I guess it would be okay." He shuffled papers around the small desk and came up with a piece of white paper folded several times over. Neal's note. "Here you go. Enjoy," he said, smiling.

"Thanks." I plucked the paper from Cody's hand before Maddie or Cynthia could comment. My first handwriting sample. I was on my way.

CYNTHIA could hardly wait for Riley, still on outside duty, to close the door to our cab. "Let's see that note, Gerry. That was brilliant of you to ask for it."

I pulled the paper from my pocket and unfolded it. Neal wrote in a tight, heavy hand, with few flourishes. Uppercase letters were almost identical to their printed counterparts; the words were slanted on the page. I was sure an expert could attach a name and a personality trait to go with these characteristics, but I doubted they pegged him as a killer. And they certainly didn't look anything like the open, graceful penmanship of Aunt Elsie's note. I put Neal's name in the NO column.

"Maybe a good idea, but not useful this time," I said, and handed the paper across Maddie's lap to Cynthia.

Cynthia gave the note a quick look, grimaced, and shook her head. "I agree. He didn't write Aunt Elsie's note. Not even close. Aunt Elsie always had beautiful, careful penmanship. You should have heard her go on and on about how schools should get back to teaching cursive." I expected Maddie to comment, but she was too busy texting. Cynthia sat back in the dark cab and blew out a long breath. Her voice sounded halting, and as we passed streetlights I could see that she was close to tears. "I think that someone"—she let out a little growl, startling Maddie—"whoever wrote that note for my aunt saw an opportunity and looked around and found the hiding place, then helped himself to what was in that box."

"See, Grandma," Maddie said, sending an email off with a *whoosh.* "You *are* still working on the case." She'd finally caught on to what we were talking about and realized she'd been left out. "You're still working with Buzz Arnold."

"Who's Buzz Arnold?" Cynthia asked, perking up.

"Are we almost there?" I asked the cabbie.

"THIS is my third-favorite restaurant for dinner," Cynthia said. "We got in only because the matinee-goers have already eaten; it's too late for the pre-concert crowd; and it's too early for the after-concert people."

"Sounds like it's tricky to get food in New York," Bebe said. I held my breath, hoping Cynthia wouldn't take the comment as a slight on her hometown. "But I read in my guidebook that Manhattan alone has more than thirty-five hundred restaurants. I can't imagine." *Whew.* Conflict averted.

"Are your first- and second-favorite restaurants really better than this, Ms. Bishop? This is delicious." Maddie made this pronouncement while sitting in front of the large appetizer plate we'd ordered to share. The dish included endive with marinated vegetables, ham puffs with olives and oranges, and flatbread with goat cheese. And Maddie had called it delicious? If I weren't so averse to attention, I'd have whipped out my phone and sent a photo of her eating potato pancakes with a pecorino crust to her parents. As far as I remembered none of us had ever seen Maddie eat any cheese other than what she called pizza topping. If I'd known that the cure to Maddie's picky eating habits was a simple trip to Manhattan, I'd have taken her here as soon as she was on solid foods.

At dinner, I wanted to keep talk of the investigation to a minimum, but it was inevitable that we'd slide into it now and then. Such as, when I turned to Cynthia and asked, "Just one more thing before I forget. Do you have anything around your house that has Ashley's or Candace's handwriting?"

"I'll look. They would sometimes leave a note for me. I'm

not sure whether it was Ashley or Candace who'd write." I drew in my breath, hoping no one noticed. I felt a long moment of sympathy for Ashley and Candace as I realized that Cynthia had just admitted to one way at least that she couldn't distinguish one young woman from the other. "I'm not sure I kept anything from them, whoever it was," she continued.

Bebe allowed a few minutes of "The Life and Death of Aunt Elsie" conversation, then cleared her throat in preparation for a new topic. "The show ends at four tomorrow. Then we have the evening, plus Monday afternoon before we leave on Tuesday. On Monday morning, I have a managers' meeting"—here she sounded proud and excited, as I knew she was—"where I'll be giving a preliminary report on the show." SuperKrafts probably had many capable managers, but I doubted they had any as enthusiastic as Lincoln Point's Barbara "Bebe" Mellon.

In other circumstances, I'd have been eager to make plans for the time between the end of the show and our leaving. But I knew that Cynthia would want stepped-up attention to her case, and that Bebe would simply want me around. There was nothing to do but work it out hour by hour.

BY the time we got back to the Lex, Maddie and I were both exhausted and full from a five-course meal. I barely kept awake long enough for what used to be a tucking-in session.

"Did you see all the samples I made from the kits, Grandma?" a sleepy Maddie asked.

"I did. They're wonderful. No wonder you sold so many."

"Kits," she said, and giggled. "We better not tell Mrs. Reed, huh?"

"Probably not." I could almost hear the disgust in the voice of my friend Linda Reed as she spoke of "anything other than DIY from scratch, don't bother."

My phone-calling time was curtailed by my drooping eyelids, but I managed a few words to Henry (I missed him, too, and was glad he enjoyed the roast pig and the hula dancing); to Skip (Buzz

Arnold was all he was cracked up to be and, yes, he was still into Yogisms); to Mary Lou (so relieved that Richard yielded to her and did not book a flight to JFK to check on his daughter); to Bev (I was glad she received the postcards already and was sorry I hadn't called more often).

I fell asleep thinking about my third-grade teacher and her cursive writing drills and wishing they hadn't been replaced by keyboard-proficiency skills.

Chapter 15

LIKE ANY OF the shows, small or large, that I've been involved in, we had shorter hours and fewer visitors on Sunday, the second day. After a leisurely breakfast at our usual place in the hotel, Maddie was on coat-check duty again, and Bebe was happily noting that we were out of a few items. No more kits on hand for a miniature gazebo or very tiny wicker porch furniture (in one one-hundred-forty-fourth scale: one inch for every twelve feet of real size, so that a six-foot sofa would be one half inch long). Only a few more holiday decorating sets and faux snow-covered trees were left in the cartons under the table.

Bebe kept herself busy spreading red-and-green foil-wrapped chocolate kisses to fill the empty spots on the table. "Wouldn't it be great if we had absolutely nothing to pack up?" she asked.

I agreed and predicted that every Christmas item would be gone before we closed shop. I fielded a call from Cynthia, who'd found a couple of handwritten notes from Ashley ("possible, but not likely") and Candace ("chicken scratches"). My hopes for a quick and easy penmanship match-up, a call to Buzz, and an entry to the NYPD were fading. I'd looked forward to at least part of a day devoted to Case-free enjoyment of the Big Apple. A stop at the Algonquin to breathe in the same air as Dorothy Parker and the rest of the *New Yorker* band; tasty cucumber-and-dill sandwiches at afternoon tea at the Ritz; a seventieth-floor view of Manhattan from the Top of the Rock; a ferry ride to Ellis Island where Ken's Irish ancestors arrived more than a hundred years ago; a few more minutes with the sounds of Grand Central Station—announcements, meetings, rolling trains, conversations both hushed and loud. Any or all would do. Maybe tomorrow morning would be free.

I was unprepared for a breathless Maddie, who'd run from the check-in counter at the entrance doors to our table in the middle of the hall. I could only hope that she hadn't knocked over anyone on the journey. "Grandma, Grandma," she croaked, and, once again, I checked for blood.

"What is it, sweetheart?" I asked.

"I know who did it." She kept her voice low, which wasn't difficult, given her respiratory state. "We have to find Mr. O'Brien." Ronnie O'Brien, the head of security. And I thought we'd been dismissed from the Case of the Missing Crafts. If there was a case. "There's a lady and a man. They just came in, and he left his jacket for us to check, but she kept her big, heavy coat on. She didn't have that big, flowery tote like yesterday. I'll bet she left it home because she knew everyone saw it, and I'll bet now she hides the stuff in her coat."

"You can't assume—"

"We need to find Mr. O'Brien. They're over at the first row now, but Mr. O'Brien has to hurry or send someone." Maddie's words came in bursts; she could hardly catch her breath. I was amazed that no vendors or customers around us noticed her agitated state. She had done well in containing herself, and anyone who did notice probably chalked it up to a preteen breakdown over a bauble that was too expensive for her allowance.

"Take some deep breaths, sweetheart. What makes you think that's the couple who's been stealing things?"

Bebe, who was finishing with a customer, had listened in and called for Security. She obviously had more faith in my granddaughter than I did. Whatever Bebe told Ronnie (maybe that a minor child was in desperate need of assistance), he was at our table in a couple of minutes. Maddie explained her findings to us all: She remembered that the woman who "fleed" (her word;

I'd work on that with her later) out the back of the hall yesterday wore a long, gray coat with a large cape attached, that came to her waist. Just like the one this woman wore. She also remembered that the man with her today, the one who checked his green camouflage jacket, was in all the footage she'd looked at where there was a distraction or disruption of some kind—something had been broken, or a table leg had collapsed, or a loud argument had caused a fracas in an aisle. Ronnie wasn't so quick to dismiss Maddie this time, leading me to believe she'd triggered his memory about the presence of the man at the scenes. He used his pager to summon his staff. I was surprised that pagers hadn't been replaced by smartphones, going the way of Christmas pins.

Maddie caught her breath. "Don't look," she said. "The lady is over at the first row, but the man is all the way over near the last row." No sooner had she spoken but a ruckus broke out in the last row. Voices could be heard complaining about soup that had spilled from a dealer's thermos onto a customer's pants. Or, by the time the news got to our table, it might have been coffee spilled over another dealer's merchandise. While many heads turned to observe the soup-or-coffee-spill incident, at our table we all looked in the other direction, toward the woman allegedly shopping in the first row. Sure enough, the woman appeared to have dropped something. She bent over to pick it up and then began a slow journey toward the front entrance of the hall. My guess was that her male partner would head out at some later time, after casually picking up his jacket. Except that my granddaughter had been on the job. Either that, or I was foolishly buying into her fantasies.

Ronnie bought it also, however. He spoke into his radio and within minutes, one uniformed guard swooped in on the woman, another on the man. It all seemed to be over before it started. Police work in action. Unlike the scene of my traffic accident. Both outcomes typical of New York City, I guessed.

"Wow," Maddie said, as if she were in the middle of a dream where she was a detective like her Uncle Skip, and she had just solved a major case that brought the uniforms in to arrest the criminals. Which, in a way, had happened.

EVERYTHING else seemed anticlimactic after the great drama of the early afternoon. Vendors breathed sighs of relief; shoppers refocused on their mission; the noise rose steadily to its normal high level. By closing time at four o'clock, we'd come close to attaining Bebe's goal of having "absolutely nothing to pack up." The leftover merchandise, which fit into one medium-size carton, consisted mostly of SuperKrafts pamphlets and a few boxed sets of dollhouse furniture.

"I'm tempted to buy the leftover dollhouse pieces myself, so I can report a complete sell-out," she said.

"Don't you think that might look suspicious? Sending only the few things we have left will look more plausible." Bebe fell for my made-up ruling and put in a call to Corporate to arrange for the carton to be picked up on Monday morning. I was glad I'd been able to spare her some embarrassment if she were ever found out.

Crystal and her parents came to say good-bye; they were headed back home tonight. Maddie had bought a small heart charm for Crystal, and the New Jersey family presented Maddie with a lovely bouquet of flowers and a box of gourmet chocolates as a thank-you for her work as a volunteer at the coat-check counter and on the lunch-running circuit.

"And for your crime-solving skills," Crystal added. "I can't believe you're, like, a real detective," she said, and the friends hugged again. "You're like the books I read. This one would be *Madison Porter and the Case of the Crafts Show Thieves*." The girls were giggly and teary-eyed, much as Maddie and Taylor were in Lincoln Point only a few days ago, and exacted the same kinds of promises to text and send selfies often. Crystal's parents and I shook hands and exchanged knowing glances, aware that once the girls returned to their homes, it would be about a week until school, after-school programs, and their local friends took over their lives again.

The janitorial crew who'd been standing by at all the entrances and exits with their barrels, mops, and cleaning supplies, moved in like infantry troops ready to do battle with the trash. I was glad that this time I wasn't the one responsible for tearing down the signs, folding the tables and stashing them away, and sweeping up droppings, from large scraps of paper and food wrappers to tiny sequins and beads. I smiled at the crew and thanked them as we left the hall.

The show was over, but kudos for Maddie had just begun, as Ronnie O'Brien and his staff invited us to an intimate ceremony in the Lex's security office. We'd deposited Maddie's flowers and candy and freshened up in our rooms before heading down to the second-floor office. Maddie was thrilled to find the room transformed into a party scene, with a small cake decorated with the message THANKS DETECTIVE MADDY (I was sure that, given a chance, Maddie would adopt the new spelling), surrounded by tiny magnifying glasses made of frosting. I was impressed with what must have been Ronnie's clout in the Lex's kitchen, pulling off such a quick turn-around. (I imagined rows of plain square cakes lined up waiting to be custom-frosted for such a moment.) Ronnie presented her with a special pen-and-pencil set with the security company logo (I suspected they purchased these by the thousands), and several toasts were made with pink punch.

With all the fanfare, it wasn't hard to keep Maddie from realizing how surprised I was that she'd been right. Ronnie wouldn't tell us much about the details of the arrest, except to say: "We call it 'booked and cooked.' The lady's coat was full of items with no receipts, adding up to a pretty penny." We'd have to be satisfied never knowing the thieves' names or why they chose to ply their trade at our fair.

Besides the principals, Cynthia responded to my quick message and came by for the little party; and Jackie Cromwell, the show's energetic organizer, made a special little thank-you speech. Maddie couldn't have been more excited if she'd been lifted onto the shoulders of an NYPD lineup (or on the back of one of their horses) and carried around town. The same might have been said of Bebe, who reminded everyone that Maddie was her special friend, from her hometown. I took lots of pictures for Henry, whose idea started the whole effort.

At the end of the mini–award ceremony, we bundled up to go to dinner. I was getting used to seeing Maddie with an added ten pounds of clothing. Tonight she wore her green knit hat pulled over her ears with the hood of her jacket on top of that, looking like a little thief herself, plus two scarves, one inside her collar, the other outside. I stuck with my standard for the week, a turtleneck sweater, a heavy wool jacket, one hat, and one scarf. As soon as we hit the other side of the turnstile doors, Maddie lifted the outer scarf to cover her mouth, then lowered it for a minute to address the Lex's doorman.

"When are we going to get some snow?"

"Maybe tonight," he said, joining us in our laughter.

SUNDAYS were easier for diners and Cynthia had made reservations at her first choice of restaurant, Due Cugine, in SoHo, the South of Houston neighborhood of lower Manhattan. Maddie ordered tuna, and if she was surprised that it neither looked nor tasted like the kind she mixed with mayonnaise and relish and spread on white bread, she didn't let on. "Mmm," she said, after a taste of the marinated turnip served with the seared tuna. In a way, I felt sorry for Taylor and for Maddie's Palo Alto school chums who were bound to be subjected to food stories they probably didn't care a whit about. I felt there was good news for her parents, however, who might be able to enjoy something other than pizza on family night out.

Dinner talk revolved around the highs of the crafts show, and, sadly, the lows of Cynthia's personal quest. After all our efforts, there remained the unanswered question—how did Aunt Elsie die? The handwriting samples from Neal, Ashley, and Candace seemed to rule them out as viable murder suspects, though I still wondered if the two lying caregivers should be further scrutinized. We enjoyed a brief moment of hope when Cynthia told us she'd found a postcard (alas, not at all the handwriting we were looking for) sent to her by Duncan after his weekend getaway to a beach in Cape May, New Jersey. We'd yet to find and examine samples of the other doormen's handwriting, and as a last resort, Philip's, but I didn't hold out much more hope for that approach.

"Does Duncan send a postcard to every resident?" I'd asked when Cynthia told me about his sample.

She'd shaken her head and explained. "He brings a bunch of cards home and hands them to the mailman, who then puts them in selected boxes. We think he has his favorites. I'm not sure that's legal, but Duncan saves postage."

Cynthia's proposal that we make a toast was welcomed. We picked up our wine, water, and tomato juice glasses and clinked them together. "To Bebe, and continued success and career growth." *Hear, hear.* "To Gerry and Maddie, for using their delightful company and excellent skills to see me through a difficult time." *Hear, hear.* Cynthia's words and manner pleased me, mostly because I sensed that she was coming around to accepting the original ruling of the NYPD in the death of her aunt. I was more than pleased when Bebe raised her glass again. "To Cynthia, hoping for comfort and happier days ahead." *Hear, hear.* I knew we'd have the morning to think more about Aunt Elsie, but I acknowledged that we might have to be content with only the solution of what I thought of as The Little Case, though I guessed the victims of the thefts wouldn't appreciate that designation. Finally, in unison, we toasted, "To us." *Hear, hear.*

We ended dinner on a happy note when the waiter, who'd been clued in to "The Case of the Crafts Fair Thieves," brought a special dessert—a decadent chocolate parfait—for Maddie, on the house. It was a good thing he also brought three extra spoons.

I WAS impressed that Due Cugine had its own doorman, or perhaps just a gentlemanly security person who hailed two cabs for us, one going up to the West Side, the other to the East Side.

Bebe, Maddie, and I were cozy, squeezed into the back seat of the cab heading up Sixth Avenue. "Cynthia's very nice," Bebe said. Startled as I was, I jumped in quickly, agreeing, before Maddie had a chance to ask why the change of heart. "I should have been a little more understanding of what she's going through. It was probably like losing a parent, and I know what that's like."

"I'm glad we had a nice dinner together," Maddie said. *Whew.* Our cab cruised up Sixth without a hitch. The only excitement was Bebe's being able to point out SuperKrafts' corporate offices as we passed it. "I'll be there again tomorrow morning with all my charts," she said, and uttered a sound of satisfaction, either for her job performance or the memory of our chocolate parfait. Initially, Bebe had wanted me to accompany her to the meetings; I hoped she saw now that it was better that she hadn't shown up with a crutch, namely me. I spared Bebe any speeches about how it might have been the best thing for her to see that she was very competent and could manage her job with great professionalism on her own.

Never the first to lose energy, Maddie kept track of our trip uptown on her smartphone, pointing out (or, at least in the direction of) Washington Square Park where, as I'd told her many times, I'd gone to college, on the right; the West Village on the left; and the Flatiron District. As we approached Bryant Park, behind the NYPL, Maddie told our cabbie, the first I'd seen without a Bluetooth attached to his head, "Take the next right." He laughed. "You better than GPS," he told her. "Sound nicer." Thanks to the two of them, we made it home to the Lex, to be greeted by a doorman who answered the usual question in the usual way.

BEFORE bedtime, Maddie and I engaged in some serious packing, which included finding room for our purchases. My carry-on was available, since we'd sold or given away the minis we'd brought from home, and I'd donated my leftover supplies to a local crafter who didn't have airline weight limits to worry about. Maddie stuffed her T-shirts and the countless leaflets, brochures, maps, and ticket stubs that she'd picked up during the week into my carry-on. I checked out a long pile of items on the narrow space in front of the television set, yet to be wedged into our luggage. A snow globe featuring the New York skyline; several green foam Statue of Liberty crowns, probably meant for her Girl Scout troup; and a collection of other I ♥ NY novelties including magnetic bookmarks, replicas of the Empire State Building in several sizes, a key chain, a small yellow metal cab, a tin of mints, a pencil case, a deck of playing cards, and a squishy red apple with bendable arms and legs and NEW YORK in silver around its body.

I picked up the last piece—an approximately two-inch-high frosted glass dish. "An ashtray?" I asked, raising my eyebrows.

"No, it's for Mom. I thought it was for artists." She ran her finger around the rim, dipping at the indentations. "She can rest her brushes in these spots."

I cleared my throat and decided to let her mother explain the main use of the object. Or not. "When did you buy all these things?" I asked.

"All in one store in Times Square when I was with Bebe. She bought a lot, too, but there was even more stuff, Grandma. I almost got a pocket knife for Dad but I was afraid they wouldn't let me take it on the plane. I got him a little notebook instead. I hope he likes it."

"I'm sure everyone will love your souvenirs." I paused. "So you and Bebe did some shopping on the side?"

"Yeah. Bebe thought I should wait and show you all this at the end, as a surprise."

I found it amusing that Bebe preferred to keep her good times from me until the last minute.

"We still were the best table in the hall, right?"

"If you say so," I said, tickling her.

I checked the closet and the dresser and was dismayed to find the LPPD patch Skip had given me stuck at the back of the top drawer. I was supposed to have passed on to an NYPD cop. I should have given it to the non-cop who tried to chase our hit-and-run cabbie. Or, better, to Buzz. I'd have to mail it to him when I got home. I decided to send Buzz an email now, confessing my shortcomings and asking for his postal address.

Ring. Ring. A call at ten-thirty. I was surprised when the hotel phone rang about five minutes after I clicked Send.

"I see you're up, too," he said.

"We're too full from dinner at Due Cugine."

"I'm surprised. Nobody goes there anymore. It's too crowded."

It took no time to recognize a Yogism and I offered up a good laugh.

I gave Buzz a rundown on the results of the handwriting project, and accepted his condolences. "Welcome to our world," he said, and I figured he and Skip went to the same school of clichés. "Say, instead of mailing me that patch, how about you and your granddaughter come down to One PP. I'm busy filling out this infernal paperwork before they'll give me any assignments, but if you get here around noon, I'll take you to the best lunch in the city."

I agreed, signed off, and turned to tell Maddie the news. No need. I caught her hanging up the telephone extension on the night table and saw her big smile. "One PP means Number One Police Plaza," she said. "It's on TV all the time. The cops and the lawyers walk out the door of the building onto this big plaza. Wow. I'm going to be there."

What better way to spend our last lunch in New York than with the NYPD at their headquarters?

I'D done a little shopping myself at the Lex's gift shop off the lobby, and picked up a book of New York history. I knew Maddie read mostly online, her preferred educational and recreational tool, but tonight I read to her about the early history of the city, how it was once the capital of the United States. We started a list of sights to visit the next time we came to New York. At the top of the list were the tenement museum, where a costumed docent helped visitors understand the early twentieth-century immigrant experience; a ferry ride from lower Manhattan so we could look back on the skyline; and Coney Island for as much junk food as we could stand. We agreed that we'd finish the list on the plane on Tuesday. For now, we were both ready to turn in, after all the heavy lifting we'd done. The good news was that all of our belongings, new and old, were in order, most of them packed. Unless we shopped in a big way tomorrow, no new luggage would be necessary.

Maddie's final words for Sunday night were in the form of a question. "Do you think Willie's will carry asiago cheese bagels for us?"

"I'm positive," I said, not bothering to tell her that Willie's has always carried asiago cheese bagels, as well as onion, pumpernickel, sourdough, and jalapeño, among others. She'd just never bothered to look past the plain bagels.

I called Henry, remembering that he was well into a two-hour time change himself. Five hours behind New York put him at an early dinner hour on the island of Maui.

"Taylor wants to know if there are hula dance classes back home," he informed me.

"Don't be surprised if Maddie expects a fresh bruschetta for dinner for a while," I warned him.

We chatted about how great it was that kids will not only adapt to changing routines, but be so eager to take on new things of all kinds: food, weather, accents, cultural protocols.

"As for me, I can't wait to get back to the old routine," he said.

"Are you saying I'm old?"

"Just old enough."

With that, we blew kisses and said good night.

Chapter 16

BEBE WOKE UP (and woke us up) in a good mood on Monday morning. She came to our room dressed for her final meeting with her crosstown bosses. She wore another blouse I'd never seen, an off-white tuxedo-front style, and I wondered if she'd sneaked in another shopping trip this week without Maddie. The Lex was within walking distance of Lord & Taylor, after all, and almost directly above the vast lower level mall in Grand Central Station. She accounted for part of her outfit before I could ask, holding up her new scarf, in brown hues, to give us a closer look. "I got this at that shop two doors down from here, 'Scarves and More.' It's, like, Manhattan's motto. Everything's 'And More.' I love it."

Maddie and I loved it, too, we said, as we piled extra pillows behind us and sat up in our beds, both in our night clothes from a suburban mall with a meager food court. Bebe had taken the only chair in the room and began an unsolicited preview of her final presentation to her corporate overlords. During their time together without me, Maddie had worked with Bebe, taking advantage of the services and equipment in the hotel's business center, and together they'd produced impressive color graphics with data on the crafts fair. I was convinced that Maddie had done more to act as Bebe's companion and assistant at the show than I had, but, as her grandmother, one who'd supplied some of her genes and paid for her airplane ticket, I felt I deserved a certain percent of the credit.

"My bosses will be so amazed at these charts," Bebe told us, holding up a graphic that highlighted the takeaways from the show. "They're not just interested in the bottom line, though the sales figures are phenomenal, but all the networking with the other vendors, making points with Jackie Cromwell, who organizes shows all over the country, plus getting to know the events coordinator and her staff, and the security staff here at the Lex."

"And more," Maddie said, clever even half-asleep.

Bebe gave Maddie a smile and a nod, and I took it that she meant to apply about ten percent of that gratitude to me, for the genes if nothing else. She took off for her meeting, seeming satisfied that we'd connect with her for dinner, but probably not before then.

"I promised we'd help Cynthia go through her aunt's closets this afternoon," I'd reminded her. "It's a tough thing to tackle, but it might be a little easier if she has company."

"I'm glad she has you," Bebe said, nodding, and I knew she really was in a spectacular mood.

For some reason, Bebe seemed on an energy high, while I was at a low point, all the busyness and the stress of the week catching up with me. Once Bebe left, I looked over at a still heavy-lidded Maddie.

"We shouldn't waste our last morning in Manhattan in bed," I said, as I slid down to a supine position under the covers.

"Uh-uh," Maddie said. "I wanted to go skating in Rockefeller Center this morning."

As soon as I could twist my body in that direction, I looked over at my granddaughter, hoping she was kidding, but she'd nodded off.

It was a good thing the knock from housekeeping came at eleven o'clock, or we would have wasted the entire morning, and, worse, missed our lunch with the NYPD at their headquarters.

I EXPECTED a strange look or comment when at eleven-thirty I asked the Lex doorman, a young man we'd never seen before, for a cab to One Police Plaza. I wasn't disappointed. "Going downtown to catch another thief, huh?" he asked, with a wink at Maddie.

She came back with "When's it going to snow?"

"Maybe tonight," he said.

Once in the warm cab, Maddie went through her ritual, removing her gloves, flipping off her hood, loosening her scarf, and taking her journal from her backpack. She found her SNOW page and added to her tally, coming up with seven separate doormen who'd given the same answer to her snow question: "Maybe tonight."

In this direction, the streets were not as well manicured as those going west toward Park, Madison, and Fifth Avenues, prompting Maddie to ask, "Is this a fringe neighborhood? Dad asks me that almost every night. I'm writing him a postcard."

I looked out at the sooty sidewalks dotted with trash that had spilled out of plastic bags, plus a few stray paper cups with fast food logos. The pedestrians, however, seemed to be the same, well-dressed professionals hurrying to an early lunch. "I wouldn't call it that," I said. "It does look a little less cared-for in these few blocks, but there's nothing scary." Never mind the narrow alleys between the buildings, that might well look threatening on a dark night. "It's just not as dazzling as the median strip along Park Avenue." I couldn't see what Maddie was writing, but assumed it was nothing to cause her father grief.

Our cab driver continued toward the East River, talking into his headset at breakneck speed, in a foreign language. Nothing new in our driver experience this week. Maddie took a picture of the green sign, FDR DR as we turned onto it. "I know what that stands for," she said, and gave me a little history lesson about the thirty-second and longest-serving president. I added my own tidbit, that FDR was born in upstate New York on the Hudson River side, and that his home there was a national historic monument. We talked about adding a visit to Hyde Park to our list for our next trip.

Once we'd merged onto the FDR, we picked up speed and
Maddie had a hard time taking pictures until we exited. She
snapped into action when she saw a sign for the AVENUE OF THE
FINEST, a clue that we were nearing police headquarters. "Wow,"
she said, clicking her camera button. "I wish we had a street
name like that in Palo Alto." I came close to asking if she'd been
keeping track of how many wishes she'd made since the beginning of the trip, when she'd wished she had a doorman that first
night as Cynthia handed over her car to Duncan in front of her
building.

Our cabbie, another fan of music that was dissonant to my
ear, complained (in English, to us, I finally realized) for about a
mile about the wide buffer zone around One Police Plaza that
forced him to spiral in toward the building. The fourteen-story,
fortress-like structure was as imposing as any other city landmark.
Block-style architecture had not been high on Ken's list of favorites. "They don't call it 'brutalist' for nothing," he'd said during its
period of increased appearance in the United States. "It's okay for
government buildings like the police headquarters downtown,
but I wish they'd kept it off university campuses." Then he'd rattle
off all the places where schools had added a brutalist touch to
their landscape, from New Haven to Pittsburgh to Chicago to
Minneapolis.

I called Buzz as we approached the building just before noon.

"Meet you"—a phrase that sounded like *meecha*—"on the
southeast corner of the plaza," he said. Maddie was turned in her
seat, looking straight out the window at the expanse of red-and-
blue brick, snapping away with her phone. I wondered again how
we would have managed in the days when we'd have had to buy
loads of film to accommodate her new obsession. I tapped her on
the shoulder. "I'm sorry to ruin your last day by forcing you to
stop at the NYPD." She giggled and snapped my picture. Served
me right.

Buzz was waiting for us at the edge of the plaza, ready to
greet us with an apology. "I realized too late that we should have

met at the Police Museum instead. You can't get very far without
a badge of your own in this building." We assured him we were
already impressed by the outside view and that we would put the
museum on our ever-growing don't-miss list for next time.

Our personal police escort (in civilian clothes) led us across a
narrow street behind the police building. Buzz continued in his
tour-guide manner as we walked to "the best pizza this side of
Little Italy," he promised. I knew from my own youth that to a
New Yorker, Little Italy was head and shoulders above "Big Italy"
as a tourist destination.

"Forensics and all the hands-on stuff like lab analysis is in
Queens, so there's not much to see here at One PP, except the
tactical response unit, the major case squad, emergency services,
and a high-tech computer center with something like thirty-
three billion public records." Maddie gasped, which, I assumed,
was Buzz's goal. "Next time, I'll be more creative and find a way
to sneak you in." He held up a tote with the NYPD logo. "But
I did manage to pick up a few souvenirs. We'll make our trade
at lunch. You give me an authentic Lincoln Point Police Department patch, and I'll give you a pile of New York Police Department junk."

Maddie beamed her appreciation, still a bit speechless at
the size of the building and plaza now behind us and what was
housed inside. "That building's on TV all the time," she finally
squeaked out.

"You watch those shows?" Buzz asked.

"I'm almost twelve," she answered.

"As long as you don't believe everything you see. Like the
crime scene guys going in with guns blazing before the cops get
there—not! Even worse, the ME starts collecting evidence—not!
The crime scene belongs to the police; the ME just gets the body.
Oh, yeah, another huge goof is how the DNA results come back
right after the commercial—"

"Not!" Maddie shouted, but even her outdoor voice was
swallowed up in the noise of the traffic speeding by and the

ubiquitous orange-vested construction workers digging up roads or putting them back together.

Buzz laughed. "You got it."

"Uncle Skip tells us that all the time. He says you hardly ever really would have, like, six or seven police cars with sirens, all pulling up to a house at the same time. And instead of, like, forty-five minutes to solve a crime, it's more like forty-five months by the time there's a trial and everything. Do you have a bullet-proof vest?"

The out-of-the-blue question, slipped in, didn't faze the retired cop. "Yes, I do. I almost wore it today, it's so cold out." From the look on Maddie's face, I thought her next question might be "Do they come in kids' sizes?"

THE majestic view of the Brooklyn Bridge, unmistakable from any angle, dominated the side windows at the hole-in-the-wall Plaza Pizza, and rivaled what we saw of Central Park from Cynthia's apartment. "Wow," Maddie said, claiming a window seat. She snapped photos of the bridge, and then of the brick walls with floating oak panels, the wood-fired stove, the friendly wait staff, and the sign over the service counter: COME FOR THE PIZZA— STAY FOR THE COPS.

"I figured you guys would be tired of all the Upper West Side class and might enjoy a simple slice," Buzz said.

"How did you know?" I asked, comfortable in this less formal environment. Paper napkins in a metal dispenser. Self-service drinks. Shakers of parmesan cheese and crushed red pepper on the linen-free tables.

Buzz ordered an extra-large New York, then switched into cop mode and said to me, "Sorry the handwriting angle didn't work out." He shrugged. "You never know. At least you gave it a shot."

I expected a Yogism at that point, but none was forthcoming. I explained that I still had a couple of doormen that I needed samples from. "But they're part-timers and not likely candidates,"

I admitted. "The handwriting we're trying to match is almost cal-
ligraphy, and I can't imagine that would be a hobby of any of the
men we've dealt with in the lobby." I took a sip of coffee. "I'm
losing heart."

"It happens. That's when you need to stick with it." Were
cops trained as therapists, also? Like Skip, Buzz had a way of im-
parting advice that didn't seem patronizing or insulting. "How's
your friend holding up?" he asked.

I described Cynthia's attitude as better than it was last
week—that I noticed she'd softened, that she was no longer as
desperate-sounding, and that I hoped she was closer to accepting
the NYPD verdict. "She was disappointed at first, but I think she
realizes that there wasn't much for the police to go on, except her
own intuition about her aunt."

"In the beginning it's always a let-down. People expect a full-
scale investigation no matter what the circumstances. Sure, every
case rates an autopsy, unlimited computer power and forensics,
and at least two detectives dedicated to it for however long it
takes. That's what loved ones expect. But, practically speaking—"

Maddie *tsk-tsk*ed like an old lady. "Like on TV, again," she
said, shaking her head, enlightened as she was.

"Exactly," Buzz said. "There are pluses and minuses to being in a big city over a small town. On the one hand, the smaller
departments don't have the resources. In a small town, you might
not even have a medical examiner, just a coroner who might also
own the local meat market, for example, and has the coroner's
job because he's the only one in town with a large refrigerator." I
gulped and put my arm around Maddie, as if to protect her from
unpleasant details of life and death. "Here we have a full-time
medical examiner with a staff and a budget, a huge department,
but we also have more cases and have to make choices. The homicide rate has been going down for sure, hitting a forty-year
low last year. We pay attention to those things." Buzz paused for a
drink of his soda. "Say, have you heard the joke? How low is the
homicide rate in New York City?"

"How low?" Maddie asked, already laughing.

"It's so low, anyone can afford one."

Maddie laughed hard. I doubted she understood the underlying meaning, unless all the crime dramas she watched and detective stories she read had taught her a few things. Talk of crime was interrupted by the arrival of the largest extra-large pizza I'd ever seen. And the largest individual slices in the country, I imagined. A thin, but not too thin, crust, fresh sauce, and an aroma to make the world seem right. "Wow," Maddie said.

"Okay, no more serious talk," Buzz said. "Except one more thing. Maddie, I'll bet you're a techie, right?" She nodded. He took a Plaza Pizza napkin and wrote in large print. "Here's a URL for you to look up. It has everything you want to know about the NYPD, including crime statistics. Charts, trends, pdfs. You'll love it. And while we're at it, we should exchange cell phone numbers."

Once we'd all entered and saved our contact information, Maddie took the napkin Buzz had written on and looked at me. "Should we analyze this handwriting, Grandma?"

Buzz guffawed. "You're related to Skip all right."

"Did you pass the test for your new assignment?" Maddie asked. My eyebrows went up. She who didn't miss a thing was once again on the verge of embarrassing me, this time with the NYPD.

"No worries," Buzz said, addressing my flushed face, no doubt. "I passed everything, but now I have to wait for a case to come up. There are quite a few of us doing this retire-then-return thing these days and we have to wait our turn."

"It must be exciting to be a detective," Maddie said.

"Is that what your uncle Skip tells you?"

Maddie grinned. "No, he says it's mostly paperwork. I was just checking."

After one (Maddie), two (me), and three (Buzz) slices of outstanding pizza, we were ready to exchange tchotchkes. I handed Buzz a small gift bag with the patch from Skip, plus a couple of treats for Rosalie. I'd brought several small holiday boxes of chocolates and California tea towels with me for just such an occasion, and was happy I had swag left for Rosalie. Maddie had made a "nice-to-meet-you" card from scraps at the crafts table.

Buzz outdid us with as many souvenirs as I'd seen lined up across our hotel dresser last night. Amazingly, there wasn't a single duplication of the items Maddie had bought in the Times Square shop. She pulled the treasures out of the tote Buzz handed her—a note cube, a lapel pin, a charm in the form of tiny handcuffs (an extra squeal for these), a bumper sticker and car-decal set, a head-band, a package of stickers, pens, and pencils, all with the NYPD logo. The funniest: a black T-shirt with white letters that spelled: SUPPORT YOUR LOCAL POLICE—LEAVE FINGERPRINTS. After much laughter from Maddie and me, she pulled out the last item, a small, fuzzy blue teddy bear wearing a badge and an NYPD cap.

"I guess I misjudged how sophisticated you are," Buzz said. "Maybe you can give that to someone's kid sister."

"I love teddy bears," Maddie said. I rolled my eyes, remembering how she'd gotten rid of every stuffed animal in her room at least three years ago, and refused to entertain the idea of keeping even one such memento from her childhood. Now, in a pizza parlor in the shadow of One Police Plaza, I'd have bet that if there were an NYPD bib in the bag, she would have embraced that, too.

ONE more cab ride to the Upper West Side, this time with a Middle-Eastern–sounding driver who engaged us with his desire to move to a warmer climate. His brother-in-law had moved his family to Florida, we learned, and as soon as he had put together enough money, our driver planned to follow suit. I'd been back in New York City long enough to suspect that this might simply be a "tip generously and send this guy south" speech, preying on the sympathetic nature of grandmothers and granddaughters.

Duncan was on duty to welcome us, for the last time, as we arrived at Cynthia's building. He touched his cap. "Always a pleasure," he said offering me his gloved hand. "I'll bet Ms. Bishop is waiting." Once in the lobby, out of the cold, Maddie handed Duncan our last box of chocolates.

"A small token of thanks," I said.

His gratitude was profuse, ending with a laugh. "I guess you haven't heard the joke? Why didn't the doorman want to go on strike?"

Maddie took the bait again. "Why?"

"Because it would be more work than when he's working."

I loved the way New Yorkers poked fun at themselves.

Chapter 17

FIFTEEN FLOORS UP, Cynthia was waiting for us in the doorway to her apartment. In spite of his self-deprecating joke, reliable Duncan had called up to announce our arrival, doing his duty as usual.

"I'm so glad you're both here," she said, her voice reaching a new level of sadness. She hugged us as if this were the last time she'd see us.

The whole apartment seemed to be sad. There might as well have been a black drape over the walls. The easy chair where Cynthia had already piled some of Aunt Elsie's coats and outerwear appeared to sag from the extra weight; Central Park was dreary under an overcast sky. How had I not noticed before how bare the trees were, how desolate the streets looked?

Behind her, the dining room table was laid out with a tea service and cookies. I wondered if Cynthia had gotten any sleep or if she'd kept herself busy most of the night.

"Ooh, can I have a black-and-white?" Maddie asked, her innocence and cheeriness barely cutting through the heavy air.

"You just had the biggest slice of pizza in the world," I said.

"But that was a long time ago," she said, her hand on her stomach, suggesting it was empty. "And remember, it's just 'slice,' you don't need to say 'slice of pizza.'"

I thought I detected a smile crossing Cynthia's lips. She'd released us and held out the plate of cookies. "Help yourself, sweetie. It's nice to see that another generation likes black-and-whites. And did I ever tell you that Aunt Elsie, as classy a lady as she always was, loved a slice?" Cynthia seemed to transport herself to another time, when she might have brought home a pizza and, for a change, passed up the matching china for an easy-care evening of paper plates and napkins.

Maddie gave me a look that said I should give her points for her own cookie- and pizza-loving classiness. "We didn't have dessert," Maddie said, maneuvering her mouth around a bite of cookie.

"Unless you count the candy you bought from the Plaza Pizza vending machine," I reminded her.

"Nah," she said, and took a bite from the white side.

"Let's get to work. We can take a full tea break later," I offered, and the room brightened a little as our team rolled up our figurative sleeves.

We started with a small closet off the foyer that held more outerwear—windbreakers, parkas, lined jackets, and coats in a wide range of lengths and weights, On the closet floor were plastic boxes of boots, scarves, gloves, and hats. So different from my outerwear wardrobe, which consisted of a few jackets (and one hat that I never seemed to locate until the end of the season) for what passed for winter in Lincoln Point. Cynthia had already moved her own coats and snow paraphernalia to the spare room, she told us, in preparation for giving the closet a good cleaning, so this part of the job was easy—all of Aunt Elsie's cold weather clothes and accessories, except for those needing a trip to the dry cleaners, would go into cartons marked for a women's shelter in lower Manhattan that Cynthia had made arrangements with.

Maddie's task was to fold each garment as neatly as possible, and fill the boxes. She accomplished this in record time, humming lines from "Rudolph the Red-Nosed Reindeer." I thought of asking her to stop but decided a little lightness might be just what we needed for the somber job. When she'd caught up with all the outerwear we'd sent her way, Maddie settled herself in the living room with her laptop to work on her journal and (finally) a few school assignments she'd left till the last minute though they'd been accessible online all week. My granddaughter was much better at making up her own homework.

Cynthia and I headed for the bedrooms where Aunt Elsie had had the use of two full closets, each one packed tightly with suits, dresses, skirts, tops, and casual clothes. I knew this would be the tricky part for Cynthia. I thought back to when I performed a similar purging of Ken's clothes. Even the most ordinary shirt seemed to be attached to a special memory, every tie reminding me of an event that meant something—an anniversary dinner, a school award ceremony, Richard's wedding, Maddie's sports team events. How could I toss anything out? It would be like removing Ken from my life. I closed my eyes for a moment and took a deep breath before returning to the task at hand. It was important to help Cynthia as she had come to my aid at that unbearably rough time.

"Some of Aunt Elsie's wardrobe won't be useful to the shelter," Cynthia said, fingering a dress-and-shawl outfit that was more suitable to a modern-day production of *Much Ado About Nothing*. "They're looking for business clothes that can be worn to a job interview or to work in an office." I made a resolution on the spot to go through my own closets at home and put my former teaching outfits to good use. Cynthia's eyes teared up as she pulled out a long silk dress in shades of pale green with a touch of glitter in the form of gold sequins at the waist.

"We don't have to do this now," I offered.

"No, I want to. Aunt Elsie wore this dress to the reception for my graduation from nursing school. The shades of green represented all the comfort my classmates and I would provide in our careers, she told me." Cynthia let out a sad, breathy sound. "I can't part with it."

I could see that it was too soon for Cynthia to be taking on this task, but I also knew that she wanted to take advantage of my presence and get the job done. "Put it aside for now," I suggested, in what amounted to a plan for performing triage on the garments. "For now, we can just pull out things you know for sure you don't need to keep."

She let out a breath. "Okay. Let's move on to the more tai- lored things, like these classic suits, probably from all the board meetings she went to until a couple of years ago. They'll be per- fect for job interviews." We assigned a place on the bed for busi- ness attire—simple dresses, skirts, jackets, and tailored blouses— and a large box for purses, shoes, and other accessories.

A knock on the door called Cynthia away. "That will be Duncan with a dolly to pick up what we have so far. I told him it would take several trips. He's going to keep the boxes in the storage area until I'm finished, then arrange for the pickup from the shelter."

As I continued sorting, I heard Cynthia's directives to Dun- can, asking him to take the large cartons of outerwear, three in total, that Maddie had packed. At the same time, Maddie came bounding into the bedroom where I was, with what she labeled a "present" from Duncan.

She showed me a small fan of papers. "Duncan thought I might want these for my journal. He copied a few pages from the reports they send to"—she paused, her thinking frown in place, then continued—"a board or the building's managers or someone." She flicked the pages in front of her. "They show what happened on whatever day you want to look up, like whether someone got flowers delivered or a man came to fix a pipe or, like, one time the basement was flooded. That almost never hap- pens in Palo Alto." For a minute I thought she was going to come up with one of her wishes, such as "I wish we had floods in the basement," or, more appropriately, "I wish we had a basement."

"That's going to be a great addition to your report," I said.

"I know. I can put all these things in the back, with the maps and everything." I saw Maddie's report growing by leaps and bounds and had in mind to save a copy for her future biographers. "Grandma, I should go downstairs with Duncan. I'm finishing the interview part of my journal and I need to clear up a few things with him. He might have a different joke or something. Duncan says it's okay."

"I'd rather have you stay—"

"It's fine, Gerry," Cynthia said, Duncan trailing her. "Duncan is very good with kids, and I think Maddie will enjoy the action in the lobby more than going through old clothes. I think we're about to tackle the musty-smelling section of the closets."

"*Eeuw,*" Maddie said, to further her agenda.

"Riley's here, too. We won't let her out of our sight," Duncan said.

"Please, Grandma?"

"It was so nice of you to copy that material for Maddie," I said to Duncan, still unsure whether to send her off with him. Not that I didn't trust him; in truth, it was Manhattan that I didn't trust. How silly.

"Please, Grandma?" Again.

My fears and resistance faded and I relented. "Don't be pesty, okay? They have work to do."

Duncan chuckled. "Not according to common wisdom."

"Take your jacket," I said. "The lobby might be cold."

"Okay, okay," Maddie said, halfway to the door, having dropped her photocopies onto a side table that already held her laptop and homework. She grabbed up her jacket, scarf, hat, and gloves and raced to catch up with Duncan. "Thanks, Grandma," came from over her shoulder.

Cynthia and I turned back to our project. "Notice how Aunt Elsie's clothes are all about the same size? She was like you, Gerry, always stayed trim and fit. Me?"—she laughed—"I have pants in three sizes."

"You always look great," I said, to a friend in large-size sweats, who needed to hear it. I lifted a couple of suits with their hangers from a closet rod and set them on the bed. As I smoothed out the jackets, I felt something in the pocket of one. "There's a note or a receipt in here," I told Cynthia, extracting a piece of paper that might have come from a small notebook. I handed her the folded paper and continued patting down Aunt Elsie's suits.

"This is weird," Cynthia said. She handed back the note and I read the short message: *Is this okay?* with an uppercase *C* as signature, all in careful cursive.

"I take it you're not the 'C' who wrote this."

Cynthia shook her head. "Well, we'll never know," she said, tossing the paper aside. We continued our sorting, discovering a few handkerchiefs (not paper tissues), a pen with a hotel logo, a café receipt, and an expired library card. Nothing interesting, until Cynthia held up a lightweight blue seersucker suit, the likes of which I hadn't seen for many years. Clearly, Aunt Elsie was not a victim of the New York City fashion scene. Smart woman.

"I wish I'd kept some of my outfits from our college days," I said. "The fabrics and workmanship were so much better. And they seemed to last forever. Or am I just getting really old?"

Cynthia didn't answer, but instead showed me what she'd pulled from the pocket of the seersucker jacket: *I hope this passes the test. C.* Again, the handwriting was clear and careful. "One note is weird," Cynthia said. "Two is really odd. Do you think there are more?"

We looked at each other and said, almost simultaneously, "The winter coats. We didn't look in the pockets."

"I'll call down to Maddie," I said, happy for a chance to check on her, since she'd been gone all of twenty minutes.

"I just got here, Grandma," she said. "I helped Twelve-B with a package and got the elevator for her."

I'd always known my granddaughter was a quick study. I could hear her telling her Palo Alto class about how she was temporary doorwoman in a fancy Manhattan apartment building. "We need to have those boxes back," I said. "Cynthia and I realized we forgot to check the coat pockets for loose change or something that might be valuable." My words came easily; Manhattan had turned me into a facile liar. Or had I always been that way?

"I already did that," she said. "Before I packed them." She sounded put out that we wouldn't have anticipated her thoroughness and, indeed, I should have. "There were a couple of quarters and pennies and some pieces that looked like parts of an earring.

I put them on the table next to the rose-colored chair. And I found a few crumpled up ticket stubs and pieces of paper and threw them away."

I'd walked over to the end table and verified that it now held scattered coins and the backs of three post earrings. At the sight of the earring backs, I immediately thought "candlesticks," the ready-made dollhouse accessory. No time for minis, though; I shifted gears back to Maddie.

"Where did you throw the papers?" I asked.

"There's a wastebasket next to the chair I was sitting in. Why do you want all this stuff anyway? Is it important?"

"Thanks, sweetheart. Are you having fun?" I really wanted to ask, "Are you safe?" though I couldn't imagine a much safer neighborhood than the Upper West Side, even if she did venture outside onto the sidewalk by herself. Still, across the street there was the two-and-a-half-mile-long Central Park, with its seven bodies of water, and acres of woodland that I couldn't begin to measure, and it was already getting dark, and I couldn't remember what, if anything, Buzz had said about crime in the park, and...

"Duncan left, but Riley and Cody said I could interview them, so I have to go now."

"Take care, sweetheart," I said, but she'd already clicked off.

Cynthia and I wasted no time removing the crumpled paper from the otherwise clean wastebasket. We ignored the ticket stubs and took three new notes to the table, taking turns reading out loud, trying to make sense of them.

I hope this will do. C., I read.

Another try. C., Cynthia read.

Try this one. I can give you as many samples as you want. C., I read.

I had an *aha* moment when I saw a reasonable time line. "This was the first one," I said, tapping the longest note. All the others are follow-ups."

"Follow-ups of what?" Cynthia asked. "I hope not pills or... something illegal. It can't be."

"I think you're right. Nothing else is involved." I tapped the table near the short notes. "These are the samples." I took a breath and it became obvious to both of us.

"Handwriting samples," we both said.

"They don't look that different to me," I said, comparing loops and uppercase swaths with an amateur's eye.

"Not to me, either. Maybe the person was just trying to fool her, playing a game." Cynthia shivered again. I didn't pursue her thought. "All we need to do is figure out who 'C' is," I said.

"Could this really be it?" Cynthia asked, her eyes wide, addressing herself more than me.

"It certainly looks like someone with an initial 'C' was auditioning for the role of scribe for your aunt," I said.

"We should check the rest of her clothes." Cynthia looked so shaky, I thought I'd have to help her off her chair. Instead, I convinced her to stay put. "Why don't you let me do a quick search of what's left in the closets?" I poured a cup of tea and set it before her. "And then we can talk about it." I hated to get her hopes up, or mine, for that matter, but a lead was a lead and we couldn't ignore it.

ABOUT twenty minutes later, I joined Cynthia, feeling as though I'd done hard labor in a work-release program for the NYPD. I'd lifted and searched and lifted some more, working as if I had a tight deadline, which, in a way, I did. "I found one more note," I said, smoothing out the paper I'd found in the pocket of a brown wool jacket with a narrow fur collar, a peplum, and a matching long, slim skirt. The outfit would have worked in any movie from the forties or fifties. I hoped the note was more recent.

"It says, '*Okay, this has to be it. C.*' Do you suppose that means it's the last one?" Cynthia asked.

"I don't know, but let's write the names of all the people in Aunt Elsie's life with names that begin with 'C,'" I suggested, thinking how ironic that the main "C" in Aunt Elsie's life was sitting at the table, a victim almost as much as Aunt Elsie.

I found a pad of paper and pen on a nearby desk and took

a seat across from Cynthia. I poured myself a cup of tea, then sipped and wrote as she talked.

"Well, first names first. Besides me, we have Candace the almost-nurse and Cody the almost-doorman." I was happy to hear a hint of humor as she drank her tea and furrowed her brow in concentration. "For last names, there's Philip Chapman. I don't think there's anyone among her theater ladies with a *C*." To be sure, she ticked off on her fingers: "Martha Wagner, Pauline Brawley, Francesca Donovan, and sometimes Muriel Roberts." Nothing there, I agreed. "Oh, and our super, Neal Crouse. That's four *C*s. How strange. I never realized all the *C*s there were in Aunt Elsie's life. Cody and Philip are the only ones we don't have a handwriting sample for."

Cynthia's eyes widened. "So either of them would be candidates for writing that note." Cynthia stood, now too excited to sit still, as if I'd mistakenly served her espresso instead of chamomile tea. "Philip. He surely knows cursive and I'll bet he still writes well enough to please my aunt." She walked a few steps away from her chair, then sat back down. "Or Cody. He's paid her a lot of attention, making sure he gets the Sunday *Times* for her on Saturday evening, picking up an extra sweet for her. I always thought he had beady, conniving eyes, trying to curry her favor. And you know, certain levels of interaction are frowned on by management. He could have been jeopardizing his job, but he still came around a lot. Why would he do that, unless…" she paused, frowned "…unless he had this plan in mind all along."

"We shouldn't jump to conclusions," I said, regretting that I'd soon have to tell Cynthia what I'd been keeping from her. While Cynthia zeroed in on Cody, all I could think of was my interview with Ashley and Candace, and the fraud they'd committed on the day Aunt Elsie died. I'd chalked it up to misfortune and bad timing, that their simple act of covering for each other became so important. Now, it seemed, it might not have been a simple act at all. "Let's go through them all. You said you had a handwriting sample for Candace?"

"Why Candace? Are we going alphabetically?" Cynthia seemed agitated. I sensed she was eager to finally have someone to blame, someone to get the attention of a homicide detective. "I told you Candace's handwriting is like chicken scratches. I looked at a couple of things she'd written. It was nothing like what we saw on Aunt Elsie's note."

"What was it that you read, on Candace's sample, I mean?"

She slapped her hands on the table. "A couple of lists. Aunt Elsie must have asked her to pick up a few things at the drugstore and the medical supplies store and she wrote them down, checked them off, and left the lists in the miscellaneous drawer in the kitchen."

"Do you still have them?"

"No, but why are we focusing on Candace, anyway, Gerry? Is there something you're not telling me?"

I exhaled a long breath and probably a sigh of pain. "Candace was here on the afternoon of Aunt Elsie's death."

"No, as I told you, I called here around three o'clock. Don't remind me." She held her hands to her head, probably remembering what she considered the worst decision of her recent life. "I talked to Ashley, and sent her home."

"You talked to Candace."

Cynthia's face turned pale; she dropped her arms and seemed to go weak at the knees. I hurried to the other side of the table and braced myself for her fall, but she collected herself and stood again, facing me.

"How could you, Gerry?"

Her look devastated me. I tried to explain, assuring her I'd gotten advice from two real cops about whether to disclose the switch to the police, whether it signaled something critical to the case.

"They reminded me that workers do this all the time," I said, "From doormen to hospital and service workers. A lie doesn't make you a murderer." If it did, there was no hope for my future as a law-abiding citizen. "Think for a minute, Cynthia. What difference does it really make whether it was Ashley or Candace who was here at three? You said you talked to Aunt Elsie herself at that time, so you know she was fine then. Telling the truth would have gotten no more attention from the police than the lie did." I continued rationalizing both the girls' lie and my cover-up, trying to remember everything I'd been told by Skip and Buzz. In my heart I knew I hadn't shirked legal responsibility, but I felt I'd done something equally blameworthy toward a friend who was counting on me.

Cynthia was disturbingly quiet while I tried to make sense. When she spoke, her comment assured me that she hadn't processed a word of my exposition. "Neither one of them knows this case firsthand," she said. She picked up her cell and scrolled through her contacts, a determined look on her face.

"What are you doing?" I asked.

"I'm calling the agency. I'll think of some reason to have Candace come here again. Maybe Ashley, too. And have the police here at the same time."

"Cynthia—"

She held up her hand. "No advice. Please, Gerry."

"What about Cody? Remember the behavior that pointed to him? And we don't have a handwriting sample from him. A minute ago, you were ready to have him arrested."

"That was when I thought you'd told me everything you knew from your half-hearted investigation."

An investigation I'd been telling her all along I had no resources for, had no time for, and was unqualified for to begin with. I swallowed Cynthia's remark, holding back a response. "At least let me give you Buzz's number. He'll be able to expedite things for you," I said.

"Who's Buzz?"

I felt my face flush, recalling another tidbit I'd withheld from my friend. "He's Skip's friend, the retired NYPD detective I told you about."

Cynthia uttered a *hmph* sound. "You never told me his whole name. I guess you never told me much of anything, now that I think of it."

I knew she had every right to be upset with me. I'd been self-ishly selective in what I shared with her. "I'm so sorry, Cynthia."

She shook her head. "I'm sure you meant well, Gerry, but this is my responsibility only. I see that I was unwise to expect you to give your full attention to my problem in the first place. You had a reason for coming to Manhattan, and it had nothing to do with me. I assumed—incorrectly, I see now—that you'd want to help me, once you knew my situation. I was so wrong." Cynthia clicked off her phone with "I'll never get anywhere this way." She stomped to the spare room for her long wool coat. She put it on, wrapped a scarf around her neck, and pulled a hat and gloves from the pockets.

"Where are you going?" I asked, confused by the unexpected turn.

"I'm going to the agency. I'm tired of their Christmas music. Or I might just go right to the precinct."

"Cynthia, can't we talk about this?"

"The door will lock automatically when you leave," she said, and walked out the door.

If I thought Cynthia was thinking rationally, I'd have been hurt. But she was upset, and with good reason. I gave in to the temptation of rethinking all my decisions—to come to New York, to call Cynthia and tell her I'd be in town, to accede to her wishes to look into things without clarifying what that would mean, to keep anything at all from her once I got involved. I couldn't wait to get home.

Give my regards to Broadway . . .

Bebe calling. I was close to hitting Ignore but decided that I might as well accept all the opprobrium that was coming to me.

"Gerry, I'm finished with downtown. I can't tell you how great it was. Well, I will tell you, but later. I'm almost packed and have the afternoon free." Another drain on my psyche? I didn't think I could handle it. I sighed, waiting for what was coming. "I know you're helping Cynthia with her aunt's clothes and all and I thought maybe I could take Maddie and treat her to something special. I checked and we can get in at the Rockefeller Center ice skating rink." I perked up. "At the same time, you'd have some alone-time with Cynthia. I'm sure it will be a while before you'll see her again."

I wished I knew where this was coming from. Very far off from what I expected from Bebe. But it was a dream offer. I could wallow in my guilt for a while, maybe over a mocha down the street, or maybe enjoy a long call to Henry for some words of wisdom. And Maddie would have another spectacular experience under her little belt. "That would be fantastic, Bebe, if you're sure you want to do that?"

"Yes, yes. It's for me, too, you know. The perfect cap to the week. I can come and get her."

"She's down in the lobby with the doormen right now. She's been there about an hour, and probably bored by now, so you could just scoop her up from there. I'll tell her you're coming."

"I'm on my way. Thanks, Gerry."

I hung up. Things were brightening. *Thank you, Bebe.* As long as I didn't dwell on Cynthia's words, I could salvage the afternoon. I still had doubts that she was on the right trail with Candace, or even a Candace/Ashley conspiracy, but it was no longer my problem. If it ever was.

I moved into the living room area and sat in the easy chair where Maddie had been working on homework with her laptop. I dialed her cell and got her voicemail. It wouldn't be the first time she'd be trying to limit her contact with me, especially if she thought I'd bring her back up here with the musty clothes. I left a message sure to please her: "Bebe's going to pick you up and take you ice skating. Call me." That should do it. At least a couple of people would have a great afternoon.

My eyes fell on the pages Duncan had copied for Maddie. The top sheet was print-side-up and I caught sight of a feature I knew was important, but couldn't remember why. I picked up the sheet. The page seemed to be a service record of sorts, as Maddie had described—a form, with blocks to write in date, time, and action or brief narrative. A new floor lamp was delivered to Four-A; a request came from 18-C to have someone check their heating unit; 17-B needed a new electrical plate for the sockets in the master bathroom. One entry read simply "Shih Tzu" and another "Turkish Van," which I took to mean pet care for absent owners.

I perked up at the idea of reading what was going on during the day of Aunt Elsie's death. I ran my finger down the columns, hoping for something to jump out at me. Nothing. My shoulders slumped. Of course not. What had I been thinking? That a killer was going to admit to entering 15-D to check on the progress of his murder project? Finally, after many false starts, it dawned on me that I had a gold mine of handwriting samples. I ignored the dates, times, and facts of the entries, and looked at the handwriting. Entries had been written and initialed by D. W., for Duncan Williams; N. C., for Neal Crouse; R. S., for Riley Simpson; C. N., for Cody Nugent.

I jumped from the seat, nearly falling over the footstool. "I found it," I said, out loud, as if Cynthia were still in the apartment, in a tone that was equal parts excitement and relief. I picked up the other sheets and began my own regime of pacing as I read Cody's entry about picking up a load of dry cleaning from 12-A; and another one, where he cleaned up a mess of mud on the lobby floor, which had been tracked into the elevator. It was Cody. The same graceful *C*. The same full loops. Whatever the technical chirographic terms were, I could see at a glance that Cody's penmanship matched that of the writer of the notes to Aunt Elsie. Aunt Elsie dictated, and Cody wrote the letter for her.

Everything went black for a moment, and then became very bright. Duncan had left early; Maddie was with Cody and Riley. "Maddie!" I screamed. Or maybe it came out as a whisper. Or maybe no sound at all emerged, pushed back into my throat from fear. Maddie! I had to find her.

Chapter 18

———❧❧❧———

I SPRANG INTO action and picked up the white intercom receiver, frozen by fear. No answer. What did it mean that there was no answer from the lobby? I couldn't let my mind go there. I called Maddie's number again, from my phone, and listened to ring after ring until her voicemail came on. Maddie changed her outgoing message at least once a week. Today's message was "Hi. Maddie's in Manhattan. Where are you?" A few hours ago, I had found the greeting funny and clever. Now it made me sad and even more worried. I hung up and dialed again, clicking off before the message, heading for the door at the same time. I hit 911 on the run.

"Emergency services. What is the emergency?" A simple question, but I couldn't think of how to answer. My granddaughter is in the hands of a killer? Would they believe me or keep me talking instead of doing something about it?

"It's my granddaughter," I managed. "I think she's in danger."

"How old is your granddaughter?"

"Eleven."

"What's your name?"

"Geraldine Porter. My granddaughter is Madison Porter."

"And where is Madison now, Mrs. Porter?"

I gave Cynthia's address, hoping at least Maddie was still in the building.

"What is the nature of the danger?"

The dispatcher was much too calm to suit me. By now, I was running down the hallway toward the elevators.

"I think she's with a killer."

"Can you tell me why you think that?"

"Can't you just send someone? She's eleven years old."

"Can you stay calm and tell me what you think is happening, Mrs. Porter?"

No! I clicked off, too frustrated to finish the conversation. She had my name and address; if she wanted to do something, she would. Meanwhile, I'd try to reach the only cop I knew who was in this time zone and would believe me without a long exposition about why I was sure that Cody Nugent had slowly murdered Elsie Bishop and now had my granddaughter in his grasp.

I flew down the maroon-carpeted hall, hitting the keypad all the way. I would never have guessed that I'd be able to punch in cell numbers with one thumb, and run at the same time. Buzz answered right away, possibly saving me from falling on my face, or from certain death due to an inability to breathe.

"Hey, Rosalie says thanks for that candy," Buzz answered, apparently recognizing my cell ID. "She fell in love with See's on our trip to San—"

I cut in with the briefest of messages, giving Cynthia's address, and adding, "Maddie's downstairs with Elsie's killer. I called nine-one-one, but if you could—"

Buzz cut in with an equally succinct message. "I'm on it," he said.

I stood at the bank of three elevators on the fifteenth floor, breathing hard, hopping from one foot to another, slapping my phone against my thigh when I wasn't calling Maddie. I blew out short, frustrated breaths as I listened to her voicemail message over and over. I stared at the elaborate plates above the elevator doors, old-fashioned dial-position indicators, until I thought my glare would melt the bronze. Two of the arrows were at *L*, the lobby; the third at I, the first floor. None of the arrows was moving.

I pushed the elevator button again. When that didn't work, I rattled it in its socket, then pounded on its rim, then leaned on its center. Nothing. I'd read that the longest period that people to-day were willing to wait for an elevator was seven seconds, before they began to get twitchy. I felt I'd already paid my seven-seconds dues. I looked up. The pointers on the dials hadn't moved.

I turned and saw the sign for the stairs. I tried to figure which would be faster, walking down fifteen flights, or waiting a couple more minutes for the elevator. What if I couldn't make it all the way down? What if the elevator never came?

The stairway won. I turned to the doorway and made a bee-line for it. On the next floor, I opened the door leading back into the hallway, giving the elevators one more chance. I looked at the position dials and saw the same immovable bronze arrows. Someone must have locked down the elevators. Back to the stair-well. Three flights down, I stopped at a landing to dial Maddie again, then Bebe. Why hadn't I thought of that sooner? I'd lost track of time. All I'd done since hearing Bebe's delightful plan to pick up Maddie and go skating was read, fret, and race down stairs. As if I could influence events from a distance, I pictured Bebe and Maddie in a cab, headed for Rockefeller Center, rent-ing skates, laughing, making their way to the ice, with cheerful music in the background, and roasting chestnuts on a nearby cart. I tried to calculate how long it would have taken Bebe to change her clothes, then get a cab from the Lex to here. Two miles, I reminded myself. Not long. And with a Lex doorman, she'd have been in a cab in no time. I dialed Bebe and got her voicemail. The ability to leave a message—"This is Gerry. Please call me"—was the only satisfaction I would have.

I continued running down the stairs, keeping track of the large painted numbers. The tenth floor, the ninth, the eighth. I took another break to check the elevators. The position pointers hadn't moved. On to the seventh, then the sixth floor. I felt a se-vere pain in my middle and had to stop. The stairwell was deathly quiet; I heard my heart pound in my neck, my thumbs, my head. Every joint was rebelling, but I had to continue. I thought by now I should be able to yell down the stairwell and reach Maddie.

I thought of calling others for support. Henry? Skip? Bev? But why upset anyone else since they couldn't do anything from three thousand miles away, except join me in my panic. Why wasn't Maddie answering her phone? Or Bebe? I told myself there was probably nothing to worry about. I plowed on down the steps. My chest hurt and I vowed to get in shape as soon as I got back to Lincoln Point. With Maddie. Maddie, my sweet, beautiful, brilliant granddaughter, would be with me and we would go to the gym together.

Fifth, fourth, third floors, and finally I heard noise. Police sirens? Fire engines? An ambulance? Or was I delirious, dreaming that someone stronger than me had made an appearance, someone able to grab Maddie away from Cody? The thought of Cody, combined with my extreme abdominal discomfort from this unwanted exercise, made me sick. All the little facts started to arrange themselves in a pattern that should have been obvious from the start. He was good-buddies with Aunt Elsie, Cynthia had said; he had money troubles; he was an art student and his talent could easily have extended to copying anyone's handwriting. And most important, he hadn't taken a day off in two weeks. I imagined him worrying that Aunt Elsie's death was close and he'd have wanted to be on hand to switch the pill bottles in the confusion of the hours after.

I saw the enormous maroon letter *L* on the wall of the landing below and moved on. The lobby was so close now. I hated the color of the *L*; it reminded me of Cody's uniform jacket. Ugly maroon. The sounds were louder now and spurred my jelly-like legs to stiffen and hold me up. I fell back onto the newel post at the bottom, rested for whatever scientists called the smallest measurable amount of time, and slammed through the heavy door, nearly landing on the homely maroon carpet.

A gigantic new Christmas tree with flashing red-and-white lights filled the lobby. Had someone added to the original decorations? I blinked. Not a tree; they'd just added strings and strings of lights. Large lights. I closed my eyes, took short, painful breaths, then opened them. Not holiday lights. Police lights. On and off, rotating.

The lobby was empty except for cops, who pushed their way through the front doors without benefit of a doorman. The sounds of the sirens almost drowned out a banging noise that seemed louder to me than the trumpets of herald angels. The uniformed officers looked around the lobby. I didn't need a sound meter to trace the thumping sound to the break room, behind the nearly invisible pocket door. I raced to open the door, braced for the worst, cops behind me. I was ready for the sight of Maddie on the floor. Maddie face down, not breathing. Bleeding. I shut my eyes. When I opened them, I saw the counter, the lockers, the old sofa, the coffee machine, the stack of folding chairs. And someone tied to one of the chairs, mouth gagged, eyes wide, breathing hard from bouncing around to get attention. Riley Simpson, steady now, not moving. Officers rushed to release him. Gag off first. Tape slit open.

"Man, oh, man," he said.

"Where's Maddie?" I asked, panting. Not "How are you, Riley? What happened? Can I get you anything?" Just "Where's Maddie?" I screamed.

"Maddie's fine." Was that my own voice? My dream? My wish?

Not Riley's voice. He was with the officers. "Man, oh, man," he said again, rubbing his wrists. "He shot out of here. When the lady came to get the kid, he tied me up then flew out the door."

"We have him." A uniformed officer. What were they talking about. Was Riley's "the kid" Maddie?

"Maddie's with Bebe Mellon." Buzz Arnold's voice now. "We traced Maddie's phone and found the two of them twirling around to 'Jingle Bell Rock.'" He rubbed my shoulder, sat me down on the sofa. The same sofa I sank into during my interview with Duncan. A more pleasant time in this room.

"I'm so sorry, Gerry. I should never have left you." Cynthia's voice. Cynthia sitting next to me on the battered beige sofa. Was everyone here? When would I hear Maddie's voice? "I saw the patrol cars all speeding this way and I ran back," Cynthia said. The room spun. Coffee spilled. Candy tumbled from the vending machine. The glaring lights crept in and covered the ceiling. Buzz sat me up and held me while someone shone a white light in my eyes.

"You're good," the man with the light said, and I believed him. I had to believe him.

"I'm so sorry, Gerry," Cynthia said again. "Buzz told me what happened."

"Where's Maddie?" I asked. I thought I knew the answer; she was skating with Bebe. She was safe. But I had to hear it again.

THE crowd sorted itself out in the lobby of Cynthia's apartment building. I learned that Buzz Arnold, though retired, was respected enough in the department to be in charge now, directing things. Although it was never clear to me whose turn it was to speak and who was taking notes, I listened and learned from everyone.

From Riley Simpson, the newbie doorman: "I don't know what got into Cody. The kid—Maddie somebody?— said something that set him off, something about notes they found in an old lady's pockets, notes Cody had sent to her. And the kid talked about copies of our reports that Duncan made for her school journal. Cody freaked out. 'I gotta get out of here. They'll know everything.' 'So, go,' I said, even though I had no idea what he was talking about. His eyes freaked me out, like he was really high, maybe. But Cody wanted to get rid of the kid first, telling her she should go back upstairs, it was so boring down here, but she didn't want to go back. She enjoyed it, she said, and it would be good for her journal. Even though today was the dullest day you can imagine. No one's home from work yet, no one goes out on a Monday night. And I guess everybody cooks on Mondays, because there was only one delivery, a deli chicken dinner. The kid wrote down that I called upstairs and then got on the elevator with curry chicken. Exciting, huh? Exciting enough for a kid, I guess. Then a short lady comes to pick up the kid and as soon as they leave, Cody rips out the intercom and shuts down the elevators and ties me up. 'What's with this, dude?' I ask him, but he gags me and says something about a murder across town that was in the newspaper. Like I knew what he was talking about. That's it. Then he takes off. That's all I know. Man, oh, man. I don't get paid enough for this."

From Cynthia: "After I left my friend in the apartment, I was going to take a cab to the agency that provides nurses and healthcare workers for my aunt, but I changed my mind. I decided to walk straight to the Twentieth Precinct building and do my best to be heard there. It's not a long walk and it's a relatively mild night and I needed to clear my head. I had been, uh, on a rampage about one of my aunt's nurses. I thought she had…well, in any case, I'd gotten a few blocks away and I heard all these cruisers roaring down Columbus, then turning on Sixty-eighth, and then down Central Park West, toward here. My building. So I came back as fast as I could. I called my friend, but I kept getting voicemail. I called Neal Crouse, our super, but I remembered that he had the day off and I didn't have his emergency information with me. It was at home where all the building numbers are. When I got here I saw the crime scene tape and nearly had heart failure. I can't believe what happened here and I'm so sorry I left my guest, my friend, to deal with it all by herself. I'll never forgive myself."

From Detective Lux, a friend of Buzz's: "We had almost closed the investigation into the death of Ian Johnson, a med student who was allegedly an accident victim last week. But then some neighbors in his building came forward, and we looked deeper, and found Johnson had been fooling around with the meds in the university lab where he had access. We started looking at his roommate, Cody Nugent, who'd been making some atypical purchases lately. Like he'd come into some money. Once the pieces fell together, Cody Nugent became a prime suspect, but he hadn't been formally charged. It looked like Johnson supplied Nugent with fake meds and when he found out what Nugent was doing with them, he grew a conscience, and that didn't work for the doorman."

From Buzz himself: "Thanks, Chris. As far as today goes, apparently, Cody took advantage of his boss's day off, which left only the newbie, Riley. Cody was about to make one last killing, so to speak, and rob one of the apartments he'd been scouting. Then, when Maddie came down and innocently told him about the notes, he realized he'd been caught for the Bishop murder, too. He had to get out of town quicker than he thought."

From Detective Lux: "We caught him heading back to his apartment near Penn Station, where he intended to pick up the stash he had left there. Bad choice."

From Buzz: "Absolutely bad choice. Oh, and about locating Maddie. When I got the call from Gerry Porter, I had my guy ping Maddie's phone and immediately beat it over to the rink and flashed my ID and they let me look at the real-time video. I saw them skating like nothing was wrong—Maddie and the woman, Bebe, on the video— then I went upstairs to the street level and made sure that I could see them the old-fashioned way. In person. There was enough of a crowd standing there, looking down on the ice, watching the skaters, so I know the subjects didn't see me. I called over to a uniform and commandeered him to keep an eye on them. Then I buzzed over here."

I FELT like I'd finished a doctoral program in criminology. Or psychology. Or both. I was exhausted. Detective Lux left, and I saw Buzz and Cynthia head-to-head in a conference. From the slope of Cynthia's shoulders when they parted, I figured she lost whatever contest they were in. She came over to me and put her arm around my shoulder. "I'm so, so sorry, Gerry. I said some things I shouldn't have, and I don't know how to make it up to you." Since I didn't know how, either, I kept silent, and Cynthia continued. "Buzz wants to take you to Rockefeller Center now and I think that's a good plan. Can I meet all of you guys later, I mean, except for Buzz? Well, unless Buzz wants to come, of course, and take you to dinner?"

Food was the last thing on my mind. Right down there with talking to Cynthia for one more minute. I wanted to see my granddaughter. "I'll call you," I said.

Buzz led me out to his car, past the few cruisers that were left outside the building. I looked at one of the patrol cars as I passed and gasped. A man in the passenger seat smiled at me. He had dark, sinister eyes, and a goatee. Cody? The man put his hat on and I saw that it wasn't Cody. The man was a cop, putting on his police cap. I needed to calm down.

"Ready to go see your granddaughter?" Buzz asked, buckling himself in next to me.

I nodded. I'd had enough of the Upper West Side for a while. "Let's leave all this to the *Stegosaurus* and the other primitive reptiles," I said.

Chapter 19

BUZZ MIGHT AS WELL have been a cabbie, with his one-armed, roughshod driving through traffic. I vowed I'd never complain again about the few cars that sometimes raced to the intersection of Springfield and Gettysburg in Lincoln Point. I wondered if Buzz thought he had blazing lights on the roof of his personal sedan. I doubted it would make a difference if he had a siren blaring; the rest of the cars' horns were rush-hour loud.

"How much does Maddie know?" I asked.

"Not a thing as far as I know."

"That means Bebe doesn't know, either."

"Right. All I did was check the camera, like I said, and then sneak a look at them for real from the top of the steps." He turned his face to me and laughed. "You'll have to forgive me, but, I was just thinking, you can observe a lot by watching."

"Yogi?"

"Uh-huh. I thought you needed a laugh." I obliged by showing him the widest smile I'd formed for several hours. "You gonna keep it that way? Not telling anyone?"

"For now, certainly. Maybe Skip. Maddie will be curious, but I'll have to let her think the police were correct to begin with. Aunt Elsie forgot to take her meds."

"Good plan."

As we approached Rockefeller Center, I took out my phone and dialed Maddie, this time with less manic key-punching. "Hey, Grandma, we're almost done. We're turning in our skates."

"Did you have fun?"

"Yeah. Wow. I can't wait to tell everyone."

"I noticed you turned your phone off."

"Uh-uh. Well, maybe I muted it for a while because I didn't want to interrupt my interviews. And at the skating rink it was too loud anyway. Did you call? You knew I was with Bebe, right?"

"No matter now. I'm glad you had a good time."

"Bebe took some pictures with my phone so I can print them and put them in the journal right away."

Buzz indicated that he was going to drop me off on the street at the back of the enormous attraction that was the Christmas tree. There was no way he'd find a parking space anywhere close.

"I'm close by," I told Maddie. I'll meet you behind the tree, across the street. Stay on the line until we find each other."

"Okay, we're going to have to walk around and it's going to be slow, because it's very, very crowded. I skated with Santa, Grandma. I think Bebe had to pay him."

Buzz leaned over and gave me a hug. I nearly cried with gratitude but held it together enough to promise him that I'd send Rosalie See's chocolates for life.

I stepped out of Buzz's car, enjoying the cold wind more than usual. Maybe because Maddie was fine. And I was alive.

I HAD no trouble convincing Bebe and Maddie, both of whom were also red-faced and exhausted (Bebe and I more than Maddie), that we should have dinner in, at the hotel restaurant we were so familiar with. We took one of our usual tables, overlooking 42nd Street, and recapped our week.

Cody's name came up only once. When Maddie reviewed the good time she'd had in the lobby, interviewing the doormen, acting as a building employee, I couldn't ignore it without arousing suspicion. "I'm glad to hear that, sweetheart," I said.

"Cody wanted to take me to Columbus Circle. He said they had this special ice cream that only New York has, but Riley made a fuss 'cause he's new and didn't want to be alone, so we didn't go."

There was no special ice cream, I wanted to tell her, and *Thank you, Riley.* But there was no point in upsetting her after the fact. "I wish I knew what he meant. I'd get some with you," I said.

"We could ask him."

"We could. Or we could get a scoop of that gelato right at the door to Grand Central for dessert before we go to our rooms."

"We can eat it in the lobby," Bebe said, "and do more people-watching."

That was an idea I could get behind. Bebe offered to pick up the gelato while Maddie finished telling me all the skating stories. Bebe was still basking in the glow of her success as a SuperKrafts manager; she couldn't have been more solicitous if she knew that I'd galloped down fifteen flights of stairs before dinner.

Between Rockefeller Center rink stories (you can skate really close to Prometheus; the skates you rent are blue; Santa fell on the ice and took a little boy down with him) and people-watching in the Lex lobby (a family of three came in, wearing matching down jackets; eleven people walked around with cell phones to their ears; one guy in jeans might have been George Clooney—to Bebe only), we passed another hour before heading upstairs to finish packing and turn in.

OUR last New York bedtime was drawing to a close.

"You've been the best roommate," I told Maddie.

"I'll bet Mom told you I'd be messy and leave my things everywhere."

"She may have had some concerns."

"Sometimes I can be messy at home. But not in New York. I was neat and orderly, wasn't I?"

I hadn't realized it was a major goal of Maddie to be neat in New York, but she had pulled it off. "I'll be sure to tell your mother."

"Good." Maddie gasped, her eyes widening. "Look, Grandma," she said, pointing to the window. Where we could see falling snow.

"Wow," I said, and Maddie laughed. What other possible surprises would this week bring? We could have used a few more happy ones like this.

"Yes!" Maddie said. She scrambled out of bed and climbed onto the heating unit, nose to the window. "We have to go down, Grandma. We have to walk in it. You have to take my picture walking in it." I pointed out that we were both in our night clothes, sweats for me and pj's for Maddie, with a top that said TWEEN AND TERRIFIC. "We can put our jackets on over these," she said, already tucking her pajama bottoms into her short boots. "No one can tell. We only have to go a couple of blocks, Grandma." She pulled my boots out of my luggage where they were already wrapped in plastic, ready for my closet at home. But what's a grandmother to do?

We dressed quickly and arrived at the hotel turnstile door, ready for our trek. "When do you think it will stop snowing?" Maddie asked the doorman.

"Maybe tonight," he said, and we all laughed.

I joined Maddie in kicking up the first flakes that had stuck to the sidewalk. I remembered other magical winter nights: Ken and I walking in new snow, with all the dirt and debris of the day hidden under a blanket of white, the bright city lights as our guide.

"This is the best trip of my life, Grandma," Maddie said. I hoped she'd be able to say that about future trips, many more times in the next years.

I HAD one more chore to do before I could turn in. I checked to be sure Maddie was sleeping, then unplugged her phone from the charger and carried it to the window. I deleted all the message-free missed calls from me. Then, I hit the camera icon and scrolled back through the photos of the week, looking for one of the first photos Maddie had taken. I saw Cody Nugent in a new light, his sinister smile and shifty eyes unmistakable now. I hit the trash can icon, then Delete and erased the biggest blight on our week.

Now I could enjoy the snow falling on Manhattan.

———

BEBE arrived at our door bright and early on Tuesday morning. The temperature had risen during the night and most of the snow was already gone, except for patches that had collected along the curbs. We'd agreed to leave for JFK sooner than we needed to, and have breakfast at the airport.

"Gerry, you're never going to believe this," Bebe announced, waving an official-looking piece of paper with the hotel logo. A bill, I figured. "They've comped your room."

"What?"

"That means we don't pay."

"I know what comped means, but why are they doing that?"

"It's you and Maddie. The Lex is so grateful for your work on the robbery case, they've comped your room. Isn't that great?"

"It's very nice of them, but why are you so happy?"

"Don't you see? My SuperKrafts contact...well, I've been asked to call him Ben...now really thinks I'm brilliant to have brought you, even saving them money, and so...more points for me." Bebe was barely intelligible, due to the broadening smile on her face. "This trip has been magic."

Maddie nodded. "That's what I say."

The rest of the morning went smoothly, if not magically. I gave a huge tip to our law-abiding (as far as I knew) Lex doorman as he helped us and our luggage into our last cab for a while. We arrived at JFK and checked in, finding a breakfast bar outside the security area.

My phone rang. Possibly my last New York call. Cynthia's ID. I wasn't sure I was ready to talk to her. She'd left a message on my phone last night, apologizing for her behavior and wanting me to know that Philip Chapman had sent her a package containing photos and memorabilia that Aunt Elsie had given him over the course of his recent visits. They'd agreed to meet and to share memories often. I was happy for them, but I ignored the call-back option.

"It's Cynthia," Maddie said. How did she know who had

called? "Over there," she said. I looked up to find Cynthia, in person, heading across the shiny floor, carrying a large basket.

"I'm here with peace offerings," she said when she caught up to us. The snacks in the basket were perfect; Cynthia's apology for her week-long hassles (her term) was accepted all around; her final gift was outstanding. She leaned in close to my ear and whispered a dollar amount that was staggering, the money in Aunt Elsie's box, I assumed. She handed me an envelope. "This is just a little token. For you and Henry. Two tickets back here, the old-fashioned kind that travel agents can prepare," she said. "And a stay at the best hotel Park Avenue has to offer, all open-ended, for your honeymoon, if you want. No strings attached. You don't even have to contact me while you're here."

How could I refuse? I was still in a New York frame of mind.

Chapter 20

IT WOULD HAVE been hard to rank the wonderful things about being home. What would be first? That Henry had flown back from Hawaii early so he could greet us at San Francisco International and bestow a lei on each of us? The little speech he made about how glad he was that I'd had a chance to return to New York alone (more or less) before taking him along? That I'd been able to disclose all the details of the frightful moments when I thought I'd lost Maddie to him and to Skip, confiding in them, thus relieving myself of any need to tell another soul (especially her father, who would have grounded her until she was forty)?

For Maddie, a post-trip thrill was seeing the door to her room at my house decorated with a strip of black-and-yellow crime scene tape and a green-and-white MADISON AVENUE street sign.

Also high on my list of favorites was the dinner show in my living room soon after our return. Gathered for the evening, featuring cheesecake shipped from a Seventh Avenue deli, courtesy of Detective Buzz Arnold and his wife, were all family members, immediate and extended, and a few, like June and Bebe, who were close enough to be included in a super-extended category.

We were treated to command performances from Maddie and Taylor, each of whom had presented a trip report to her class, in Palo Alto and Lincoln Point, respectively. Taylor's graphics included magnificent sunsets, swaying palm trees, a volcano or two, and a few stills of the guests and the unfortunate pig at a luau. Taylor wore her I ♥ NY T-shirt for the Hawaiian presentation.

Maddie's graphics included views of One Police Plaza, photos of six or seven doormen in various uniforms (if she noticed that one had been deleted, she didn't say), and a striking picture of a pile of droppings from the horses that pulled carriages around Central Park. "I was trying to get their hooves," she explained with a grin. Maddie wore a genuine aloha shirt for her New York report.

An extension of the show, set up in my crafts room, was a miniature row of brick storefronts Maddie and I had put together, with colorful graffiti, bars on the windows, trash on the sidewalk, stacks of newspapers tied with string, junk food wrappers, and a few grimy puddles (resin, laced with brown and black paint) from last night's mini-world rain.

"Did you see a lot of this kind of street?" Richard asked.

"Of course not," I said.

"Nah," Maddie said.

As at our bon voyage party, a symphony of several conversations flew around the room.

"I wish we could all go on a vacation together," Taylor said, with a sweep of her little arms to take us all in.

"Anywhere," Maddie said.

"I loved the postcards you sent, Gerry," June said. "For the first time, I think my mail was almost as exciting as yours. Thanks."

"Why am I the one who got the police car?" asked Bev, who'd been a civilian volunteer with the LPPD for years.

"I now have seven new blouses," Bebe said. "I kept all the shopping bags, too. Lord and Taylor, Bloomingdale's, Eileen Fisher, Saks Fifth Avenue, Strawberry, Macy's, and of course one from Bebe."

"The tree at Rockefeller Center has forty-five thousand lights," Maddie said. "I counted them." She waited for someone to laugh, but, alas, I was the only one who responded.

Nick had a story, as usual. "I read that a couple of guys from an electronics company pulled this prank on an elevator in New York. They were trying to show how realistic the images on their new hi-res screen were, so they installed the monitor, face up, as the floor of an elevator. Then they played a video on it and made it look like the floor tiles were cracking and falling down the shaft. It was just a video, but it was such a clear picture that the people on the elevator thought they were going to fall through the floor."

"Must have scared the heck out of potential customers," said my son, Richard, the glass-half-empty guy.

"You should have seen the people grabbing onto the wall of the elevator, pulling their feet in close. It was hilarious."

"I love all my presents," Mary Lou said, wearing her new green foam Statue of Liberty crown.

"I read about that elevator prank," June said. "No one was hurt, but I think it was in the UK, not New York."

"I'm glad you never took the subway," Richard said. "Bad things can happen. You wouldn't believe it."

"The tree really does have forty-five thousand LED lights," Maddie said, "even though I was kidding about me counting them."

"I've just been promoted to Nephew of Police Detectives Everywhere," Skip said, holding up a special patch Buzz had sent him.

"They didn't have cheesecake like this in Hawaii," Taylor said. "But the banana coconut cream pie wasn't too bad."

"Gerry and I have an announcement," Henry said.

"We've set a date," I said.

All other conversation stopped.

Miniature Tips

Gerry and Maddie love to share creative tips for making doll-house furniture and accessories from everyday objects.

Room Non-boxes

Here's a variation on the room boxes Bebe and Maddie make at the workshop in Chapter 12. Instead of using an ordinary wooden room box, try making a scene in a bag or a hat or an object that fits the theme. For Christmas, for example, use a Santa hat; for Fourth of July, a Revolutionary War soldier's hat; for Thanksgiving, a pilgrim's hat. Fabric stiffener will keep them firm (or you can make the hats from stiff paper) and you can build a tree-decorating scene, a fireworks display, or a turkey feast, a few inches in from the edge of the hat. Variation: Eat a whole tub of ice cream (!), cut a door on the bottom or tip it on its side, and use it to house a mini–soda fountain. And more!

Luggage Cart and Accessories

Have you made too many suitcases (Chapter 5)? Make a luggage cart to hold them all. Use a piece of sturdy cardboard for the bottom. Cover one side with felt of any color, cutting to size (not folding over). Use buttons for wheels. Bend wire (or paper clips) into shape for the sides of the cart. Don't forget luggage tags! Make them out of card stock, any shape you like, then glue a favorite theme picture on one side. Punch a hole in one end and use thread or single-ply yarn to tie the tags to the suitcases. For an antique look, add a steamer trunk. The small boxes that come with new jewelry are often just the right shape. Paint to suit.

Wire Power

Many items can be made using (1) wire (2) wire cutters/pliers and (3) a good eye for shapes. Think of things that are mostly wire—grocery carts, baskets, whisks, eyeglasses. Try cutting a piece of wire and bending it into the shape of any of the articles above simply by following the lines of a life-size piece, or a picture of one.

Stickers Again

You say you've already combed the sticker aisles for useful items? Now make your own stickers for accessorizing your dollhouse or room box. Cut a picture from a magazine or a photo, scan it, and print on adhesive-backed paper such as the kind you use for printing mailing labels. An example: scan a picture of a heating vent from a catalog or ad; print to size on adhesive paper; cut out; and stick to the wall or floor of your "home." You can also make dimmer switches and outlets/sockets this way. The look will be smoother, and there will be more substance to the item than if you simply glue the cut-out pictures directly onto to the walls or floors.

Springs Again

The small springs found in ballpoint pens have many uses, as listed in accounts of earlier Gerry and Maddie adventures. Here's a new one: Cut the springs into segments the size of hair curlers in the scale you're working in. You can glue them to the head of a doll who's in your mini-salon, leaving a few scattered around the floor. If your doll is at home, wrap a piece of netting over the "curlers" and have her answer the door in her housedress.

For the Wall

Decorate walls with photos and certificates, the easy way. No more struggling with your printer to get it to reduce the image by 80 percent. You don't even need to search for just the right "printies." Simply go through your own collection of photos for snapshots you intend to throw away some day. Maybe you have three or four shots of the same group of people, with almost the same background. Is there something on the wall in a picture that can be useful in a dollhouse or room box? A diploma? A favorite calendar? A portrait? An academic or military award? Cut them out and glue to the dollhouse/room box wall. Done!

More from Photos

You want to toss that three-by-five photo of you and your sister at the beach, but you love the sand castle you made together. Cut out the castle and make a frame for it by tracing its dimensions on card stock of the desired color. If it's big enough, skip the frame and use it a poster. Glue it to a dollhouse/room box wall and discard the images of you and your sister having that bad-hair day.

By Candlelight

This might be the easiest of all dollhouse DIY accessories (Chapter 17). Materials: the backs of earrings, the kind of metal back that goes with the posts for pierced ears, and toothpicks. Place the back, wide side down, on your worktable. For candles, place colored toothpicks in each hole. Or, you can paint them yourself. Place them on your mantel or dining room table and you're done. (Probably best not to light them!)

About the Author

Margaret Grace, author of seven previous novels in the Miniature series, is the pen name of Camille Minichino. She is also the author of short stories, articles, and twelve mysteries in two other series. She is a lifelong miniaturist, as well as board member and past president of NorCal Sisters in Crime. Minichino teaches science at Golden Gate University and writing at Bay Area schools. Visit her at www.minichino.com and on Facebook.

More Traditional Mysteries from Perseverance Press
For the New Golden Age

Diana Killian
POETIC DEATH SERIES
Docketful of Poesy
ISBN 978-1-880284-97-1

Janet LaPierre
PORT SILVA SERIES
Baby Mine
ISBN 978-1-880284-32-2

Keepers
Shamus Award nominee, Best Paperback Original
ISBN 978-1-880284-44-5

Death Duties
ISBN 978-1-880284-74-2

Family Business
ISBN 978-1-880284-85-8

Run a Crooked Mile
ISBN 978-1-880284-88-9

Hailey Lind
ART LOVER'S SERIES
Arsenic and Old Paint
ISBN 978-1-56474-490-6

Lev Raphael
NICK HOFFMAN SERIES
Tropic of Murder
ISBN 978-1-880284-68-1

Hot Rocks
ISBN 978-1-880284-83-4

Lora Roberts
BRIDGET MONTROSE SERIES
Another Fine Mess
ISBN 978-1-880284-54-4

SHERLOCK HOLMES SERIES
The Affair of the Incognito Tenant
ISBN 978-1-880284-67-4

Rebecca Rothenberg
BOTANICAL SERIES
The Tumbleweed Murders
(completed by Taffy Cannon)
ISBN 978-1-880284-43-8

Sheila Simonson
LATOUCHE COUNTY SERIES
Buffalo Bill's Defunct
WILLA Award, Best Softcover Fiction
ISBN 978-1-880284-96-4

An Old Chaos
ISBN 978-1-880284-99-5

Beyond Confusion
ISBN 978-1-56474-519-4

Shelley Singer
JAKE SAMSON & ROSIE VICENTE SERIES
Royal Flush
ISBN 978-1-880284-33-9

Lea Wait
SHADOWS ANTIQUES SERIES
Shadows of a Down East Summer
ISBN 978-1-56474-497-5

Shadows on a Cape Cod Wedding
ISBN 1-978-56474-531-6

Shadows on a Maine Christmas
ISBN 978-1-56474-531-6

Eric Wright
JOE BARLEY SERIES
The Kidnapping of Rosie Dawn
Barry Award, Best Paperback Original. Edgar,
Ellis, and Anthony awards nominee
ISBN 978-1-880284-40-7

Nancy Means Wright
MARY WOLLSTONECRAFT SERIES
Midnight Fires
ISBN 978-1-56474-488-3

The Nightmare
ISBN 978-1-56474-509-5

REFERENCE/MYSTERY WRITING

Kathy Lynn Emerson
How To Write Killer Historical Mysteries:
The Art and Adventure of Sleuthing
Through the Past
Agatha Award, Best Nonfiction. Anthony and
Macavity awards nominee
ISBN 978-1-880284-92-6

Carolyn Wheat
How To Write Killer Fiction:
The Funhouse of Mystery & the Roller
Coaster of Suspense
ISBN 978-1-880284-62-9

31901056171608

Available from your local bookstore
or from Perseverance Press/John Daniel & Company
(800) 662–8351 or www.danielpublishing.com/perseverance